THE
ROSES
OF MAY

THE
ROSES
OF MAY

Book 2 in the Collector Trilogy

DOT HUTCHISON

Text copyright © 2017 by Dot Hutchison
All rights reserved.

No part of this book may be reproduced, or stored in a retrieval system, or transmitted in any form or by any means, electronic, mechanical, photocopying, recording, or otherwise, without express written permission of the publisher.

Published by Thomas & Mercer, Seattle.

www.apub.com

Amazon, the Amazon logo, and Thomas & Mercer are trademarks of Amazon.com, Inc., or its affiliates.

ISBN-13: 9781503939509
ISBN-10: 1503939502

Cover design by Jae Song

Printed in the United States of America

To the dangerous girls with sharp-edged smiles

Her name is Darla Jean Carmichael, and she's your first.

But then, you don't know that yet.

What you know, on this fine spring day, is that it seems even God himself has gone out of his way to make her look more beautiful. She's all innocent beauty, no artifice or vanity; it's why you love her the way you do. Her shining blonde hair hangs down her back in heavy waves and she's wearing her old-fashioned white Easter dress again, even has the lace gloves and starched lace hat on. Have you ever seen anything so wholesome? So pure?

Even nature agrees with you today. Along either side of the bare, dusty path to the church, the grass is thick with jonquils, all yellow and white, like they could never aim higher than to match Darla Jean. Even the wild daisies are yellow and white, and most years they're ribbons of pale lavender through the fields.

This year there's only Darla Jean.

Except . . . not just Darla Jean.

Her hand is looped through the arm of a young man, tucked into the crook of his elbow like it belongs there, and it doesn't. Her hand doesn't belong there because he isn't you. Darla Jean is yours.

Has always been yours.

She's never needed you to tell her before; she's always just known it, the way she should, because the two of you are meant to be together, whatever others would say if they knew.

Furious, heartbroken, you follow them to the small brick church, set against such an explosion of flowering trees it looks like a needlepoint. Somehow, despite the rush of emotions pounding in your ears as another heartbeat, you notice other things. In his free hand, the young man carries the basket of treats her mother asked her to take to the church, each individually wrapped for sale because the church needs a new roof before storm season.

He leans into her every time she laughs.

She's laughing a lot.

But that sound is yours, just like the rest of her is yours, and how could she share it with someone else? That laugh has always soothed you, teased you away from the rage that stays far too close to the surface. Now each time you hear it—high and soft, like the wind chimes on the back porch—you feel a sharp pain in your chest, a throbbing echo in your skull.

They walk together into the church, and it takes you a minute or two to find a window that lets you see them clearly, without being seen in turn. She shouldn't have to know you're there to know what she owes you, how she ought to behave. The interior of the church is dim, full of shadows and starbursts after the bright sunlight, so you don't immediately realize what's happening.

And then you do.

All you see is blood.

He's kissing her, or she's kissing him, faces tilted toward each other's, the rest of them nearly a foot apart. It might be his first kiss.

You know it's hers.

The first kiss that was supposed to be yours—that you've been waiting for all these years. But you've cherished her instead, knowing she's too pure, too innocent to be sullied with such things.

She was too pure. Was too innocent.

You slide down the outer wall of the church, the bricks rough and painful, scraping and digging through your clothing. You're shaking—you might be weeping. How could she? How could she do this to herself, to you?

How could she let herself be tarnished?

She's worthless now, just like all those other whores out in the world, always flaunting their bodies and their smiles and their cruel, knowing eyes. You would have worshipped her to the end of your days.

You love her, though. How could you not, even still? You love her enough to save her, even if you have to save her from herself.

You hear the boy leave, an apology tumbling from his lips—he has to help his brothers get ready. You hear the pastor greet Darla Jean with good cheer. He tells her he has to run into town to buy cups for the lemonade— will she be all right alone? But of course she will. She's grown up in this church. It's never been anything but a safe place. She can't imagine a world where that won't always be true. As you watch the pastor walk down the path—away, and farther yet—you hear her start to sing.

Her songs are yours, too, and there's no one else to hear them now.

She greets you with a smile and a laugh when you walk inside, her eyes bright. You can't call them guileless. Not anymore. Not now that she's lost her innocence. Her smile falters as you approach.

She has the nerve to ask you what's wrong.

You know you don't have much time—it's less than two miles to town, and the pastor walks there and back frequently—but there's time enough to show her. You show her everything.

You promised her a life together, that you would always be there for her. You promised her the world.

She threw it away.

This is all her fault.

You leave at a run, still seething with hurt and betrayal.

Darla Jean stays behind, sprawled on the stone, her Easter dress just tatters and rags soaking up the pool of red. The jonquils you'd picked for her—a gift, and look what she's done with it—lie scattered around her. Her eyes are wide and empty, an echo of confusion, and you've given her a jagged smile she can share with the world if she wants to.

She can't laugh anymore, can't sing, can't taint what's yours.

She can't do anything anymore. Perhaps you didn't mean to. Perhaps your hunting knife slipped and cut too deep. Perhaps you forgot there's so much blood so close to the surface. Perhaps you did exactly as you meant to.

She's just another whore, after all.

Now Darla Jean is dead.

You didn't know she'd be your first.

You don't know yet, but she won't be your last, either.

FEBRUARY

Paperwork will, if left unattended, multiply exponentially, much like rabbits and wire coat hangers. Scowling at the newest stacks on his desk, Special Agent Brandon Eddison can't help but wonder how they would look on fire. It wouldn't take much. Just a flick of a match, the snick of a lighter, the corners of one or two pages in the middle so it would catch nice and evenly, and then all the papers would be gone.

"If you set them on fire, they'll just print them off again and you'll have all of it plus the paperwork about the fire," says a laughing voice to his right.

"Shut up, Ramirez," he sighs.

Mercedes Ramirez—his teammate and friend—just laughs again and leans back in her chair, stretching into a long, slightly curved line. Her chair creaks in protest. Her own desk is covered in papers. Not stacks. Just covered. If he asks her for any specific piece of information, she'll find it in under a minute, and he will never understand how.

In the corner, facing their angled desks, is the lair of their senior partner, Supervisory Special Agent in Charge Victor Hanoverian. To Eddison's disgust and amazement, all the paperwork on that desk seems to be done, sorted into colored folders. As the leader of their intrepid trio, Vic has more paperwork than either of them, and he always has it finished first. Thirty years in the Bureau does that to a person, Eddison supposes, but it's a terrifying thought.

He looks back at his own desk, at the newest stack, and grumbles as he reaches for the top pages. He has a system, one that baffles Ramirez as much as hers unnerves him, and despite the height of the pile, it doesn't take him long to move the papers to the appropriate columns at the back of his desk, sorted by both topic and priority. They align neatly with the back edge and corners of the surface, alternating portrait and landscape within each stack.

"Has a nice doctor ever talked to you about that?" asks Ramirez.

"Has A&E ever staged an intervention about yours?"

She snickers and turns back to her desk. It would be nice if, just once in a while, she rose to the bait. She's by no means unflappable, but she's strangely impervious to teasing.

"Where is Vic, anyway?"

"On his way back from a deposition; Bliss asked for him to be there."

He wonders if he should point out that, three and a half months after they rescued the surviving girls from the burning Garden, she's still using the Butterfly names, the names the victims were given by their captor.

He doesn't point it out. She probably knows. The job is easier, most of the time, if they can put everything in neat little boxes in their minds, and who the girls were before they were taken is harder to integrate.

He needs to get to work. It's a paperwork day, or mostly, and he really should make at least one of those piles disappear by the end of the day. His eye falls on the colorful tower of folders that lives on the back-right corner of his desk, growing over the years with more folders but no answers. That stack never disappears.

He leans back in his chair and studies the two framed photos atop the squat filing cabinet that holds his office supplies and blank forms.

One is of him and his sister on a long ago Halloween, one of the last times he saw her before she got snatched off the street on the way home from school. She was only eight years old. Logic tells him she must be dead. It's been twenty years, but he still finds himself examining any twenty-something woman who resembles her. Hope is a strange and fickle thing.

But then, so was Faith, strange and fickle, back when she was just his sister rather than a missing-child statistic.

The other photo is newer, just a couple of years old, a souvenir from the most disturbing and unexpected day trip he's been on that didn't involve work. Priya and her mother dragged him on a number of strange sightseeing trips during the six or so months they lived in D.C., but that jaunt was the stuff of nightmares. He's not even sure how they ended up in a field full of massive presidential busts. They did, though, and at one point Eddison and Priya had climbed up onto Lincoln's shoulders, both pointing to the very large hole in the back of the statue's head. Realistic? Yes. Intentional? Judging from the battered condition of the rest of the twenty-foot-tall busts . . . no, not so much. There are other pictures from that day—safely tucked away in the shoe box in the crawl space in his closet—but this is his favorite. Not because of the thoroughly discomfiting bust of an assassinated president, but because it's the one where Priya surprised herself by grinning.

He's never known the Priya who grinned without thinking. That Priya shattered just days before he met the girl who grew from those broken pieces. The Priya he knows is all sharp edges and snarls and smiles that slap you in the face like a challenge. Anything softer—anything kinder—is accidental. Her mother may see some of that softness still, but no one else does, not since Priya's sister was reduced to photos and facts in one of the colored folders on the back corner of his desk.

Eddison is fairly sure he would never have become friends with the old Priya. He's still startled to be friends with this one. She should have only ever been the sister of a murder victim, a girl to interview and feel sorry for and never really know, but in the days after her sister's murder, Priya was so damn angry. At the killer, at her sister, at the police, at the whole fucking world. Eddison is very familiar with that kind of anger.

And because he's thinking about her, because it's a paperwork day after a string of bad days fighting to contain the media on the Butterfly case, he pulls out his personal cell, snaps a picture of the framed photo, and texts it to her. He doesn't expect a response—the clock tells him it's only nine where she is, and without school to wake her up, she's probably still burrowed in her blanket burrito.

A moment later, though, his phone buzzes with a reply. The photo is a long shot of a red-brick building that should be stately but just looks pretentious, one stretch of brick covered by rusting iron lattices that probably hold ivy in the warmer months. Tall, medieval-looking narrow windows are scattered through the brick.

What the hell?

His phone buzzes again. *This is the school I almost got stuck going to. You should see their uniforms.*

I knew you were only doing online classes so you could stay in pajamas all day.

Well, not ONLY. You know the headmaster protested when Mum told him we wouldn't be enrolling? Told her she was doing me a disservice by allowing me to slide by with an inferior education.

He winces. *I can't imagine that went well.*

I guess he's used to flexing his dick and getting what he wants. Mum's dick is more impressive.

A weight drops onto his shoulders and he flinches, but it's just Ramirez. Her concept of personal space is drastically different from his, in that he actually has a concept of what it should be. Rather than argue, because it never seems to do any good, he tilts the screen so she can read it.

"Flex his . . . Eddison!" She flicks his ear hard enough to hurt. "Did you teach her that?"

"She's almost seventeen, Ramirez. She's perfectly capable of being crass all on her own."

"You're a bad influence."

"What if she's the bad influence?"

"Who's the adult?"

"Certainly neither of you," observes a new voice.

They both cringe.

But Vic doesn't remind them that personal cells aren't supposed to be out during work hours, or that they have things they really should be doing. He just walks past them, the smell of fresh coffee wreathing around him, and calls back over his shoulder, "Tell Priya hello."

Eddison dutifully taps it in as Ramirez slinks back to her desk. He laughs at Priya's instant response. *Awww, did you get detention?*

What are you doing awake, anyway?

Wandering around. The weather finally turned.

Isn't it cold?

Yes, but it is no longer snowing, slushing, or otherwise shitting cold wet things from the sky. Just seeing what's here.

Call me later. Tell me what's there.

He waits for her affirmative, then slips the phone back into the drawer with his gun and badge and all the other things he's not supposed to play with when he's at his desk. In the damn-near unrelenting slog of horrors that is his job, Priya is a prickly spark of life.

He's been in the Bureau just long enough to be grateful for that.

Huntington, Colorado, in February is freaking freezing. Even layered up enough to feel three times my size, the cold has a way of creeping between fabrics. We've been here a week, and this is the first day it's been almost nice enough to explore.

So far, it all feels very much like any of the places we've lived in the past four years. Mum's company shuffles us all over the country so she can put out fires, and in three months we'll be leaving again, maybe even for good, so she can take over Human Resources in the Paris branch. Not that France is necessarily final, but I think we're both hoping it will be. *Priya in Paris* has a lovely sound. In the meantime, Huntington is close enough to Denver for Mum to sensibly commute, far enough that it's supposed to feel more like a community than a city, according to the company agent who let us into the house our first day.

After five days of slushing, it snowed over the weekend, leaving the lawns fluffy and white and the borders nasty and grey. There is very little uglier than plowed snow. The roads are clear, though, and all the sidewalks are tinted blue from the salt. It feels like walking over the remnants of a Smurf slaughter.

I shove my hands into my coat pockets as I walk, partly for warmth on top of the gloves, partly to keep my fingers from itching for a better camera than my phone's. I left my good camera at the house, but Huntington is a little more interesting than I expected it to be.

Passing the closest elementary school reveals a squirrel winter home set up to one side of the playground; it's basically a high-stilted chicken coop painted bright red. There's a hole in the bottom so the squirrels can get in and out, and the blinking red light of a camera inside that must let kids in the school keep an eye on the rodents through the winter. Currently, a few are sleeping peacefully on what look to be semi-shredded quilts and sawdust. Yes, I totally peeked. It's a squirrel home.

A mile or so on, there's a bare space set back from one corner of an intersection, too small to be a park of any kind, but with a gorgeous wrought-iron gazebo in the middle of it. Sort of a gazebo—it doesn't have a floor, just the posts digging down into frozen earth, but for all the strength of the metal, the supports are intricately wound together and the almost onion-top looks lacy and delicate. Like an outdoor wedding chapel, but surrounded by fast food joints and a stand-alone optometrist's office.

Starting a wide loop back home, I have to cross a seven-road intersection, half the roads one way only and all the signs pointing the wrong way. There isn't a single car in sight on any of the seven roads. True, it's only half past eleven in the morning, and most everyone is at work or school, but I get the feeling this intersection is braved only by those drivers filled with resignation at the inevitability of certain death and doom.

I take pictures of everything anyway, even though they'll mostly turn out crap on the phone, because taking pictures is just what I do. The world seems a little less frightening, somehow, if I can keep the camera lens between me and everything else. Mostly, though, I take pictures for Chavi, so she can see the things I see.

Chavi's been dead almost five years now.

I still take pictures.

Chavi's death is how I met my FBI agents, and they are mine in an important way, Eddison and Mercedes and Vic. She should have been just another case to them, my big sister just another dead girl in a file, but they kept checking in on me after. Cards and emails and phone calls, and at some point I stopped resenting the reminders of Chavi's murder, was grateful that as we moved from place to place, I had my strange group of friends in Quantico.

I walk past a library that looks more like a cathedral, complete with stained glass and a bell tower, and a liquor store bookended by law offices specializing in DUIs. A little bit farther on, there's a plaza anchored by an enormous twenty-four-hour gym on one end and an educational afterschool care facility on the other; between them are seven different types of fast food. Weirdly enough, I kind of like that, the contradiction and messiness, the awareness that our intentions tend to go fuck themselves and our vices are right there waiting.

A much bigger plaza—two stories and with way more elaborate decoration than any outdoor shopping center should have—houses what has to be the nation's fanciest Kroger. A sign outside advertises a Starbucks inside, but there's another Starbucks in the plaza and one just across the street, and it's supposed to be a joke but so, so isn't.

I should probably get lunch, but I try not to eat out on my own if I can help it. It's not a health thing; give me takeout with Mum, and I am all for it. It's the on-my-own bit. After a few years of trying to balance what my body needs against what my emotions insist I need, I'm still not great at it. Sometimes—mostly only on bad days, anymore—I still eat myself sick at the realization that Chavi isn't here, she's not *here* and it just hurts so fucking much in a way that doesn't make any sense, because anything that hurts this much should be able to bleed out, should be able to be *fixed* and it can't be, so eating Oreos until I'm bloated and cramping and vomiting just gives a way for the pain to make sense.

It's been a few months now since I teetered over that line I drew for myself and collapsed in front of the toilet—and Oreos definitely don't taste good the second time—but I'm still . . . *aware*, I guess, that my control isn't what it should be. Mum has always been significantly less concerned about the weight than about the eating-myself-sick part, but between the two of us—her iron will and my relief at her iron will—we've managed to stabilize things so I'm no longer swinging wildly between the worrisome extremes of bony and round.

That my current weight makes me look more like Chavi than ever . . . well. On good days, it's a shudder and carefully avoiding pictures, or mirrors larger than a compact. On bad days, it's needles crawling under my skin and my fingers twitching for Oreos. Mum calls me a work in progress.

I head inside the Kroger. I'm pretty sure I can't feel the tip of my nose, so a hot drink wouldn't be the worst thing. If I don't eat until I get home, it's harder to get myself in trouble.

The barista is a tiny, sparrow-like lady who must be eighty if she's a day, her lavender-tinted hair poufy in a Gibson Girl bun with bright purple bobby pins. Her back and shoulders are bent and her hands arthritic, but her eyes are sharp and her smile welcoming, and I wonder if she needs this job or if she's just one of those people who gets a part-time job after retiring because the house or her husband gets too irritating over long periods of time.

"What name, sweetheart?" she asks, Sharpie in hand as she reaches for the cup.

"Jane."

Because watching people butcher *Priya* sucks.

A few minutes later, I have my drink. There are tables and chairs packed together here in the corner of the grocery store, and there are speakers in the ceiling pumping out some corporate CD of smooth jazz, but it's all but buried under the sounds of the rest of the store: squawky calls over the intercom, crashes of carts and cans and boxes, screaming children, the pop rock soundtrack—it's chaotic and clashy and makes the whole café-in-a-grocery-store thing a bit weirder.

So I head back outside, into the cold and the shred of a breeze that's picked up, and wander off into the parking lot. I came from the back of the plaza, but the road fronting it will take me straight home, and it's probably about time I headed back.

Instead, I freeze at the sight of a strange little pavilion. It's up on a grassy island, one of several splitting the parking lot into sections, the iron covered on three sides by what looks to be heavy white canvas. Space heaters, coils glowing cherry-red, hang from the struts, safely above the heads of a collection of mostly older men in similar ball caps, dark blue or black with yellow embroidery, all of them layered up against the cold that slams in from the rolled-up side of canvas. They're seated at stone picnic tables, boards and pieces spread between them. It shouldn't be anything, but it is, because it's achingly familiar.

Nothing looks quite the same as old men gathering for chess.

Dad and I used to play chess.

He was terrible at it and I pretended to be, something that bothered him a lot more than it did me, but we played every Saturday morning in the park near home, or in the adjacent empty church during the long Boston winters. He sometimes wanted to play during the week, too, but there was something about the Saturday tradition that appealed to me.

Even after Dad, I keep looking for chess gatherings everywhere we move. I lose every game, at least half of them on purpose, but I still want to play. Everything else that was Dad is neatly packed away, but convincing others I suck at chess, that I get to keep alive.

A car door squeaks as it opens nearby, pulling my attention away from the old men and their boards. A few feet away, a young woman, maybe midtwenties, sits in the driver's side with a lapful of knitting, and she smiles at me. "You can go talk to them, you know," she says. "They don't bite. At least not with teeth."

I'm not very good at smiling anymore—it comes off a little frightening—but I try to muster an appropriately friendly expression. "I didn't want to intrude. Do they let others play with them?"

"Sometimes. They're pretty particular about it, but it can't hurt to ask. My grandfather's up there."

That explains the knitting. Thank God—a parking lot Madame Defarge would be pretty creepy.

"Go and ask," she urges, her thumb absently petting the loops of red yarn around her pinky. "The worst they can do is say no."

"You encourage everyone who stops and stares?"

"Just the ones who look lonely." She closes the door before I have to come up with a response to that.

After a few more moments of standing there like an idiot, an ache building in all the parts of me that aren't frozen through, I walk up onto the grass and into the mostly warm pavilion. The players all stop their games to stare at me.

Almost all the men are older, clearly veterans, based on the operation and unit designations on their hats. Chess parks are common places to find vets, so while I don't know all the operations, I know enough to lump them into groups. Most of these guys served in Vietnam, a few in Korea, a couple in Desert Storm, and one very old man, bundled in scarves and blankets and seated nearest the space heaters, wears a hat with Operation Neptune embroidered on it, the thread faded to a weary mustard.

Holy shit.

This man stormed Normandy Beach before my grandparents were even born.

One of the Vietnam vets, a saggy, pouch-faced man with a bulbous, broken-veined nose that suggests chess may be the way he keeps himself from day-drinking, scowls at me. "We're not looking for donations, girl."

"Wasn't offering any. I was going to ask if you allow others to play with you."

"You play?" He doesn't sound like he believes me.

"Badly, but yes. I look for a place to play wherever we move."

"Huh. Thought that's what you young people use the Internets for."

"It isn't the same."

The oldest man clears his throat, and the others all turn to look at him. Every group has a hierarchy; groups of veterans are really no different, and actual rank aside, World War II trumps all. This man lived through hell and has carried its scars with him a lot longer than anyone else here. That kind of rank doesn't retire or get discharged. "Come here, please."

I walk around the table and perch on the tiny sliver of bench sticking out beside him. He studies me—for what, I'm not sure—and the sickly sweet smell of his breath makes me wonder if he's diabetic, if he's actually okay sitting out here in this weather, space heaters and layers aside. His skin looks parchment thin, folded over itself in soft wrinkles, unevenly discolored with age and wear and thin blue veins spider-webbing his temples and under his eyes. Thick, pale scar tissue knots around one temple, digging back over and behind that ear. Shrapnel from Normandy? Or something else entirely?

"You've got your own war, don't you, girl?"

I think about that, letting the question beneath the words take shape. It takes the shape of Chavi, all that rage and sorrow and hurt I've carried since her death. "Yes," I say eventually. "I just don't know who's on the other side of it." A war needs an enemy, but I'm not sure anyone can sabotage me as well as I do myself.

"We've all wondered that a few times," he agrees, his eyes flicking to the other men. All but one are watching us; the exception is studying his board with a faint frown and the dawning realization that his king's about to be cornered. "What's your name, then?"

"Priya Sravasti. Yours?"

"Harold Randolph."

"Gunny!" Most of the men cough into their hands. Only one refrains, and he doesn't look like a veteran. He's younger, softer, and there's something in his eyes—or rather, something *not* in his eyes—that says he doesn't belong the way the rest of them do.

Gunny rolls his eyes. He slowly peels off a knit glove to reveal a second below, this one fingerless and a yellow as faded as the letters on his hat. His hand shakes slightly as he lifts it—a palsy, I think, more than cold—and he touches the tip of my nose with one finger. "Can you feel that?"

I almost smile, but I don't want to scare him, make myself less welcome. "No, sir."

"Then get on home for today, and come back whenever you want. We don't play much on weekends. Too many folk."

"Thank you, sir," I tell him. Impulsively, I drop a kiss on his cheek, soft whiskers tickling my lips. "I'll be back."

The bulbous-nosed man snickers. "Look at that, Gunny's got a new future ex-wife."

Most of the others nod at me, acknowledgment rather than friendliness, but that's okay. I have to earn a place here, show them I'm not just bored or flighty. I stand up and walk along the back of the pavilion, soaking in the warmth before I head home, and glance at the man at the far end of the tables, the one who doesn't seem to belong. He's not wearing a ball cap, just a knit cap pushed back far enough to show light-colored hair that's impossible to describe as blond or brown.

He smiles blandly at me.

"You look familiar," I blurt.

His smile doesn't change. "I get that a lot."

No shit. He doesn't look like anyone, so he must look like nearly everyone. There isn't a single distinguishing feature on him, nothing to say yes, I'd absolutely recognize him out of context. He isn't handsome, he isn't ugly, he just . . . is. Even his eyes are a murky, indistinguishable color.

And his smile doesn't change the look of his face. It's strange, that. Smiles change you, the tilt of your cheeks, the shape of your mouth, the crinkle around your eyes. But his face doesn't look any different than it did before he smiled. It's not that it looks fake exactly, it just doesn't look . . . well, natural. But let's be honest, chess parks are a haven for the socially awkward. Maybe I should just be impressed he's making eye contact.

I nod, still feeling somewhat unsettled, and head home. I'm not feeling the cold as much, which is less a sign of the day warming up than a hey-idiot-get-inside-before-you-get-frostbite warning.

Once in the neighborhood, I stop at the large overhang sheltering the wall of mailboxes for our street. There's even a trash can chained around one of the posts for all the junk mail. In my more sentimental moods, I miss our mailbox in Boston, with the brightly colored handprints across the cheerful yellow surface. Dad didn't want to put his handprint—he thought it was undignified—so the three of us attacked him with paintbrushes and ended up with a beautiful multicolored moustache print on the front flap.

I wonder if we still have that box. I haven't seen it in a couple of moves. Then again, that's the case for at least half of everything we own—unpacking and packing again hasn't seemed worth the effort.

I pull out a double handful of circulars and oversize postcards addressed to "Our Neighbor" and "The Residents of . . ." and flick them into the bin, along with the dental appointment reminder postcard forwarded from Birmingham. There's a greeting-card envelope in a cheerful shade of green, a very spring kind of color, with Mercedes's handwriting on the front. It's not all that surprising; technically I start virtual school today, taking online classes with a tutor in France so I get used to thinking and working in another language, and Mercedes *always* has a card waiting for my first day of school, no matter how many there are in a year.

What's surprising are the other two envelopes, nearly identical in size. One is labeled all in caps, the writing effortlessly neat and legible, the kind that holds up well even as the paper and ink start to fade, the black print stark against the hot-pink card stock. The pale blue envelope has a mostly tidy scrawl, readable after a blink or two.

Mercedes's card is right on schedule, but Vic and Eddison usually space theirs out a bit differently.

These are nothing like the card they'll send in May, the one all three of them will sign. That one won't have a note, not even a preprinted one. Just their signatures. Just a reminder that my sister's murder hasn't been forgotten. It takes some careful planning and an awareness of the postal service to make sure that one doesn't arrive with my birthday cards.

Because nothing says happy birthday like the reminder that the FBI still doesn't know who murdered your sister and a string of other girls over the years.

Inside the house, I strip off the outside layers to hang in the front closet, then head up the stairs to my room, peeling off the rest on the way. The cards get dropped onto my bed, the clothing onto the chair I dragged up from the neglected dining room to contain the chaos. After a hot shower that has my nose and fingertips painfully aware of returning sensation, I go back down to the kitchen and make packaged oatmeal, adding in cinnamon and honey and milk, and take it upstairs with me.

It's only once I'm settled on the bed in pajamas, the oatmeal working its magic to warm my insides, that I reach for the envelopes.

Mercedes's card is exactly what it should be, a cheerful back-to-school message in neon pen, half of it in Spanish because it cracks her up when I write back to her in French. I pull out Vic's next, a black-and-white photo of three cats in massive sunglasses. The note inside is nonoccasional, a few lines about his oldest daughter's college letters and the miserably rainy weather in northern Virginia. Eddison's, with a picture carefully straddling the line between gross and funny, doesn't have anything written in it at all.

Why all three?

But then I look at Mercedes's card again, the front decked out in enough glitter to make a unicorn shit itself in glee, and realize some of the glitter doesn't belong. The rest of it is superfine, pastel in tone. Here and there, though, are swirls of what look to be glitter glue, thick and a little gloppy and dried into little ridges of bright color. I slide a thumbnail under one of those swirls, gently prying it away. The paper tears on one curve, then releases. A moment later, I've got a rough circle of glue on one finger and an unobstructed view of part of the original card.

She covered over the butterflies.

Her name is Zoraida Bourret, and it's Easter Sunday.

You like Easter in the more traditional churches, when the girls and women still wear white dresses and lace, and hats with ribbons or flowers. There's something about sitting near the back of the church and seeing the sea of Easter hats.

And this year, you see Zoraida.

You've seen her before, of course, helping her mother with a horde of younger siblings. You've listened to the gossip, and that subtle something other that isn't gossip but isn't quite news. Her father was a police officer killed in the line of duty, and even though Zoraida was a sure shot for college and great things, she's dropped all her extracurriculars and probably her chance for higher education in order to help at home, and no one even had to ask it of her.

What a good girl, the women say.

What a sweet child.

What a wonderful sister.

She doesn't look anything like Darla Jean, but there's something there that reminds you. It's been almost a year since Darla Jean betrayed you, and even still you love her, miss her, mourn her.

But Zoraida really is a good girl. You've watched her enough to know that. She comes straight home from school, picking up her siblings on the way, and gets them all sorted with snacks and homework and activities, and almost always has dinner nearly done when their mother gets home from work. She helps with the baths and getting all the younger ones in bed, and only then does she sit down at the kitchen table and start on her own homework. It takes her late into the night, but then she's up early again, making sure everyone gets breakfast and gets dressed and gets off to school.

And when the boys come round—and they do come round, because she's a beautiful girl, and Lord, but the world lights up with her smile—she politely sends them away, because her family is more important.

Because she's a good girl.

When the service lets out, it's easy to steal the cute plastic purses a couple of her younger sisters have left on the pew. They forget them all the time, the twins, remembering them only halfway home, and because it's a long walk to the church to save gas on the weekends, it's always Zoraida who comes trudging back for them. She shakes her head at it every time, but she smiles, too, because she loves the twins and would do anything for them.

And you know you have to help her.

You have to make sure, for her sake, that she's always this good, this pure.

So you steal the purses, knowing the twins will forget, and wait for her to come back. The church empties faster than usual, everyone heading home to egg hunts or dinner or extended family. You sit in the shadows and wait, and there she comes, fanning herself with her hat. It's starched white lace, stiff and inflexible, with peach-colored ribbons woven through the brim and base of the crown. The peach and white look so soft against her dark skin. A single purple-throated lily is pinned like a corsage to her dress, almost high enough to be her shoulder.

You come up behind her, steps soft on the thin carpet, and cover her mouth with your hand. She draws a sharp breath, starts to scream, but your arm comes up against her throat. She struggles, but you know how long to keep the pressure firm, and she falls unconscious.

Her dress is so white, so clean. So innocent. You can't bear the thought of ruining it.

So when one of her brothers comes by a bit later, worried when she didn't return home right away, he finds her laid out before the altar, purple-throated white lilies in a halo about her head, her clothing neatly folded and stacked on a pew, the hat atop the pile and her plain buckle shoes beside. The gash across her throat is a clean line, because she couldn't struggle while unconscious.

No pain, no fear.

She won't have the chance to fall like Darla Jean, won't face that temptation and betrayal.

Zoraida Bourret will always be a good girl.

Eddison's apartment will never win prizes for decorating. It's not homey, nor is it particularly cozy. If it has an aesthetic, it would probably be vaguely institutional. It's tidy—even the dishes in the sink are rinsed and neatly stacked, waiting for him to empty and reload the dishwasher—but it doesn't contain much that makes it feel personal. The walls are the same eggshell they were painted before he moved in. He did add curtains over the windows, partly because the blinds let in too much light and partly because he really doesn't want anyone looking in. With the exception of the dinner table, a gaily colored tile-topped monstrosity Priya and her mother rescued from a closing Mexican restaurant and gave him as a joke, the furniture is dark and utilitarian. His movies and books live in the random extra closet near the television.

Generally Eddison prefers it that way. When he comes back from assignments where he's been in people's homes, seen all the personal ways people shape the places they live, he's grateful to have a fairly neutral space where he can center himself again. And perhaps there's a bit of paranoia to it. He's not sure he knows anyone in law enforcement without the lingering, nearly-always-unspoken fear that one day someone might go after their loved ones in revenge. If he doesn't have his loved ones out on display, if he doesn't leave clues to his vulnerabilities lying around in open sight, even in his own apartment, it makes him feel safer.

He didn't lose his sister because he joined the FBI—he joined the FBI because he lost his sister—but he can't bear the thought of endangering his parents, or the various aunts and uncles and cousins he still keeps in contact with.

Today, though, when he's spent the entire day staring at paperwork that will probably fill the rest of the week, he can't help but realize that the place he calls home is downright sterile.

Changing out of his suit, he settles down on the couch with a box of takeout. Vic's wife and mother, saints that they are, have offered many times to teach him how to cook properly, but the best he can manage without mayhem is ramen and blue-box mac and cheese. Contrary to Ramirez's mockery, it has nothing to do with being male and everything to do with getting bored halfway through preparations.

He's pretty sure the landlord would not be pleased to paint over smoke stains on his kitchen ceiling again.

His personal photos, anything with him or a loved one or a location connected to him, are packed away in shoe boxes hidden in a crawl space in the bedroom closet. There when he wants to look through them, hard for anyone else to find. A few photos are safe to put up, though, and he looks at them rather than try to find a game on the television.

He doesn't remember telling Priya why there were no pictures displayed when she and her mother came to pick him up for a barbecue at Vic's house those months they lived in D.C. He almost remembers mentioning it to her mother, though not any of the reasons. Then again, Deshani Sravasti is a formidable woman with a keen (and somewhat terrifying) ability to read people. She probably noticed the lack of photos even before he said anything about it, and made a fairly accurate guess as to why. So maybe she was the one to mention it to Priya.

Thus began the adventures of Special Agent Ken. He's not sure where Priya got the Ken doll—he suspects one of Vic's daughters—but she sewed it a suit and a little navy blue windbreaker with *FBI* in big yellow letters on the back. Now wherever she and her mother go, Special Agent Ken goes along with them, and gets his own photos with famous or interesting backdrops. The handful Eddison has framed are arrayed in an arc over the television.

His favorite is from Berlin; the doll is bent almost in half, face-down on a table next to a quarter-full glass of beer bigger than Ken would be standing. He can just see the tiny lederhosen peeking out from under the windbreaker. He's pretty sure Priya is the only person he knows who would be completely comfortable making a doll look drunk for a photo session in a public space. She doesn't sign or date the backs of the photos, just writes in a location for the more obscure backdrops. Personal in sentiment, impersonal in appearance.

Safe.

His phone rings, buzzing and dancing against the coffee table. He eyes it warily until he remembers that Priya was going to call. "So is your new town full of interesting things?" he asks instead of saying hello.

"*Interesting* is a good word for it," she agrees. "The plazas are the weirdest mix of good intentions and resignation."

"I finally got a chance to read the profile on your mother in December's *Economist*," he says. "It's an impressive write-up."

"The interview started out a bit rocky; he kept asking about Chavi and Dad, and Mum was less than pleased."

Less than pleased for Deshani Sravasti normally means her victim is lucky to escape without pissing himself. Clearly the *Economist* sent someone made of sterner stuff, given how the rest of the interview turned out.

"It got better once he got less personal," she continues. "Mum loves talking about putting out fires in the different branches."

"I'm glad they're recognizing her for it." It had been startling to walk into the bookstore and see Deshani on the cover of the magazine, her gaze direct and challenging even in a photo. More pictures accompanied the article, one in her Birmingham office, the other with Priya on their couch.

He wasn't surprised to see the tiny print that credited Priya as the photographer for the ones she wasn't in.

There's a pause then, less a second of silence than a hesitation, and the one thing Priya has never done is hesitate. This is the girl who, within ten minutes of meeting him, threw a teddy bear at his head and told him not to be such a fucking coward. They've been friends ever since.

He generally prefers not to examine what that might say about him.

"What is it, Priya?"

"Are you guys okay?"

The question makes him cold, for no reason he can name, and he jabs the plastic fork back into the noodles. "What, the team? We're fine."

"Are you? Because I got cards from all three of you today."

Shit.

He had no way of knowing that Vic intended to send a card, but he should have remembered Ramirez. Would it have been less noticeable if only two of them had arrived?

But this is Priya, and she is her mother's daughter, and neither of them has ever needed all the facts to get correctly from point A to point M.

"You don't have to tell me what's going on. I know you might not want to, or might not be able to. I'm just worried." That hesitation again, that testing the ice before the step. "Mercedes glittered over the butterflies on her card."

Fuck.

But last Tuesday—the day he'd sent the card—was a bad day for all of them. He shouldn't be surprised.

"So let me rephrase slightly," she continues. "Will you all *be* okay?"

Eddison sits on that a moment, lets it sink down to his bones as if there's an answer to be found there. Priya doesn't say anything else, doesn't push or prod or rush him to a response. She's gotten good at waiting.

The Butterflies were good at waiting, some better than others. Most of those who are left aren't good at it anymore.

He wasn't at the Garden when they pulled out the bodies of the girls who'd died in the moments leading up to the explosion, or in it. He was on his way back to Quantico, rage seeping into the places hollowed out by what he'd seen.

As they learned what had happened to those girls, he'd been filled with the horrifying realization that this case would never go away. Not that it wouldn't be legally resolved; it would. Eventually. But this wasn't a case to solve and put away, move on to the next. It wasn't even one to idly look back on while reflecting on the course of one's career.

This was a case to ruin you, to utterly wreck you for the rest of your life because how can people do this?

And because this is Priya who's asking, Priya who knows better than most what it means to not be okay—knows that it's all right to not be okay—he considers the limits of what he can and cannot tell her and decides it's going to get out in the news anyway, but she won't be the one to share it.

"One of the Garden survivors killed herself last week."

She makes a small sound, thinking rather than responding.

"It wasn't really a surprise," he continues. "Not with this one. We were more surprised that she hadn't done it earlier."

"Family?"

"She broke while she was still inside there. Her family broke her the rest of the way. But she makes . . ."

She says it so he doesn't have to. "Three," she says simply. "That's three suicides in less than four months."

"There are two others the psychologists have issued warnings for. 'More likely than not' was how they put it."

"And the others?"

"Time will tell." He hates that phrase, hates its truthfulness more. "A few of them will be . . . not fine, I guess, but as fine as they can be. Anything tries to destroy them, they'll burn the world to take it down with them."

"Four months isn't much time."

"Less than four."

"Less than four," she agrees peaceably, not because the correction is important but because he's still raw, and she knows it. He should be less okay with that than he is. He's an FBI agent, damn it, and if he must be vulnerable he doesn't need anyone to see it.

"Did you ever think about it?" he asks suddenly.

"No." The answer is prompt, but not immediate. Not defensive, not reflexive. "Chavi was a very large part of my world, but she wasn't all of it. However heartbroken I was, and am, I was equally pissed off. That makes a difference, doesn't it?"

"Does it?"

"Even if it doesn't, other things do. My sister was taken from me. But I didn't lose my freedom. I didn't lose my identity. I didn't have a set day to die."

An expiration date, one of the Garden survivors calls it. Like a gallon of milk.

He can feel his shrimp lo mein churn in his stomach.

"I lost my sister. Your Butterflies lost themselves. There's a difference in that, at least."

"We knew she was going to do it. We warned her parents, begged them to let her get the help she was offered."

"Vic begged."

"And Ramirez," he says without shame, because begging isn't a thing he does.

He's always been better with suspects than with victims. Another thing that probably says more about him than it should.

"Knowing doesn't change how you feel once it happens."

But doesn't it? Then again, that's not a question she'll hold too close. The man who murdered her sister is still out there; even if they learn who he is, it won't bring Chavi back.

"So do I ever get to meet them?" she asks.

He blinks, almost pulls the phone away from his ear to stare at it. "Who?"

"The ones who'll set the world on fire if they have to burn. They sound like my kind of people."

It startles a laugh out of him. "Oh, they are, they—no. No, absolutely not, you are never allowed to meet them," he says sternly, brain catching up to the implications of that statement. Christ, Priya would get along with Inara and Bliss without question. Like a fucking house on fire. No.

Her soft huff of laughter, little more than a breath, eases some of that knot in his chest, and it's bizarre how he can feel simultaneously better and worse.

But for his own well-being, as well as the state of the world at large, he very much needs them to never meet.

Oh-shit-thirty Wednesday morning, I snap from sleep to panicked flailing as the bed drops out from beneath me. Or seems to. I bounce against the mattress, slapping at my eyes to get rid of the crust. My room is still dark, but there's enough light from the hallway to silhouette my mother, standing over my legs with her hands on her hips in a Superman pose. The bed frame creaks under her added weight.

I groan and flop back, yanking a pillow over my face. "What the hell, Mum?"

She laughs and drops down next to me. I can smell the coffee on her breath, warm and familiar on my neck, as she wraps an arm around me. "Just because you can stay in pajamas for class doesn't mean you can avoid getting up at a reasonable hour."

"Is it still dark outside?"

"Yes."

"Then it is not a reasonable hour."

Mum just laughs again and lifts the pillow to plant a kiss on my cheek. "Up, my love. I'll make you breakfast."

She does make amazing waffles. They might even be worth getting out of bed for.

Mum leaves for work right after breakfast, and I spend the rest of the morning trying to pummel my brain into thinking in French for math and science and history. So much history—it never occurred to me how US-centric even my world history classes were until I had to start playing catch-up to the kids I'll be in a classroom with this fall.

When my head starts aching from the language overload, I put everything away and bundle up in eight or ten layers to brave the world outside. It's a clear day, but cold. Oh my God, so cold.

Part of me wonders why the vets bother with the space heaters rather than going inside. It's still cold enough to freeze a tit off just outside the pavilion and they've got three different Starbucks in spitting distance, after all. But I'm not going to ask. This will be my first time actually playing with them, and I have to earn my place. It's the same with any group.

"Here, Blue Girl, you're playing with me today," announces the red-nosed Vietnam vet before I even get up onto the grass.

Some of the others snicker at the name, but it's apt enough. The bindi between my eyes is blue crystal set in silver, same as the stud at my right nostril, and as soon as I pull the knitted cap off, the royal-blue streaks in my hair are bright and clear. The one who named me blinks at the hair, then laughs like he's acknowledging a point.

"So what do I call you?" I ask, climbing over the bench.

"You call this ugly son of a bitch Corgi, you hear?" howls the man next to him, ignoring the elbow Corgi digs into his ribs. Their hats are identical, and I wonder how it must be to go through hell with someone and have each other to lean on after.

Well, a different kind of hell, anyway. Loss is loss, and my mother and I have each other, but we didn't come through their kind of war.

Some of the others introduce themselves while Corgi and I place our pieces—Steven and Phillip and Jorge, and next to Corgi, Happy, who may be a little bit drunk. The others are intent on their games. From what I suspect is his customary corner, Gunny gives me a small smile and a wave, then looks back to his game with the bland-faced man I spoke to last time.

As Corgi and I start to play, Happy and Jorge pay more attention to our game than to theirs, both of them coaching me with often conflicting advice. Except for Happy's initial outburst, they're on their best behavior, which is to say, they alternate between extreme and sometimes awkward courtesy and the kind of crassness that probably made their sergeants cry with pride back in the day. They stumble over apologies as soon as they remember I'm listening. But I laugh with them, and gradually they relax into something that must be closer to their usual dynamic, or at least as close as it can be with a female intrusion.

"I thought you said you loved to play," Corgi says suspiciously after his second easy victory.

"I didn't say I was good at it."

"Good thing," notes Jorge.

Dad was so genuinely bad at the game that losing to him was more challenging than beating most casual players. Once I realized other people were more likely to let me stay and play if I wasn't a threat to their pride? Well. Maybe part of me keeps the losing streak alive for Dad, but it's also a strange form of pragmatism. Playing to lose lets me keep playing without any kind of pressure or drama.

We reset the pieces for the next game, and Happy comes around the tables to take my place, threatening to beat Corgi black and blue for some perceived insult. Corgi's grinning.

Men say *I love you* in the strangest ways.

"Come play with me, Miss Priya," Gunny invites, nudging his pieces back into starting position.

Everyone rearranges, finding new partners and squabbling over colors. I take the nothing man's seat, but he just slides down one to face a (relatively) young Desert Storm vet who introduces himself as Yelp.

I managed not to ask with Corgi and Happy, but Yelp?

He grimaces, cheeks pink and stretched in a sheepish smile. "Got the name in Basic," he mumbles. "Sarge would sneak up behind and bellow orders in my ear. Jumped a foot damn near always. Named me Yelp."

And those kinds of names stick.

The nothing man looks at me with a small smile, but doesn't offer his name. I don't ask—there's something about him, and I don't want to risk him conflating courtesy with interest.

Gunny's focus on the game isn't great. He loses track of moves, forgets whose turn it is. Sometimes he gets caught up in a rambling story and doesn't realize he hasn't made his move yet. I don't try to remind him, unless he looks confused. To be honest, I'd much rather be hearing about him and his buddies getting blitzed on fine wine in an abandoned chateau and trying to teach a cow to ski. It's a little hard to picture this old man having that kind of energy, but he couldn't have been much older than me when he got shipped out.

Every now and then Yelp looks at our board and shakes his head, giving me a wry look. I shrug, but don't try to explain. My reasons are my own.

Gunny dozes off halfway through our second game. One of the Korea vets, who introduces himself as Pierce, drapes another blanket over the older man's shoulders, tucking it up under his chin and over his hands. "Store offered to let us use their café," he says gruffly, embarrassed, I think, by his own kindness. "Gunny said he's old, not dead, and we'll be out here or nowhere."

"Nothing wrong with a little pride," I reply. "At least not when you've got brothers to temper it with a bit of sense."

He blinks at me, startled, and then smiles.

"I should probably head out anyway. There's schoolwork I need to look over before tomorrow." I ease off the bench, stretching stiff, aching muscles. "I'll be back on Friday, if that's okay."

"Come on back whenever you want, Blue Girl," Pierce says. I have a feeling Gunny will be the only one to call me Priya. "You're welcome here."

A little bubble of warmth blooms beneath my sternum. I've been allowed into a number of chess groups over the years, but this is the first time I've been truly welcomed since Boston.

I fix my coat, pull my hat back on, and head across the parking lot into the Kroger to get a hot drink. The space heaters keep the pavilion comfortable, if a bit on the chilly side, but the walk back home is long enough I'd rather have cocoa to keep me company.

It's a pretty long line in the café, which seems to be the result of a new barista, working solo, trying to fill the constantly changing orders of a horde of older women in purple and red.

Is there a collective noun for the Red Hat Society ladies?

Next to the line, just a few feet away from me, someone settles into a chair, draping his heavy brown coat over the back of another chair. It's the nothing man from chess. He pulls a book from the pocket of the coat, a large paperback so battered and busted it's impossible to know what it is. The pages curl at the sides, the spine is cracked in too many places, and the front and back covers are gone. Just gone. He opens the book, but he's not looking at it.

He's looking at me. "A drink does sound just the thing."

Then why isn't he in line?

I shift my weight, sidling a few inches away. He's not even that close, really, it just feels invasive. And I probably shouldn't keep calling him *the nothing man*; that's the kind of thing that spills out by accident and causes problems. "I don't think I ever got your name."

"I don't think I ever gave it."

I shuffle forward as the line moves. One of the red-and-purple ladies is scolding, and the barista looks about to break down.

"It's cold outside," the man says after a little too long being silent.

"It's February in Colorado."

"It makes for a cold walk," he continues, either missing or ignoring the sarcasm. "Would you like a ride?"

"No, thank you."

"You like the cold?"

"I need the exercise."

I don't turn, but I can feel his eyes move down, then back up. "You don't, not really. You're fine as you are."

What the hell is wrong with people?

I move forward again, a little too far away for him to politely speak, and after another couple of minutes, up to the register. "Venti hot chocolate, please."

"And your name?"

"Jane." I pay, get my change, and slide along the counter to the pickup spot. The Red Hat ladies are flocked around the condiments bar, gradually migrating to a corner where they push all the tables together.

"Jean!" calls the barista. Close enough.

I wade through the last of the purple-and-red horde, doctor my drink, and start toward the door.

"It gets dark early; are you sure you don't want that ride?" offers the nothing man as I pass him.

"I'm sure, thank you."

"My name is Landon."

No, his name is Creep.

But I nod to acknowledge and walk off.

Creepy men are an unfortunate fact of life. I watched Chavi get harassed from a young age, and I had to put up with it myself even before I got walloped with the puberty stick. I've never seen anyone brave enough to be inappropriate to Mum, but I'm sure it happens. It probably just comes out in more subtle fashion.

There's only one surprise when I check the mail: a plain white envelope with a return address I don't recognize, but my info is written out in Vic's blocky print and the frank is from Quantico. Inside the house, I peel off layers and hang them in the front closet, then turn to the spindly, tile-topped table at the base of the stairs. A butterfly with open wings spans the four tiles, all soft, dreamy greens and purples, but it's almost completely covered with a circle of yellow silk chrysanthemums, a fat red candle, and a picture frame.

That's where Chavi lives now, in that frame and others like it. The frame is coated in gold glitter, worn away to the gold paint beneath in the upper left corner. The three of us spent a long time deciding which picture to put in there. We knew which one we wanted, which was the most quintessentially Chavi, but it was also the one the police and media used, the one that was plastered all over the Web and the papers and the posters asking if anyone had information. Eventually, we went with it anyway. It was Chavi.

It was her senior photo, and even against the standard mottled-grey background and the self-consciously awkward chin-on-fist pose, the things that make her *her* blaze out. There's a light in her eyes, framed with heavy black wings and shimmering white-and-gold shadows, with a bright slash of red at her mouth to match the streaks in her hair. Her bindi and nose stud were red and clear crystal, set in gold, bold and warm like the rest of her. Her skin was darker than mine, dark like Dad's, which just made the color stand out that much more. What made the photo most Chavi, though, was that she'd completely forgotten that was the day of her appointment. She'd spent the morning playing with a new box of oil pastels, then had to rush to get ready, and she managed to look flawless—save for the rainbow smear of pastels on the outside of the fist propping up her chin.

Digging out the box of matches from the tiny drawer under the tabletop, I light the red candle and lean over to kiss that worn corner. This is how we keep Chavi with us, part of our lives in a way that doesn't feel too clingy or creepy or crazy.

We don't have a picture up of Dad, but then, Chavi didn't choose to leave. Dad did.

Settling onto the couch, I turn the envelope over in my hands, looking for clues about the contents. I don't really like mystery mail; I got too much of it after Chavi died, people all over the country finding our address and sending us letters or cards or flowers. Hate mail, too; it's astonishing how many people feel the need to write complete strangers to tell them why their loved one "deserved" to die. Vic's handwriting is reassuring, but also strange. For anything more than a card, he usually warns me to keep an eye out for it.

And it is definitely not Vic's writing inside. The script matches the return address, the letters elegant but simple, easy to read. There isn't a greeting, just a launch straight into:

Victor Hanoverian tells me you know what it's like to put yourself back together after terrible things.

I do too, or I used to. Maybe I still do, for myself, but there are others now, and I'm not sure what to tell them, or how to help them. Not the way I used to know or be able to guess.

My name is Inara Morrissey, and I'm one of Vic's Butterflies.

Oh holy shit.

I glance over the rest of the letter, not even skimming so much as checking the handwriting to see if there's a note from Vic, something to indicate why he decided to mail this. Doesn't that break a rule or something? I know her name, of course—the Butterflies have been national news for almost four months now—but our cases are only connected through the agents. Isn't there some Bureau regulation about keeping things separate?

But then, Vic was careful, wasn't he? He didn't give my address to Inara; he mailed it himself. I don't have to reply, I don't have to give her my information. How does she even know about me, though?

I go back to where I left off.

I saw your picture on Eddison's desk a few weeks ago, and Eddison being the prickly bastard that he is, I was curious. I didn't think he even liked people. Vic was the one to tell me who you were, or rather, what you were, at least when they met you. He said you lost your sister to a serial killer, and my first thought was "Huh, me too."

I think that's the first time I ever called any of the girls my sister, and I was surprised by how much it hurt. To lose them again in a new way, maybe, or that I felt that way about them and I never said.

I'm not asking what happened to you. I know I could look it up, but I don't want to. To be honest, I'm far less interested in what happened to you than I am in what you chose to do after.

It was easy to be strong in the Garden. The others looked to me and I could let them because I knew how to tread water and I could hold them while they learned. We're out now, though, and they're looking to me to be as strong as I was in the Garden, and I don't know how to do that with everyone watching.

I don't know how to do any of this. I was always broken, and I was always okay with that. I was what I was. Now people are clamoring to see how I'll fix myself, and I don't want to fix myself. I shouldn't have to. If I want to stay broken, isn't that my choice?

When Vic mentions you, or just hears your name, he looks like it's one of his own girls being talked about. Eddison actually seems to like you, and I was fairly convinced he hated anything with a pulse. And Mercedes smiles, and looks a little sad, and I'm coming to understand that she'll smile at anyone, but she's only sad for the people she loves.

They adopted you, in their way, and now they've adopted me and I'm not entirely sure how to let them.

You don't have to write back. I find I can't talk to the other girls about any of this because they need me to seem stronger, and I don't want to let them down. But Vic smiled when I asked if it would be okay to write, so I'm hoping it's a better idea than it feels.

How do you put yourself back together when the pieces permanently lost are the only reasons anyone's looking at you?

Um.

She's asking me how to do something I'm not sure I've actually done. If I had to guess, that's exactly why Vic sent the letter: because she's right. We shouldn't have to fix ourselves if we don't want to. We shouldn't have to be strong or brave or hopeful or any such bullshit. Mum has always emphatically stated that it's okay to *not be okay*. We don't owe that to anyone else.

I need to sit on this for a few days.

When Mum comes home a few hours later, laptop bag and briefcase in one hand, bags of takeout in the other, I have my journal out, searching for a way to explain how much it meant when Pierce said I was *welcome* at the chess pavilion. "Get the plates?" she asks, leaning down to kiss the frame and almost lighting her scarf on fire. She drops the bags beside her, the takeout with more care than her computer.

She looks beautiful and fierce in her work clothes, the grey pencil skirt and blazer severely tailored and not much softened by the lavender silk blouse and patterned scarf. Her long hair is pulled back into a tight twist and pinned to within an inch of its life, and her heels are just high enough to be authoritative, just low enough to still kick your ass. The only things that seem out of place are the things that carry over with her to after-work, the emerald-and-gold bindi and nose stud, and the slim gold hoop curving over the middle of her lower lip.

Mum very purposefully left her family and most of her culture behind in London when we came to America twelve years ago, but she kept the bits she liked. Mostly she kept the things that kept people from assuming we were Muslim. Mum didn't much care if she was being somewhat sacrilegious as long as it kept her brown daughters safe. The bindi, the jewelry, the mehndi when we do it, they're all supposed to have more weight than we give them.

I get up and get the plates and silverware. After bringing the takeout bag into the living room, I head back and grab a couple glasses of milk and some clean Tupperware. I wait, though, to let Mum dish out. It's that self-control thing. I just feel better letting her control the portions.

She comes back downstairs in yoga pants and a loose, long-sleeved T-shirt that used to have the logo of Chavi's high school printed across the front. You can still see bits of it, if you squint and already know what it's supposed to say. The rest is faded and peeled and comfortably worn. Her hair is out of its pins, twisted into a haphazard braid down her back. This is the Mum who likes to bury her fingers in soil and help things grow, who's always been as quick as her daughters to launch a pillow fight.

Plopping down onto the carpet so we can treat the coffee table like an actual table, she reaches out for the boxes and starts dishing out.

Orange shrimp and lo mein noodles for her, sweet-and-sour chicken and white rice for me, each meal split about evenly between the plates and the Tupperware containers. She parcels out the sack of egg rolls but doesn't try to separate the bowls of soup—wonton for me and egg drop for her. Takeout soup just doesn't reheat well enough to bother. Tomorrow, we'll both have the leftovers for lunch and some other kind of takeout for dinner.

Most of the kitchen is still in boxes, something that is unlikely to change in the coming weeks. Cooking is just not a thing that's going to happen.

"How was chess?" she asks around a shrimp.

"It was good. I'm looking forward to going back."

"Get a good feeling from everyone?"

"Almost everyone." Her gaze sharpens on me, but I shrug and bite into a piece of sauce-covered chicken. "I'll avoid the exception."

"You'll take your pepper spray just in case?"

"It's on my keys. Outer pocket of the coat."

"Good."

We eat in silence for a while, but it's not awkward or uncomfortable, just a way to let the day process and filter out so we can enjoy the evening. Eventually she turns on the TV to a news channel and mutes it, skimming the headlines on the ticker and under the inset photos. When we're done eating, we both stand to clear the table. She grabs the leftovers and trash, and I take the plates and silverware. We have a dishwasher, currently blocked off by two stacks of boxes, but there's not really a reason to use it, not for only two of us. I rinse and wash everything and pop it on the drying rack next to the sink.

Mum settles back onto the carpet after, turning on the Xbox and a Lego game. I curl into the couch with my current journal.

For a long time, the only words on the page are *Dear Chavi*.

Chavi started the journals even before I was born. She took plain composition books and decorated the covers, and started writing me letters so she could prepare her baby sister for life. When I got old enough to learn how to write and start keeping my own journals, it just made sense to write back to her. We didn't exactly read each other's books. Sometimes we'd copy out sections or entries for the other, or read a bit aloud. We used to sit next to each other on one bed or another and write after Dad shooed us to bed—because if Dad was tired, we must all be tired—and I can't even think how many times I fell asleep with my face on the page and a pen in hand, and woke up to my sister tucking me in next to her.

"Are we leaving Chavi behind?" I ask suddenly.

Mum pauses the game and looks over her shoulder at me. After a moment, she sets the controller on the table and leans against the couch.

"Going to France," I clarify. "Are we leaving her behind?"

"Did we leave her behind when we left Boston?"

Her ashes are in a subdued urn that looks a bit more like a wine tube than anything else. Dad insisted we keep it on the mantel, but Mum and I keep it packed away, waiting for France and the chance to spread the ashes in lavender fields. Not that Chavi ever asked for that, because how many seventeen-year-olds have to think of funerary wishes, but it feels appropriate. She loved excursions to the Loire Valley when we used to visit, back when we lived in London.

But Chavi isn't really her ashes. She's more her photo in our chrysanthemum-and-candle shrine than she is her ashes, but it's still not . . .

"Is France going to be home?"

"Ah. Now it takes shape." Twisting around to face me, Mum wraps her arm around my ankles so she can comfortably rest her chin on my fuzzy socks. "We've had houses since Chavi died, but we haven't really had home, have we?"

"You're home."

"And always will be," she says easily. "But that's a person. You're talking about a place."

"Is it selfish?"

"Oh, sweetheart, no." Her thumb rubs the hollow behind my anklebone. "Losing Chavi was terrible. That wound will be with us, always. I know we've been in a bit of a holding pattern, with all the moves, but when we settle in France, can you even imagine how pissed she'll be if we don't make our home there? If we always make ourselves feel transient?" Her chin digs into the top of my foot. "Five years ago, it would have been impossible to imagine a life without Chavi in it."

"But that's our life now."

"But that's our life now," she agrees. "And once we're in a place for longer than five months, once a place is ours, we owe it to ourselves and to your sister to really make it ours. To make it home. It's a terrifying thought, isn't it?"

I nod, the world blurry.

"We love her; that means that it isn't possible for us to leave her behind."

I nod again.

"There's something else." When I don't answer immediately, Mum walks two fingers up my leg until she can poke the ticklish spot near my knee. "Priya."

"Another girl is going to die this spring," I whisper, because it seems a terrible thing to say out loud. "He'll kill again, because as long as they don't catch him, there's no reason for him not to keep going. So how do you make a man stop killing?"

"Personally? String him up by his balls and skin him with a dull, rusty knife. I hear the police frown on that, though."

And maybe that's the thing still niggling at me about Inara's letter. Everything about the Garden is caught up in a media shit storm, and that's not going to change anytime soon. Everyone has an opinion, everyone has a theory. Everyone has their own notion of what justice means. I used to think I wanted nothing more than to see Chavi's murderer get arrested, but the older I get, the more I see the appeal of Mum's more straightforward approach.

So what does that make me?

The morning of the funeral, Eddison picks Ramirez up from her tiny house (which she insists is properly called a cottage) and drives over to Vic's place. It's obscenely early, the sky not even grey yet, but it's a long drive to the Kobiyashis' home in North Carolina. He parks on the curb so he doesn't block in Vic or either of the Mrs. Hanoverians.

The front door opens before they even get to the porch. Mrs. Hanoverian the elder, Vic's mother, steps back to let them inside. "Look at you two," she sighs. "Crows, the both of you."

"It's a funeral, Marlene," Ramirez reminds her, dropping a kiss on her cheek.

"When I eventually kick it, none of you are allowed to wear black. I'm writing it into my will." She closes the door and tugs Eddison down by his coat so she can kiss his cheek. It's only been an hour since he shaved, so for once he isn't stubbled and scruffy. "Good morning, dear. Come into the kitchen and have some breakfast."

It's on the tip of his tongue to say no—he doesn't like eating this early; it just sits in his stomach and makes him feel ill—but Marlene Hanoverian had her own bakery until she decided to retire, and he'd have to be much more stupid than he is to turn away anything she's made.

They walk into the kitchen and he stops short, staring at the already occupied table. Two young women, both eighteen, look back at him. One of them twitches her lips in acknowledgment. The other grins and flips him the bird. Both have cinnamon rolls dripping with icing on small plates before them.

He's not sure why he's shocked. Of course some of the other sur-vivors might want to be present for the funeral. While it would be too traumatic for some, he can well imagine some might come purely to see their fellow former captive safely lowered into the ground, rather than preserved in glass and resin in the Garden's hallways like most of the others had been.

"Morning," he says warily.

"Vic offered us a ride," says the taller one. Inara Morrissey—he seems to recall hearing that the name change is official now—wears a deep red dress that should probably clash with her golden-brown color-ing but doesn't. She looks elegant, and entirely too put together for this early in the morning. "We took the train down yesterday."

They live in New York now. Well, Inara did before she was kid-napped. Bliss lived in Atlanta, and moved in with Inara and the various other roommates as soon as she was out of custody. The rest of her family migrated to Paris for her father's job, and if Eddison occasionally wonders whether or not that particular set of relationships is mending, he's not going to poke the bear by asking.

He knows he shouldn't call her Bliss—that was the name the Gardener gave her, and it's both painful and wildly inaccurate—but he can't call her Chelsea. Chelsea is such a normal name, and Bliss is such a hellion. Until she tells him otherwise, she's Bliss. She's tiny, barely coming to Inara's shoulder even when they're seated. Her wild black curls are caught back in combs and she's wearing a bold blue dress a few shades richer than her almost violet eyes.

He's not surprised that neither of them is wearing black. He knows they don't avoid it in general. Both are fairly well-adjusted (though he sometimes has his doubts about Bliss) and both work at a restau-rant that requires them to wear it. Their only clothing in the Garden, however, was black. Black, and open-backed to show their wings. To honor one of their own, they would never choose it. He just hopes the Kobiyashis won't think it's rude.

45

But then, Bliss *is* rude. It's not the first time she's said hello by flipping him off.

"Is anyone else coming?" he asks, exercising healthy caution by letting Ramirez slide in first on the curved bench seat. He can respect the hell out of both girls for coming through what they did more or less intact, but he's never quite sure if he likes them. That ambiguity is entirely mutual. Any time he can keep at least one person between him and them, he does so, and doesn't feel like a coward for it.

"Danelle and Marenka might," Inara answers, licking icing off one finger. Small remnants of discoloration on the backs of her hands mark the worst of the burns and gashes from the night the Garden exploded. "They hadn't decided yet when we spoke to them on Wednesday."

"They're worried the Kobiyashis will be assholes to them," adds Bliss. When Ramirez glances at her, questioning, Bliss draws the shape of a butterfly over her face.

Both agents shudder.

Because somehow, the case kept getting worse. Some girls, either because they were already broken or because they thought it might help them escape, had cozened up to their captor, and he'd mark them with his favor by tattooing another set of wings on their faces, to match the ones on their backs. Everyone else could cover up their wings, once they were out of the Garden. Danelle and Marenka, the only survivors to have gotten that second set of wings, have to rely on a hell of a lot of good makeup.

Even with the smaller sets on their faces covered, those who know they're there treat the girls differently. Treat them worse, as if sucking up to try to stay alive longer makes them evil.

He hopes they decide against coming. He actually likes Danelle and Marenka, both of them calm and steady and less sharp-edged than Inara and Bliss. Better for them to grieve Tereza—Amiko, he reminds himself, her name is Amiko—without her parents being hateful.

Marlene sets plates before him and Ramirez, then pours out mugs of coffee. Despite the hour and the fact that she's not going to the funeral, she's fully dressed, a single strand of pearls soft and prim against her dark green sweater set. "That poor girl," she says. "At least she's at peace now."

That rather depends on what you believe, doesn't it? Ramirez touches the crucifix at her throat and doesn't say anything. Inara and Bliss both take over-large bites of pastry, chewing to keep from speaking.

Eddison's not really sure what he believes when it comes to death or suicide or any of that.

Vic comes into the kitchen then, adjusting the knot on his dark brown tie. Eddison and Ramirez are both dressed for a funeral; Vic is dressed for a Butterfly's funeral, in brown and ivory somber enough to be respectful to grieving parents and far enough from black to be comforting to survivors. It's exquisitely sensitive and intuitive and a number of other adjectives Eddison is decidedly not, even on his best days.

"Sit down and eat, Victor," his mother tells him.

He kisses the top of her head, safely away from the tidy coils of silver hair that have been pinned in place. "We have to head out, Ma, it's almost—"

"Victor, you will sit and eat and start this terrible day off right."

He sits.

Inara covers her mouth with one hand, but her pale brown eyes are bright. She's a very contained young woman, restrained in expression around most. The survivors are somewhat exceptions, but he has a feeling she's only truly relaxed around the girls she lives with. "Mrs. Hanoverian, please tell me you used to write notes in his school lunches."

"Let's see, Mondays I told him to make good choices; Tuesdays I told him to make me proud; Wednesdays I told him . . ." But she trails off, smiling as the girls dissolve into almost silent laughter, leaning against each other.

"And you doubted me," Vic chides around a mouthful of cinnamon roll.

It's strange to be laughing before they head out to a seventeen-year-old's funeral. Sixteen. Her birthday would have been in a few weeks.

Inara catches his eye and shrugs. "You laugh or you cry. Which would you rather do?"

"Yell," he says succinctly.

"Me too," Bliss replies, teeth bared in a snarl. A bit of cinnamon-heavy bread is caught between two of her teeth.

He figures Inara will eventually tell her about it.

The seven-hour drive to North Carolina is quiet, but not silent. Ramirez stretches out in the very back seat, because if she's a passenger without paperwork to keep her busy, she will fall asleep before the next exit, every time. Inara and Bliss sit in the middle, the radio turned down to allow conversation with Vic in the driver's seat. Eddison listens but doesn't particularly contribute. Most of his attention is on his phone, skimming through Google alerts for bodies found in churches. It's a little early in the year yet for Chavi's murderer to strike again, but he checks regularly, just in case.

Bliss is taking classes, filling in gaps in her education so she can take her GED this summer. Neither she nor Inara has decided yet about college, it seems. He gets it. If they know what they want to do—and he doesn't think they do—why throw themselves into it now when they know the eventual trial is going to take up so much time? They're already down in D.C. fairly frequently to answer more questions in pretrial. They'll both be called to testify if the case gets to the courtroom before they're eighty, and Inara has already promised the other girls she'll be there when they take their turns on the stand.

No matter how often he hears proof of Inara as housemother, he still can't wrap his brain around it. It's like a pit bull in a tutu.

A Butterfly with boxing gloves.

After two stops for gas and a meal, they pull up to the church for the funeral. There aren't many cars in the parking lot.

"Are we early?" Ramirez asks groggily, reaching for her purse so she can fix her makeup.

"A little," Vic answers.

Ramirez isn't awake enough, but Eddison hears the layer tucked into the simple words: Vic doesn't expect there to be many people.

Bliss releases her seat belt with a click and a heavy thunk of the latch hitting the door. "Told you. The Kobiyashis are assholes. They probably wouldn't hold a funeral at all if the suicide hadn't hit the news."

Eddison glances back at Inara, who knew Tereza better than Bliss did, but she's looking out the window at the white-boarded church.

They all get out of the car and stretch, and Vic takes Bliss's hand and hooks it around his elbow as they walk ahead to the double doors. Part of it is manners—Marlene raised a gentleman—but Eddison's willing to bet a month's pay that Vic's hoping to keep a leash on Bliss's idea of small talk. Ramirez double-checks her face in the tinted window and hurries after.

Eddison's in no hurry. He leans against the side of the car, looking up at the Baptist church. Except for the space in front of the doors, the building is lined with thick, dark shrubs in beds of reddish mulch. There's extra space in front of the shrubs, a stretch of pine chips before the faded grass picks up. Flower beds? The church probably looks rather charming that way, all abloom, but that makes him think of the Garden, of how he's told it looked before the explosions, and fuck, is there anything this case doesn't touch?

He's gone to more funerals than he can count, and yet every single one is just . . .

Inara settles next to him against the car, hands clasped at her waist. A black-and-gold wristlet dangles from her hooked pinky. "You don't *have* to be here, you know."

"Yes, I—" But he stops, swallows back the reflexive indignation, because this is Inara. Inara, who always means what she says, but usually not in the way you first expect.

And he realizes that no, he doesn't *have* to be here. There's no Bureau requirement, no order, no generally agreed guideline, nothing official that mandates his presence at the funeral of a girl who killed herself because the seams where she broke the first time were too fragile to stitch together a second time. It's his personal code that has him here, his principle that keeps him facing terrible things because it's the right thing to do.

It's his choice.

He looks over at her, unsurprised to find her watching him, her thoughts on the matter neatly tucked away and impossible to read. That's not something she learned in the Garden, or after. That's always been her life. "Thank you."

"Careful, Eddison," she teases, her hands lifting in mock surrender. "Someone might hear and think you almost like me."

"Almost," he agrees, just to see her startled smile.

He doesn't offer her his arm, and she doesn't expect it. They push off from the car and walk together into the church, shoulders tight with the shared awareness that this almost certainly won't be the last Butterfly funeral, but it might be the worst.

For Inara, it might be the worst funeral, full stop, but Eddison is far too aware that spring is coming. Whoever killed Chavi Sravasti and so many other girls will kill again, responding to triggers the FBI can't name, and Eddison will stand next to Vic and Ramirez at yet another funeral and feel like a terrible person, because he'll be grateful it isn't Priya.

I've had five years for the reality of Chavi's death to seep into my bones, but that doesn't keep the memories from bleeding sometimes, doesn't prevent the nightmares that wake me in a sweat, throat raw from screaming. I don't know that anything will ever actually stop them.

Mum wakes me with a firm shake, her arms around me before I can open my eyes, before I can properly recall that I'm safe, in my bed in our rental house in Huntington, far away from the neighborhood church outside of Boston where I last saw my sister. The nightmares don't fall into any sort of pattern—there's no way to guess what will trigger one—but they happen often enough that we've developed a routine for dealing with them.

While I take a cool shower, Mum strips my bed of sweat-damp sheets and heads downstairs to the laundry room. When she comes back, two mugs of tea in her hands, I'm already in fresh pajamas and settled in her bed. Neither of us wants me alone after one of these dreams, but I won't sleep again and I don't want her to lose sleep staying up with me, so this is our compromise. We pop in a DVD and Mum is out cold halfway through the first episode of one of the BBC Nature programs.

I brought my journal to Mum's room, but I'm not really feeling it. There are years of nightmares across dozens of journals; telling Chavi about another one won't help anything.

Maybe telling someone else might.

Inara's letter sticks out from the top of the notebook, where it's been living for the past week. Maybe I finally know how to answer it.

Dear Inara,

My sister Chavi died on a Monday, two days after my twelfth birthday. She was seventeen.

We spent all weekend celebrating my birthday. Saturday we spent at the nearby park. Technically it was a churchyard, but the church was tangled in taxes and repossession, and our neighborhood just sort of . . . took it over. Everything was blooming, and the day was filled with laughter and games and food. Not everyone in the neighborhood got along, but most did. Sunday was for family, for favorite meals and movies. Our only trip out was when Mum and Chavi took me to the mall to get my nose pierced.

Dad stayed behind in protest. My parents were both born in India and raised in London, and he always argued that leaving behind a community of culture meant giving up the signs of it, too.

Monday, though, we were back to school. Usually, Chavi would bike from the senior high to the junior, and we'd head home together, but I had a yearbook meeting and she had a study group. Chavi had more freedom than a lot of her friends and classmates, mostly because she didn't abuse it. She let Mum know when she arrived or left places, always updated her if plans, locations, or people changed. Always.

When Chavi texted to say she'd be home by nine, we had every reason to expect she would be, but nine o'clock came and went, and Chavi didn't.

Ten o'clock came and went, and Chavi didn't.

She didn't answer texts or calls, and that just wasn't Chavi.

Mum called the others in the study group, but they all said the same thing: she left the coffee shop around eight, biking the same direction as always. One of the boys offered her a ride, but she said no. Chavi always said no when he offered her something, because he had a crush on her and she didn't feel the same way. Dad laughed at Mum and me for worrying. Chavi was just being a teenager, he said, and when she got home, she'd be grounded and she wouldn't ever do it again. That wasn't Chavi, though.

The disc menu pops up on the television, tinkling music on a twenty-second loop. Rather than get up to change the disc, I hit "play all" again. I take a moment to shake out my hand, rubbing out the cramps starting to form.

Chavi going missing is easy to talk about. What followed is less so.

But Inara's nightmares are out there for the world to see; until the next girl dies, mine are on the page only for her. I can do this.

Mum called the police. The dispatcher listened and agreed it was out-of-character behavior, and started asking questions. Where was she last seen? What was she wearing? What color was her bike? Could we email a recent photo? We lived outside of Boston back then. Chavi was off to college in the fall, but she was still seventeen, so she was still a child. The dispatcher said one officer would come to the house, in case Chavi came back, but others would be out looking.

By then, Dad was pissed. At Chavi, for making people worry. At Mum, for causing such a fuss. At me, even, for insisting on going out with Mum to search. I missed most of their argument, because Mum sent me upstairs to dress in something warmer, but when I came down, the newly arrived officer was standing in the doorway looking profoundly uncomfortable while Mum told Dad to stay and wait if he couldn't be bothered to break a sweat for his missing child.

You don't fuck with Mum.

It was late enough that none of the patrol cars had their sirens on. Their lights flashed, though, and it brought neighbors out of their houses and more people joined the search. It's something to see, really, everyone throwing coats over nightclothes and pairing off with flashlights and whistles.

Josephine—Chavi's best friend and girlfriend, though most only knew the first bit—went toward the school to look. Her mother had to hold the flashlight because Josephine was shaking too much. She knew the same thing Mum and I did: Chavi would never just go off or stay out.

Mum and I went to the church. It hadn't actually been a church since just after we moved there, but everyone still called it that. A few members of the former congregation even donated a salary for Frank, the Desert Storm vet who lived in a studio at the back of the lot and kept everything up. One of the side doors was always unlocked in case of bad weather or a need for shelter. Maybe Chavi had fallen from her bike and couldn't get all the way home. Maybe her hypothetical fall had broken her phone, so she couldn't call for help.

We looked through the park first, but when she turned toward the trees at the back of the property, Mum told me to wait by the church. Whenever the weather got warm, transients started camping there overnight, so she didn't want me back there even with her. She told me again to wait, promised she'd wake up Frank so she wasn't alone.

I didn't follow her, but I also didn't wait. Couldn't wait, not if there was a chance my sister was inside that building. It didn't occur to me for a second that it could be dangerous. The church was safe, not because of any religious sensibility but because it was always safe. Chavi and I were always safe there.

We could spend hours at a time there on sunny days. She'd sit on the floor, sketch pad on one knee, puddles of colored light on the grey stone around her. We were so in love with the stained-glass windows. She kept saying she couldn't get the drawings right, and she'd try again and again and again, and I'd stand off to one side with my camera to capture the dust that danced in the sunbeams, the color on the stone, the way the light and motes made Chavi glitter.

On the good days, that's the Chavi I see when I close my eyes: light and color and glitter.

I push "play" again on the disc menu and press my hand flat against the blanket, willing it to stop shaking.

I can do this.

I don't even have to send it, if it's too overwhelming. But I can finish this. How many times has Inara had to tell her story to strangers?

She was out in the open in the T of space between the altar and the discolored portions of floor where the pews used to be. She was stark naked, but my mind latched less on to the fact that she was nude—she was my sister, I'd seen her naked before—than on the fact that her clothes were neatly folded and stacked on top of her backpack a few feet away. Chavi might as well have been allergic to folding her clothes for as often as she did it. But seeing how utterly clean her favorite shirt was made me realize how much blood was on the floor around her, and I dropped to my knees beside her, pushing at her to wake up, please, wake up. I was still screaming.

I'd never seen so much blood before.

I didn't hear Frank come in but suddenly he was there, half-dressed and carrying a paint gun. He took one look at Chavi, turned grey, and whirled around in a wild circle. Looking for whoever did it, I realized much later. Then his arm came around me and he tried to tug me away. I think I remember him speaking? I've never been sure.

But I wasn't going to leave. I fought his grip, and truthfully he was too shocked to put much strength behind it. I was still screaming at Chavi, poking at the ticklish spot on her ribs because she could never sleep through that, and she still didn't move.

There was a sound at the door, followed by Mum's yell, my name sharp and shrill and scared, and Frank ran to her. He kept her from coming in, physically barring the way, and he begged her, weeping, to call me to her. Just call me away from Chavi.

I'll never forget the flowers around Chavi, and in her hair: yellow chrysanthemums like suns.

You know how big news tragedies or events have that one pivotal, iconic photograph? So that years or even decades later, people can instantly recognize the picture?

When a reporter broke the story, they didn't have a picture of Chavi's body, just a yearbook shot and whatever they could find on Facebook. So they used a photo of me.

Twelve years old and covered in blood, still screaming and sobbing, and reaching for the church—for my sister—as a grim-faced paramedic carried me away. For months, that picture was everywhere. I couldn't escape it, and it crops up again every spring when another girl dies with the flowers and a slit throat and someone calls the FBI with the theory that it's the same guy.

I wasn't there when they told Dad. It must have been the officer waiting at the house. Dad came to the hospital, where a doctor gave me a mild sedative against the shock, and he moved so slowly, like his whole body ached. Like he'd aged centuries. He'd laughed at our worries.

I don't think I ever heard him laugh again.

Chavi died, declared the official report, between nine and ten Monday night.

The rest of our family died around midnight, only it took a while to know for sure. Mum and I were phoenixes, rising in our own way. Dad just burned and burned until he didn't.

The public steals tragedies from victims. It sounds strange, I know, but I think you may be one of the few people who'll understand what I mean by that. These things happened to us, to our loved ones, but it hits the news and suddenly everyone with a TV or computer feels like they're entitled to our reactions and recoveries.

They're not. It takes a while to really believe it, but you owe them nothing.

Our agents are good at adopting strays, but we don't actually have to let them. They make the overtures, sure, but we're the ones who allow it to become a real thing. There's comfort in that, in knowing we can at any moment choose to walk away and they will absolutely let us.

There's more comfort in realizing we want to stay, that this is a good thing we're allowed to have.

That we're allowed to be happy.

I'm still working on that, but in the meantime? We're allowed to be broken. We don't have to feel ashamed of that.

Write back, if you'd like. I don't know that I have any wisdom to impart, but your letters are welcome.

She's only a year and a half older than me.

I guess it isn't the years that matter.

Hours later, when Mum leaves for work, I retreat back to my room and wrap myself in my comforter like a burrito. I don't sleep exactly, just sort of drift until my bladder is bursting and shrieking at me to get out of bed, and it's probably for the best if I don't crawl back under the covers. Hunger curls and crawls low in my belly. The thought of eating is . . . worrisome.

I know this mood. If I start eating, I won't stop. Not even when I'm full and stretching and pained, because that kind of pain makes more sense than this grief and rage that bleed under my skin.

I shower and dry my hair, make a note to ask Mum to refresh the streaks because there's almost half an inch of root growth, and draw on eyeliner and lipstick with a heavy hand. Chavi taught me all the small tricks that make the difference between a challenge and a tease and a snarl. She always fell somewhere between challenge and tease, softened with shimmering white and gold powders. I usually brush on silver and white, but not today. Today is black and red and about as pissed off as you'd expect from that.

Once I'm dressed and I'm sure I've got the pepper spray easily accessible in my outer coat pocket, I leave the house for the chess island. The air's so dry it hurts, and I have the feeling I'll be using the tissues in the other pocket for a nosebleed sometime in the next couple of hours.

When I walk up onto the dead grass, Corgi looks up and whistles, soft and impressed. "You really do belong with us, don't you, Blue Girl?" At my smile, sharp and brittle, he nods. "Come on, then. Happy hasn't had a victory in weeks. Let him live up to his name."

So I sit down opposite Happy, who looks sober and haunted, and play until he claims he's pulled so far ahead of Corgi in their never-ending tally of victories that his friend will never catch up.

Corgi's a good player, even against people who know what the shit they're doing. If the tally is anything honest, Happy hasn't got a chance.

But Corgi smiles, scratches the side of his nose, and says Happy shouldn't sit too easy.

Landon starts with Yelp, down on the far end of the tables from me. When he shuffles down to take Steven's challenge, it puts him next to me. I'd more or less decided to give him the benefit of the doubt going forward, and assume that he doesn't mean to be creepy. Maybe he doesn't even realize he's doing it. I'm just not going to engage.

Today, though, I'd really like to pepper spray him on principle, so I should probably go back to the instinctive plan of avoid, avoid, avoid.

Bracing my hand on Corgi's shoulder, I clamber over the bench and stretch out the kinks and aches of sitting in the cold. "Come on, Corgi, show me how it's done."

He and Happy give me nearly identical grins, and he scoots over to take my empty seat. I hover over his shoulder for a while, watching the beginning of the game—I can tell by the fifth move that Happy is going to lose—until the men at the other end shuffle around. It's easy to casually plop down across from Pierce, who tends to stay close enough to Gunny to keep an eye on the old man.

I play Pierce for a couple of games, then Yelp for one while Gunny naps into his hands in the corner. The girl in the car—Hannah, I learned my second day, Gunny's youngest granddaughter—comes up once to check on him. She has a blood sugar strip in her fingers, and she slides her hand up under his sleeves to get the stick from his forearm. The device in her other hand is barely the size of an egg, but it reads the bloodied strip and gives her a number, which she notes into her phone.

I like Hannah, I think. Not that I've gotten to know her—she tends to stay in the car except when it's time to test Gunny's blood sugar—but because she never acts like this is a chore or an imposition. She bundles up and waits with her knitting or a book, occasionally looking up toward the pavilion to check on Gunny, and she seems to enjoy the other vets. They call her Miss Gunny, and she just rolls her eyes and tells me sensible people call her Hannah.

When Gunny wakes up with a start, he looks at me, his face still soft with sleep. "In the trenches today, Miss Priya?"

"Yes, sir. It happens sometimes."

"It does." He turns the board sideways so he can reach between the ranks of pieces. My heavy gloves are in my pocket, but it's still cold enough that I've got a pair of knit arm warmers over most of my hand. I give it to him anyway, his skin coarse and paper-fine as his fingers close around mine. "You're too young to stay there, though."

He's not asking. If I don't want to tell him, I absolutely don't have to, and he will not hold it against me in the slightest.

But Frank's on my mind, Frank who had a hard time coming home after his war but was always unfailingly generous and wanted to help. Some days he couldn't really deal with people, and that was fine, we let him be those days. He had a lot of those days after that night in the church.

"My sister was murdered a while back," I whisper, hoping his ears are still sharp enough that I won't have to repeat myself. Yelp and Jorge are focused on their game next to us. "I found her. Last night was a bit more . . . more present than past."

He nods and gives my hand a gentle squeeze. "And now that you're awake?"

"It's still a bad day."

"But you came out."

"All of you know that kind of bad day, or you wouldn't be here, either."

He smiles, his entire face disappearing in crinkles and wrinkles and folds. "Thank you for coming on a bad day."

I stay long enough to have a complete game with Gunny, then head into the store to get a drink for the way home. Landon follows me in.

Yay.

He stands behind me in line, and my discomfort ratchets up to anger when I realize I've got my thumb on the trigger for the pepper spray, my fingers wrapped around the leather case. I don't like feeling vaguely endangered. I want a specific threat, something I can point to and say *this* and everyone understands, not a number of impressions that make women nod and men shake their heads.

"You look sad today," he says eventually.

"I'm not."

Sadness and grief aren't the same thing. It's why they have different words. Maybe it's a subtle distinction, but we don't keep a word in a language if it doesn't still have a purpose of its own. Synonyms are never exact things.

"Are you sure?" he asks, stepping almost beside me.

"Yes."

"It's getting dark outside."

"Yes." And it is this time, the sky streaking indigo and the temperature dropping. I stayed later than I meant to, but it helped. The vets all helped, but I think I needed Gunny to reassure me that I wasn't bringing them a burden.

"You shouldn't be walking home all alone in the dark."

I turn toward him a little and smile, too many teeth and not enough sweetness. "I'm fine."

"There are bad people in the world."

"I'm aware."

I was only sort of aware of that before I was twelve. I don't think I'll ever be able to forget it.

The sparrow woman behind the counter doesn't ask for my name this time. She just takes my payment and starts making the hot chocolate, adding more syrup than she's probably supposed to.

"What if someone hurts you?" Landon presses, following me to the other end of the counter without ordering a drink.

Eddison sometimes jokes about getting me a Taser for my birthday. I'm starting to think I should take him up on it.

I ignore Landon and accept my drink from the barista, whose name tag is always hidden under her apron. I don't bother to add vanilla or sugar this time, preferring the bitterness to continued interaction. But he still follows me between the tables, and my keys—and my pepper spray—are now outside my pocket.

Then I hear him yelp, and turn around to see him dripping with what used to be a large, very hot coffee, most of it up near his face and the open neck of his heavy shirt. Another man, taller and in a cable-knit sweater, apologizes profusely but in a way that sounds just a little insincere. He brushes at Landon's shirt with a tiny napkin that soaks up nothing.

"I've got it!" snarls Landon, and stalks away still dripping.

The other man turns to me and smiles, and I can place him now, a handsome guy who sits in the corner with a book and sometimes a stack of paperwork. He's probably in his upper thirties, well put together without seeming vain about it, and he's not trying to hide the way his dark auburn hair is silvering at the temples. "I'm sorry, but he seemed to be bothering you."

I let my hand slide back into my pocket, hiding the pepper spray from sight, but don't let go of it quite yet. "He was."

He pulls a handful of actual napkins from his pocket and kneels down to sop up what coffee didn't cling to Landon. Rubbing another napkin over his hands to dry them, he pulls out his wallet and holds a card. "I recently designed the website for a shuttle service here in town. It's mostly to help homebound folks to the store or doctors or other errands. If you ever feel uncomfortable, think about giving them a call."

It's a straightforward card, a simple logo centered along the top with the information printed neatly below. It includes a phone number and website, something I can at least research.

"Tell them Joshua sent you," he adds.

"Thank you. I'll keep it in mind." I let go of my keys to take the card, tucking it into my opposite pocket with the tissues. I glance around for Landon, but he must still be in the bathroom or wherever he stalked off to, so I nod in place of goodbye and walk off.

I'll have Mum check out the card later. It might be a good number to know if the weather turns while I'm out. There's a bus system on the other side of town, but it doesn't stop near enough to home to be useful, and a cab seems a little too self-indulgent.

I take a different way home than normal, my hand back on the pepper spray, and look around me before entering the neighborhood. Mum taught us caution from a young age, and she's worked to make sure good sense doesn't turn to paranoia. I've got a strong instinct for creeps, but she's better at deciding whether or not to trust a good thing.

To make myself feel better, once my nose is unthawed I dig out Special Agent Ken from the suitcase where he usually lives and set him up against the window in the breakfast nook with a tiny plastic coffee mug. The snow outside is old and will probably be gone in a couple more days, but the street lights reflect rather nicely off of it, and it makes Special Agent Ken look about as wistful as a male Barbie can manage. He's in the tiny version of the ugly Christmas sweater Mum and I sent Eddison last year, and the tiny one is actually a lot less ugly. There's not enough space for the horrific details.

I snap a couple of shots with my camera, so I'll have a good photo for later, but I take one with my phone, too, and send it to Eddison.

Half an hour later, when I'm back in my pajamas and ready to dig into schoolwork for the couple of hours before Mum gets home with dinner, I get a message back.

He wouldn't think that white shit's so pretty if he'd ever had to walk in it.

It makes me laugh, something I know I don't do enough anymore. Eddison's breed of comfort may be strange—and not at all comforting to most—but it's familiar, acknowledging the bad day without pressing.

I used to wonder if the Quantico Three catching Chavi's killer would end the nightmares. Now I think it won't matter, that the nightmares will always be mine.

Eddison should be headed home. He's already left the office, after an overlong day of sifting through paperwork and assessing new information from the ongoing investigation into the Garden and the MacIntosh family's crimes. He can feel the dull heaviness in his bones, somewhere beyond tired but not quite to exhausted.

It's not the hours, or even the deadening boredom of the paperwork that fatigues him so. It's the content.

Some days it's just a job. Other days . . . there are reasons so many good agents burn out. Most do, eventually.

He should be heading home, to rest, to fill his head with something other than images of dead girls in glass and resin. Instead, fresh coffee in hand from the shop down the block, he walks back to the FBI building and takes the elevator to his floor. It's quiet there, the sea of cubicles empty except for one man snoring softly. It's tempting to wake him up, but he's got a pillow stuffed between his head and his desk, a blanket draped over his shoulders and chair like a cape.

You don't prepare like that for sleeping at your desk unless there's a reason you can't go home. Eddison leaves him alone, and spares a hopeful thought that the poor bastard can work it out, whatever the problem is.

From the back corner of his desk, he grabs the stack of colorful folders that never gets put away, the binder clips straining to hold the papers and photos. The conference room will let him spread them all out, sixteen victim files and one that holds all their notes on the case as a whole. Sixteen is too many—far too many—but spring is coming, and another girl will die if they can't find something to lead them to the killer.

He doesn't want to see seventeen.

He grabs the first folder, flips it open, and starts reading to refresh all the details he can never quite forget. Maybe this will be the time he finds something new, something that connects in a way it didn't before. Maybe this is the time he finally finds a lead.

"Looking for trouble?"

The voice makes him flinch, his elbow knocking against his cup. He makes a frantic dive for it as it tilts and wobbles, but he misses.

Aaaand there's nothing in the cup.

Jesus, how long has he been here?

Looking up, he sees his partner's amusement and scowls at him. "What are you doing here, Vic?"

"Came back to do some paperwork. Saw the light on." Vic settles into a rolling chair, taking in the expanse of folders. They've migrated across the table, overlapping edges but kept carefully distinct. The only one out of order is Chavi's, just to Eddison's left.

"That's how you always have your paperwork done?" Eddison asks. "You come back?"

"I go home for dinner so I can spend time with all my girls. Then, when the evening dissolves into homework or dates or movies on the couch, I sometimes come back to get some extra work done. You don't need to sound so betrayed by it."

Does he sound betrayed by it? Eddison reflects on that, then reluctantly decides that yes, yes, he probably does. Sometime over the past years, it might have been nice for the more experienced agent to give him that hint.

Vic reaches for the folder nearest him, gathering the photos into a neat stack and turning them facedown. "Do you really think you're going to see anything you didn't see the last twenty times you did this?"

Rather than answer, Eddison just looks at the folder in Vic's hands.

"Fair point." After a moment, Vic shuts the folder and slides it back in place. "Let's try this a different way."

"Meaning?"

"There are things that we take for granted because we already know the cases are connected. Let's try to remove that bias. So. Here we are, slow day, an analyst researching on ViCAP brings us these folders and thinks we have a serial killer." He looks expectantly at Eddison.

Eddison glowers back.

Sighing, Vic grabs the file with just their notes and sets it in the chair next to him. "I know you hate role-play, but it's a useful investigative tool. Indulge me."

"None of the cases share the same jurisdiction," Eddison says, and his partner nods. "Different state every time, no geographic cluster or apparent comfort zone. The victims all live in or around cities, rather than more rural areas, but there's nothing on a map to link them."

"All right. What does link them?"

"Age clusters; they're all in a four-year range, fourteen to seventeen. All in school, all female."

Standing to stretch out over the table, Vic pulls the headshot to the top of each stack. Most are yearbook photos, though a few are posed at other occasions. Candid shots may say more about a person, but posed ones are more identifiable. "What else?"

Eddison tries to pretend he hasn't seen these pictures so many times they're emblazoned on the back of his eyelids, tries to pretend he doesn't know anything about them. "They don't fit a type," he says eventually. "They're all young and objectively pretty, but hair color, skin color, racial background, they're all over the spectrum. Whatever makes them attractive to him as victims, it's not how they look. Or not only how they look."

"So we dig deeper."

"I'm not at the academy."

"I know." Vic taps at a bright green folder. "And I know we did all this seven years ago with Kiersten Knowles. We came into this because someone else connected these cases, so there were things we simply assumed to be true because they were presented to us that way. What if finding something genuinely new means tucking into the things we don't even realize we're not seeing?"

"I need more coffee."

"I'll get it. You think."

As Vic leaves the conference room, Eddison pulls one of the candids out of Chavi's file and props it up against his empty cup. It's almost the last picture of living Chavi, taken just two days before her murder. Priya's twelfth birthday. All the girls and women at the neighborhood party, and some of the more obliging men, had flower crowns on, colorful ribbons spilling out from silk flowers and wire. Priya was all skin and bones then, near the end of a growth spurt that gave her height but not weight, her hips and ribs pressing against her clothing. Her too-sharp face was alight, though, bright and joyful, with her sister's arms draped across her chest from behind. Whoever took the photo caught them in motion, their dark hair swinging around them, the red and blue streaks bold as the ribbons. Priya wore a crown of white roses, Chavi one of yellow chrysanthemums, the long petals almost like a fringed headband. Both wore cheerful sundresses and open sweaters, their feet bare in the grass.

Two days later, Chavi was dead.

So was that version of Priya.

Vic comes back and hands him a mug that says *you're my superhero*. Eddison isn't sure if that's meant to be funny or if Vic just didn't pay attention to what he was grabbing. The break-room kitchenette is home to any number of orphan mugs.

Lack of attention, he decides after a glance at his partner's hand. Vic's mug says he's *the world's gratest mom,* with a hunk of swiss cheese next to the words.

"Cause of death is the same in every case," Eddison says, taking a cautious sip. It's stark and bitter, definitely microwaved dregs, but it's got a kick. "Slit throat. Most are clean, single cuts that run deep, a few are choppy, probably indicative of a higher level of rage. Multiple medical examiners suggest it's most likely a smooth-edged hunting knife. Angle of the wound changes depending on the height of the victims, but all point to an attack from behind by someone around six feet tall. Left-to-right directionality says someone right-handed."

"Before we get into the disposition of the bodies, what else is the same about the attacks? Physically, I mean."

"That's where we see two distinct victim profiles." Eddison looks for his notes, realizes Vic still has the folder, and glares.

Vic just shakes his head and uses his mug to gesture at the spread of files on the table.

"Of the sixteen, one, two, four, seven . . . no, eight were raped, and beaten to varying degrees. Their clothing was torn, and either left on them or in a heap next to them. The other eight were not raped, no signs of sexual assault. Hints of bruising around their necks indicate they were probably choked to unconsciousness. Clothing was carefully removed and placed at a distance. To keep it clean?" Eddison skims quickly through the relevant medical reports. "No other signs of physical trauma on those eight."

"And after death? What did he do with the bodies?"

"That's what spurred the initial theory they were connected." He pulls photos out of each file, still feeling like an idiot making a class presentation, but layers them so Vic can see. "Every victim was found in a church, even those who weren't religious or overtly Christian. The churches themselves span a number of denominations. ME reports say the victims were not moved. Arranged, yes, but they were killed where they were found."

Eddison thinks of the plain white Baptist church for Tereza's funeral, the icy politeness with which the Kobiyashis greeted the agents, the outright rudeness they offered to Bliss and Inara.

Bliss snarled back, but it was Inara who *opened the casket* to set a few pages of folded sheet music under Tereza's crossed hands.

Eddison runs a hand through his hair, scraping his blunt fingernails against his scalp. He needs to get a haircut soon; it's getting long enough to curl. "They were all in roughly the same part of each church: between the altar space and the seating. They all had flowers on or around them, a unique flower for each victim."

"Where did the flowers come from?"

There are pages upon pages of police interviews with florists in every folder. Some flowers were local to the area and in season, and could have been gathered in the wild by the killer. Others had to have been purchased, but were likely bought out of town to avoid suspicion. A few local flower shops had records of cash sales for the particular type of flower, but not enough to account for the number present at the scene. Even if he buys some in town, the rest are bought or found elsewhere.

But there was one exception. "Meaghan Adams, victim number fourteen, was found with camellias almost certainly purchased from her mother's shop. Cash, no security cameras, and the clerk wasn't paying enough attention to give a description other than 'male, tall, and somewhere between thirty and sixty.'" He tries not to be irritated by that. Most people aren't trained to actively observe, to notice and remember details of strangers.

"What else?"

"The murders all take place within a two-month period. The earliest is in mid-March, the latest almost mid-May. There's something about the time of year, something about spring that sets this guy off."

Standing up with a muted groan and a stretch, Vic reaches for the bowl of dry-erase markers on the table. Most of one wall is a whiteboard, currently taken up with bullet points of what appears to be a sexual-harassment seminar. Vic wipes off all of it with quick strokes and tosses the eraser to the floor. "All right. Let's chart."

It must be nearly midnight, but Eddison nods and opens the first file, clearing his throat to read aloud. "First known victim, Darla Jean Carmichael, age sixteen. Killed in Greater Glory Southern Baptist Church in Holyrood, Texas, outside of San Antonio, on the twenty-third of March. Zoraida Bourret . . ."

As Eddison reads off names and dates, along with any other details that jump out, Vic copies it onto the whiteboard, color coding the information. Green for locations and dates, blue for officers and agents on the cases, purple for family statements, red for the victims' details. They've done this before, on this case and others: put everything up on a single page and hope to see something that gets lost in the shuffle of papers.

There's a question the instructors pose to every cohort at the academy: why is it more difficult to find someone who kills less often?

The answer has a lot of parts. A pattern that's spread out is harder to identify. Pieces of the signature get lost. A spree killer rushes and leaves clues behind. A serial murderer might take longer to make mistakes.

In Eddison's mind, it always comes back to control. The more time passes between kills, the more in control of himself a killer is, the more likely to plan, to be careful. Someone who only kills once a year isn't in a hurry, isn't desperate and likely to fuck up. A patient man isn't worried about getting caught.

Eddison is not a patient man. He's waited too long already to tell Priya—to tell all the victims' families—that they've got the bastard who killed their girls. He doesn't want to add another folder to the pile, another name to the list.

He's just not sure there's a way to avoid it.

It's practically March.

69

Her name is Sasha Wolfson, and you see her for the first time when she nearly crashes her uncle's convertible. The top is down and the crisp spring wind rips through her hair, waving it all around and into her face. She pulls over abruptly so she can knot it back, but she's laughing.

She has a wonderful laugh.

Her uncle is laughing, too, even as he hands her a scarf to tie over her hair, and he patiently explains things like lane changes and merges and blind spots. He's teaching her to drive.

You follow that laugh for weeks, through driving lessons and after-school walks and the weekends she spends working with her family's land-scaping business. She's so good with the flowers; there are always some in her hair. Her parents nearly always give her the delicate work to do, twin-ing slender, fragile vines through latticework and repotting the less hardy plants. She loves the butterfly gardens best, and sometimes she makes a coronet of honeysuckles.

You can smell them in the air when she walks by, the tiny flowers bright against her red hair.

Her sister is a wild girl, you learn. Off at college, screwing everything that will stand still long enough. Her poor parents, you hear, and the midnight calls from policemen. Drugs, and car crashes, and drinking. At least they have Sasha.

At least they have a good girl they can be proud of.

But you know how girls can get as they grow older. Darla Jean was a good girl, until she wasn't. Zoraida withstood temptations, and is protected from them now, but Leigh . . . Leigh Clark was always a vicious girl, and the world is well rid of her. When Sasha gets her license, when she can go off on her own in a car, who knows what she'll get up to?

No. Her parents may have failed their elder daughter, but they've done well by Sasha, as she does well by them. They deserve to know that Sasha will always be a good girl.

It's almost summer, and her coronet of honeysuckle is a thick crown today, her hair woven through it in places until it's all up, precariously balanced, somewhere between elegant and untamed. This is a fairy-tale maiden, and all nature bends to please her. You've read fairy tales, though. You know the prince comes, and the princess is no longer pure. There's a kiss to wake, a kiss to cure, a kiss to keep. Princesses become queens, and there's never been a queen undeserving of burning.

Red tendrils, dark with sweat, escape from the crown and plaster to her neck, her throat, as she tends the flower beds outside the church. She stands and stretches, heads into the dark, quiet church for a drink, a chance to cool off.

And you follow, because you know what happens to princesses who aren't protected from the world.

After, you pluck a single flower from the disintegrating crown and place it on your tongue. Under the copper shock of blood, you can taste the sweetness of honeysuckle.

MARCH

The temperature isn't so much warming as it is getting incrementally less cold. It's the kind of change you don't actually notice, because cold is cold until it drops to freezing or climbs to chilly, so does it really matter where in the range it falls? But the numbers insist it really is getting warmer.

Burying her face in the high collar of her coat until her eyes barely show, Mum swears the numbers are lying.

I've gotten used to it, though, because of chess and the walks, and a few more explorations with my camera. I'm still layered enough to feel like matryoshka dolls, but it takes longer for the tip of my nose to go numb. I wrap myself around Mum's arm, leaning into her to give her whatever warmth I can share.

"Remind me why I'm doing this?" she asks, voice muffled by her scarf.

"Because it was your idea?"

"Well that's stupid. You know better, why didn't you stop me?"

"If I know better, why do I do this multiple times a week?"

"Fair point. We're both idiots." She dances in place as we wait for the crosswalk to flash go, making me sway with her. "I miss green things, Priya-love."

"I offered to get you a plant."

"If it's made of fabric or plastic, it isn't a plant." She looks down at her heavy gloves and sighs. "I need dirt under my nails again."

"We'll stock up on seeds for France." On second thought . . . "After we check and make sure we're legally able to carry seeds into foreign countries."

"That's a silly law."

"Invasive species, Mum. It's a very real problem."

"Marigolds are a problem?"

"Marigolds are always a problem."

We stop at the grassy island in the middle of the parking lot. The pavilion is still there, one side rolled up and lashed. Probably so horny teens and twenty-somethings can't crawl under and make use of privacy. The space heaters are gone, though, and the little generator they all plug in to. It's a Sunday afternoon, so none of the vets are there.

"You sit out here in this weather?" Mum asks incredulously. "You don't even like getting dressed."

"Pajamas are clothes."

"For going out of the house?"

"Well, no, but that's not about the clothing, that's about the people."

"Oh, my dear antisocial girl."

"I'm not antisocial; I'm anti-stupid."

"Same thing."

"How are you in Human Resources?"

"I lie well."

I don't tell Mum stories about chess because at her most supportive, she has exactly zero interest in the game. I keep her updated when and where I'm going, and that's about the extent of that topic of conversation.

I have told her about Landon, given that he's still following me into Starbucks. Not out of it, at least, which is something. I suspect she told Eddison about Landon, because I got a text asking if blue is actually my favorite color or if I simply felt it was representative, which would normally be weird except that it was followed by him making sure I was still right-handed. I told him sunshine yellow, not because it is, but because I'd really love to see him try to find a bright yellow Taser.

"I think my nipples are about to freeze off."

Snickering, I pull Mum down the grass and aim us at the storefronts. "Come on, then. Food."

After lunch, we head over to Kroger to pick up a few things. She's considering making a treat to take into the office for her minions, which is fine so long as it's nothing that requires the oven, mixing bowls, measuring cups, or tins.

Chavi and I were always close with Mum. There was a line there, firmly drawn, between friend and Mum, and if a situation ever neared the line, she was always going to come down on the Mum side. But up until that line, she could be—and was, and is—both. After Chavi, or maybe more importantly after Dad, the line shifted a little bit. It's still there, still as firmly drawn and nonnegotiable as ever, but there's a lot more territory where she's as much friend and sister and instigator. I don't think Vic believes me half the time when I swear my mother is the biggest reason I get in trouble at school. He likes to say it's her influence, not her.

I know better. At least seven times out of ten, it is literally my mother at the school, raising hell. I'm usually willing to let insults slide; Mum isn't, especially if the insults come from teachers.

But at the end of the day, one of my absolute favorite things about Mum is—

"Two ladies as beautiful as you should be smiling!"

"A man as interfering as you should go fuck himself!"

—she doesn't tolerate bullshit. Not from anybody else, and not from herself. It's not about being an asshole, though she can be if she thinks it's the right response, but about being honest.

Mum is the biggest reason I can say I'm broken, and the reason I know that's okay.

We pick up Oreos, sugar, cream cheese, chocolate chips, heavy cream, and parchment paper, then decide okay, we can buy one new mixing bowl without feeling stupid for not digging out our own, and then compromise further and pick out an enormous popcorn bowl with a lines-and-dots color scheme designed by someone who was clearly tripping. It is the ugliest goddamn bowl we have ever owned, and I'm including the handmade day-camp ceramics in there.

It is kind of amazing.

We get more milk, too, even though we're going to regret it as soon as we start walking.

Mum complains the entire way home, putting the whine in her voice that always reduces me to giggles and coming up with more and more ridiculous things to say. I think I was eight the first time she did that, when we were at a restaurant and listening to a monstrous little darling having a meltdown. Dad made some comment about the girl's parents needing to exhibit better control of her, and Mum went to town with the fake whines, until Dad finally gave up and ordered a drink.

Their marriage didn't always work, but even when it did, it was always a mystery as to how.

The mailbox—because neither of us felt like going out to check it yesterday—is mostly junk, but it has a large envelope of paperwork from the school I'll be attending in Paris, plus a normal-size envelope from Inara. I shove that one into my pocket to read later. I haven't mentioned the letters to Mum yet, because she would probably tell Eddison, and that would give him a solid shove in the direction of a breakdown.

When he said a couple of Butterflies would destroy the world rather than be destroyed, I'm comfortable assuming Inara is one of them.

"Priya, look."

Mum and I both stop short on our walk up, staring at the front step. There's a bouquet of jonquils there, wrapped in spring-green tissue. They're a mix of types, some of them yellow straight through, others yellow-throated with white petals like a fan behind. They're tied with a bit of white curling ribbon near the base, a looser sheer white ribbon in a large bow up where the bouquet gains some width. There looks to be a half-dozen stalks, but multiple blooms add some size.

It's not the first time flowers have just shown up at our door. After Chavi died, our step used to be full of them. Everybody brought flowers and food. As if we could ever eat that much food before it went bad. Most of the flowers we just threw out, because even with the few we kept, the scents got so heavy and they clashed and it got hard to breathe. Harder. It was always hard to breathe, those first few weeks. The perfumed air made it worse.

It's been about a year, though. The last time we got surprise flowers, it was in Omaha, and someone in Mum's office there found out about Chavi. That person was very quickly dissuaded from discussing it with anyone, least of all me or Mum. But the only person here I've told is Gunny, and he doesn't have my address. Wouldn't send flowers anyway, I don't think. Before that was . . . San Diego. There were jonquils then, too.

"Mum, wait."

She pauses in reaching forward for it, her eyebrows lifting when I pull my phone out of my pocket. "Seriously?"

"Humor me."

She rocks back on her feet, making a go-ahead motion with the bag of milk.

The groceries get carefully placed on the walk. I drag off one of my gloves so I can take several pictures before crouching down next to the bouquet. There's a card threaded between some of the stems. Almost a card; it's nothing more than a small sort-of rectangle of white card stock, poorly cut. I yank it out with my hand still gloved. All it says is *Priya*. The ink is bright blue. The handwriting doesn't look familiar, but it's indented slightly into the card stock and has the kind of glisten I usually associate with cheap pens, the kind you get three bucks a dozen on the expectation that they'll be lost or stolen.

There's no delivery tag. When florists deliver flowers, there's some kind of card or tag from the florist with the delivery instructions. That's how we identified the sender in Omaha.

I take some more pictures, holding the card in front of the bouquet, then scoop up the flowers and groceries. Mum still looks bemused until we get to the kitchen and I can show her the card.

Then her face goes very still, everything tucked away until she decides what she thinks about it. "So he's here."

"Maybe," I murmur. "We've gotten jonquils before."

"Yes, in San Diego," she replies, one eyebrow tilted. "I'm sure you remember what else happened in San Diego."

I give her a nasty look.

She just shrugs. Mum saves tact for work, and even then only when she absolutely has to. She doesn't much bother with it in her personal life.

"We got them in Boston, too," I remind her. "Once Chavi was connected to the other cases, we got a slew of the earlier flowers."

"So you think it's a murder groupie."

"I think we have to concede the possibility."

She frowns at the flowers as I dump them, wrapping and all, into the sink. "Do we tell the Quantico Three?"

"Is there something to tell them yet?" I rub my thumb along the edge of the phone, trying to think my way through the options. Just like in chess, you can't think only of the move you're making. You have to think three, five, eight moves ahead, to place each play within the context of the full game. "We don't know that it means anything."

"Could it be Landon?"

"Maybe? I guess the jonquils could be a coincidence."

"That would stretch the definition, wouldn't it?"

"Your daughter was murdered by a serial killer less than a mile from home."

"Point," she sighs. She starts putting away groceries, giving herself the chance to think. Mum is nearly never without something to say, but if she has the chance to consider things first, she'll always take it. "Tell Eddison," she says when everything is either put away or stacked next to the stove for us to use. "Stalker or killer, the FBI will have to get involved anyway. If they're here from the beginning, so much the better."

I lean into her, using her shoulder as a pillow, and wait.

"If it is him," she says, "if he really has found you again . . . it's one thing to leave it unresolved when it's out of our hands."

"What makes you think it's in our hands now?"

"I don't think it is, yet, but if it is him, this is our chance. We're more likely to succeed if the Bureau's in the loop. Partial loop," she corrects herself. "I'm quite sure they don't need to know *everything*."

That's because Mum's idea of resolution is seeing the bastard who killed Chavi dead at her feet. Mine usually involves hearing *you're under arrest*, followed by a recitation of Miranda rights.

Usually.

A certain awareness of the other cases was inescapable, partly due to the questions the FBI asked us about Chavi and partly because the media seemed to insist we had to know. For a while, we didn't want to know more.

Then San Diego happened.

I supposed we could have maintained ignorance, but at that point, it seemed not just stupid but actively harmful. So Mum and I researched the other murders, painstakingly sorting out what was true from the theories of the armchair detectives or fans.

It wasn't that we were hiding what we'd learned from our agents; it was more that . . . well. They've always been so careful in their questioning not to give us the weight of those other deaths. Chavi was ours to carry, but it's so easy in a serial case to feel like you have to hold the entire string of victims to your heart. It's easy to feel guilty for the deaths that happen after your loved one's—we got cards from the families of Zoraida Bourret, Mandy Perkins, and Kiersten Knowles when Chavi's murder hit the national news—and there's this sense, irrational but strong, of *Why couldn't I provide the information to catch him?* It's not so much *What did I do that my daughter/sister got murdered for it?* as it is *What did I do wrong that he wasn't stopped?*

Guilt doesn't have to make sense; it just is.

I carry the names of those other victims, but it's not from guilt. From sorrow, usually, and from rage. Our agents tried to protect us from the extra wounds that come with serial cases, but it isn't their fault we're broken people who don't always react the way we're expected to.

"How are you going to play it?" Mum asks.

"It doesn't really matter what kind of flower it is; the fact that whoever delivered them knows where we live is problematic."

"So you're telling the truth. Novel way to go about it."

Only Mum would consider sharing a fraction of the available information to be telling the truth.

I pull up the clearest of the photos, with both the flowers and the card, and text it to Eddison along with *These were at the door when we got home from errands.*

When there's no immediate response, Mum and I both go get changed and come back to the kitchen to start the Oreo truffles. About an hour later, as we're on the couch waiting for things to chill enough for the next step, my special Eddison-only ringtone goes off. "Bad Reputation" by Joan Jett; it felt appropriate.

"Hey."

"Are those jonquils?" he asks, sounding out of breath.

With a glance at Mum, I put the phone on speaker. "Yes, yes they are. Is that important?"

"Maybe."

"You're panting."

"I was out running. Has anyone sent you jonquils before?"

He's got the Agent tone in his voice, the one that says to let him ask his questions before I try to get clarification. I don't always like that tone, but I get why it's important.

"San Diego and Boston."

"Did you get any other flowers in San Diego?"

Mum and I trade looks. "Yes. I can't recall what they were, though."

Mum's eyebrows inch toward her hairline, but she doesn't contradict me. I've never outright lied to Eddison before; I don't think I like it.

"Would you have written about it to Chavi?"

"Yes, but I'd have to dig through the journals to find which one they're in."

"When you get a chance, do that, please. And there was no delivery tag?"

"Just the bit of card stock. I still had my glove on," I add.

"I'm going to send someone out from the Denver office to pick the flowers up, just in case. You didn't throw them out, right?"

"No, they're in the sink."

"Is the sink wet?"

Mum snorts. "Please. Like we do dishes."

There's a short pause that I think is Eddison trying to decide whether or not he should respond to that. He doesn't; it's probably the right choice. "How long do you think it would take you to find the right journal?"

"I don't know. We've got boxes and boxes of journals, and they're not in any sort of order."

"Any particular reason?"

"Chavi and I read back through them from time to time, so they got put back very haphazardly. There were some we liked to keep closer than others. I still do."

Bless his compulsive heart, I think I just broke him, if the very long silence is any indication. I've seen his desk—seen Mercedes's and Vic's desks, too—and while the boxes may not be quite the breed of hell that Mercedes engenders, it must be close. "Try to find it quickly," he says finally. "If you can send a list of the flowers you received before back with the agent, that would be helpful. Otherwise just get it to me as soon as you can."

"Going to tell us what this is now?"

"Five years ago, you said you didn't want to know about the other cases. Still true?"

Mum's hand wraps around my ankle, squeezing a little too hard. I don't tell her to let go.

I'm not sure why I'm hesitating, except that I'm worried telling him a little bit may translate to telling him everything, and there are things he really doesn't need to know. There are things Mum and I need to figure out, plans we need to make, and we thought we'd have more time.

We expected something to happen—maybe hoped for it—but we didn't expect it to be this soon after we moved.

"Let me talk to Vic," Eddison says when I've been silent for a little too long. "He needs to know about this new development anyway. You think about it, tell me when you're ready. If you decide you want to know, we're doing this in person. Nonnegotiable."

"Understood," I whisper, playing up the scared little girl I should be. Would be, maybe, if I were a little smarter.

"As soon as I have the name of the agent they're sending out, I'll text it to you. Make them show their credentials. And find that journal."

"We thought it was a boy in San Diego," I tell him, hating how small my voice sounds. "I was tutoring someone, and he had a bit of a crush, and we thought he was being creepy-sweet. He said he wasn't, but we didn't think it could be anyone else, and they stopped when we moved. We didn't think it was important, or connected, or—"

"Priya, I'm not accusing you of anything." His voice is soft, gentle in a way he swears he's not capable of being. "You didn't have any reason to know it could be something. But I am very glad you told me about this. I need to call Vic and the Denver office. I'm going to text you that name, okay? And I'll call you later tonight?"

"Okay. Yes."

The call ends, and for a while, Mum and I stay on the couch, staring at the phone, Leonardo DiCaprio drowning in the background movie. Then Mum shakes her head, hair sliding out of her loose braid to frame her face. "It's just about time to make a decision, Priya-love. In the meantime, let's haul those boxes down and start getting them organized. They'll need the dates of delivery, at the very least, if they don't just ask for copies of the entries."

"What do you think I should do?"

Mum's silent for a long time. Then she gets off the couch, pulls me up after her, and hugs me so hard we're rocking in place just to keep breathing. "I am never going to make that decision for you. You are my daughter, and I will always be your sounding board and give you advice, but I can't just tell you what to do. Not like that. You are your own person, and you have to make the choice you can live with."

"I think we need to know exactly what this is before we decide. There's too many other things the flowers could be."

"Then we'll wait." She kisses my cheek, almost by my ear. "We'll gather all the information we can, and make a decision then."

85

There are all kinds of stalkers; the fact that I'm sort of hoping this is a murderous one disturbs me in ways I can't even name.

He can feel Vic's eyes on him, heavy and concerned and thoughtful and just a little bit amused. No matter how grave the situation, Vic always seems to be entertained by Eddison's pacing.

But then, Vic's never seen himself go completely still when an important piece of information shifts into place, or almost does. Vic goes still, Eddison paces.

Ramirez taps her pen against the table in a frantic tattoo that starts pounding directly into his goddamn brain.

He pivots a little too hard when he reaches the wall, sees Ramirez cringe and carefully set her pen down beside her legal pad. Later, he'll feel bad about whatever expression he must be wearing. He might even apologize. For now, he's just grateful that the sound has stopped.

They're all up in the conference room, waiting to hear back from the Denver office. Eddison is still in the sweat-stained tee and track pants, his windbreaker thrown over the back of a chair. Vic is in jeans, more casual than usual, but traded out his paint-spattered flannel for a clean polo within minutes of arriving at the office. Ramirez . . .

Hell, he'll really feel bad for her later, because she was very clearly on a date, even if it was the middle of the afternoon when Vic called her. She must have curled her hair, because he can see the natural wave fighting against the neat spirals, and she's wearing a dress and the spiky kind of heels she doesn't ever wear to the office even if it's just supposed to be a paperwork-and-phone kind of day. She hasn't complained, though, hasn't made a single mention of having to ditch her date in the middle for what may be Eddison overreacting.

Please let him be overreacting.

The phone console in the middle of the table rings shrilly, and Vic leans over to stab at the speaker button. "Hanoverian."

"Vic, it's Finney. They're okay. Little shaken, maybe a little pissed if I was reading it right, but okay."

All three let out a breath. Of course they're okay. It isn't a threat yet, just the possibility of one.

And it is not at all surprising that, having had time to think on it, one or both of the Sravasti women might be pissed.

"What's it looking like?" Vic asks a moment later. He's the one who actually knows Finney, who is, in fact, his former partner. Eddison hadn't realized it, but as soon as the Sravastis knew they were relocating to Huntington, Vic had briefed Takashi Finnegan on the case, just so there'd be someone close enough to help if it came down to it.

Clearly, neither of them expected it to come down to it.

"The card is clean for prints. Same with the outside of the tissue paper," the other agent reports. "Now that it's to the lab, they'll unwrap it and check more. The flowers could have come from anywhere, unfortunately: florist, grocery store, private greenhouse, different city, who knows. Check your email for a picture of her journals."

Ramirez reaches out to spin her laptop around toward Vic so he can sign in. Eddison stalks around the table to lean over. "Holy shit, she wasn't kidding," he mutters once the picture loads.

He's pretty sure he's never seen so many composition books in one place in his life.

"Those are just hers," Finney says, and even Vic chokes a little on that one. "They've got the sister's stacked off to the side."

"So you don't have the list of other flowers she received," Vic surmises.

"No, but she's getting the journals in order. Not even sure how. Every notebook looks different, and no labels I saw. No dates, either, except for the beginning of each year."

"Not each notebook?"

"Each year."

"Can we set up a camera for their front door?" Ramirez asks. Her fingers touch the pen, but then she looks at Eddison and puts her hand in her lap.

"Ms. Sravasti is going to put in a request. Her company owns the house and makes it available as a short-term residence, so she has to get permission to make changes. In the meantime, there is a basic windows-and-door alarm system in place, and they'll start using that."

"Start?" Vic echoes with a frown.

"It's a low-crime area; most folks feel safe enough with just locks. One of my agents commutes from Huntington; I'll have him introduce himself to the Sravastis and check in on them. If they get approval for the camera, he can help them install it."

Vic coughs into his hand. "Be very careful how you phrase that offer with Deshani."

"Already offered," chuckles Finney. "Archer worked as Geek Squad all through college; he can get things installed and set up before most people can finish reading the instructions. You told me yourself the Sravastis have been through hell and are still standing. I'm not going to assume they're anything less than capable." Over the line, the Quantico agents can hear the click of tapping on a keyboard, the ding of a computer registering new emails. "Next time she's at chess, Priya's going to try to get a picture of the guy who's been creeping on her. We'll run it as soon as she gets it to us. Hopefully we can get a last name and some background on him."

"See if he's been anywhere near San Diego?" Vic asks dryly, and Finney wheezes a laugh.

"Exactly. Your ladies have cool heads; I'm impressed."

Vic smiles and shakes his head. "They won't start the fire, but they'll dance around it if it will keep them warm."

"Deshani would start the fire," Eddison and Ramirez correct in unison.

Their partner's indignation is drowned out by another wheezy laugh from the speaker. "You know, I got that impression. Terrifying woman, and she knows it."

Scrubbing his hands over his face, Eddison finally sinks down into a chair. His skin itches, sweat from his run long dried into salty, irritating streaks.

"There is something else you need to be aware of," Finney says more seriously.

Vic groans. "Nothing good has ever followed that sentence."

"Of course not; that's why I use it as a warning." The speaker crackles with the sound of shuffling papers.

"Out with it, Finney."

"I was able to get the ball rolling today because it's a Sunday and I didn't ask for permission, but I'm going to catch hell for it, and we're going to hit some blocks moving forward."

"Why?"

"Did I happen to mention we got a new section chief a few months back?"

"What does—"

"It's Martha Ward."

"Shit."

Eddison and Ramirez both stare at their senior partner. It's very rare to hear Vic swear, even at work; he mostly stopped when his daughters got old enough to innocently repeat interesting words.

"All right," Vic sighs. "I'll talk to our chief, see if there's any push we can give on this."

"You think it'll accomplish anything?"

Vic hesitates.

"I'll keep you updated," Finney says. "Good luck."

The call ends, and all three sit for a time in the strange silence that follows. Finally, Ramirez picks up her pen and does something complicated that somehow ends with her hair twirled and pinned mostly neatly on the back of her head, the pen cap sticking out like an ornament. "Martha Ward?" she asks delicately.

Vic nods.

"So . . . why is she an obstacle? I mean, her reputation says she's pretty much a badass."

"Hard-ass," Vic corrects. "Martha Ward is a hard-ass, who regards profiling as a religion and refuses to accept any deviations. The pattern is paramount."

Eddison's the one to connect the dots, muttering curses under his breath until Ramirez launches a dry-erase marker at him. "Our killer has never sent flowers to a girl before he kills her; Priya getting a delivery is a deviation from the pattern. Ward's not going to be easily convinced that it's our killer."

Vic nods again, his expression grim. "Fourteen years ago, Finney and I were pursuing some missing kids in Minnesota. Different ages, boys and girls, but they all had brown hair and brown eyes and light-colored skin. Only three had been found."

"Dead?"

"Wrapped in heavy-duty plastic, then in blankets, and partially buried. They were curled on their sides, like they were sleeping, and small stuffed animals were tucked in with them."

"Remorse?" asks Ramirez.

"That's what we figured. Our initial theory, because all the kids looked alike and were apparently being kept for some time, was that our kidnapper was trying to create a family. That kind of profile leans slightly more female, but not enough to make assumptions."

"Ward insisted on gendering the profile?"

"Not exactly; she was on a completely different case in roughly the same area. Light-skinned brunettes in their thirties were going missing, one at a time, and showing up dead, dumped in or near construction sites."

"They were connected, right? They have to be connected."

Ramirez, for all she's been through in her life, is still an optimist. Eddison is not. "Ward wouldn't investigate the possibility," he guesses, fairly confident he's right. "You had to go over her head?"

"We didn't have a choice." Settling back into the padded chair, Vic frowns at the memory. "She insisted the cases had nothing to do with each other. Our subject was obviously female where hers was male; kids versus adult women; entirely different causes of death and postmortem rituals."

"The kids who died were accidents, but he was auditioning the women, wasn't he? Trying to find the perfect mother for his perfect family." Ramirez sighs at Vic's nod. "So the best way to find him is to investigate the overlap."

"While we argued with Ward, another woman turned up dead, and another went missing. Two kids were taken, and a different one was found. Finney and I went up the chain of command, got approval to take her case, and solved it. What we didn't take into account was that our boss's boss was good friends with Ward. When she got put on desk duty pending a case audit, he promoted her. Finney was transferred to Denver, and three days later, Eddison came out of the academy with a chip on his shoulder and my name on his papers."

Eddison refuses to give Vic the satisfaction of seeing him blush. "So you're saying I was punishment?"

"Not at all; you were already assigned to us. Finney getting transferred was the punishment. Ward's politically savvy with great connections, so she keeps advancing, but if she can make our lives hell, she will. Finney getting her as section chief is very bad luck."

"So she'll punish Priya just to make things difficult for you."

"Truth be told, she won't give a shit about Priya; Ward has all the empathy of a dead fish."

Ramirez tilts her head to one side. "Ward versus Deshani: who wins?"

Vic blinks, thinks about it, then shudders.

Anything that can make Victor Hanoverian cringe is something Eddison never wants to see.

The stack of multicolored folders is on the table near Ramirez's laptop, ready for fresh notations. Next to it, an empty folder sits and waits. Pretty soon there'll be a name on the label, probably Vic's writing because Ramirez's is a little too pretty for labels and Eddison's requires a minute to decipher.

PRIYA SRAVASTI.

He wonders if it's an accident that the folder is blue.

None of them are red, but Chavi's is a bright yellow, and that makes him think of the Taser and whether or not Priya's screwing with him on the color and the heels of his hands dig into his eyes as if the pressure could just drag all his thoughts to a stop. Just for a breath, even, because he stopped running hours ago but still feels like he's panting.

When he pulls his hands away and looks up, Vic's watching him. "We'll make sure your schedule is flexible."

"How do I tell her that the people responsible for protecting her are getting blocked by politics?"

"Just like that, at a guess."

"She's going to be pissed."

"Good. If she and Deshani get angry enough, maybe they can push the case to Ward's boss."

He can still remember the first time he met Priya, how *relieved* he was at her fury, that it meant she was that much less likely to cry, because he stopped being good with weeping girls the first time he was faced with one who wasn't Faith. But it's been five years since they met, and while pissed-off Priya is a decidedly entertaining thing to watch, he doesn't want that fury to focus. Not when he knows what it takes for her to flare from irritation (default) to rage (exhausting). Not when he knows how badly she comes down from that kind of anger, how fragile it can make her and how long it can last.

He promised her he'd never lie, not even to make her feel better, and she said she didn't want to know anything about any of the other girls, but somewhere along the way, honoring that request started to feel like a lie. Two years ago, it started to feel like lying, but he kept his silence, because she didn't want to know and he didn't want to scare her, not when some of that anger had finally started seeping away.

Vic's battered loafers nudge his ankle. "She'll be okay. She always is."

But he knows better than Vic what Priya struggles with when she tries to make sense out of all of this, when she tries to frame her sister's murder into a bigger picture. Because Vic already had so much to worry about, and Eddison not enough, so he's kept that secret for Priya and Deshani, and has never mentioned the food binges that leave the girl sweating and vomiting on the bathroom floor because her sister is gone—just gone—and there will never be a way to make sense of that.

When Faith got taken, he started smoking, not in spite of the surgeon general's warning but because of it, because he knew it was slowly killing him and that made more sense. He didn't try to stop until a couple of years after Vic took him under his wing, didn't actually stop until Priya wrinkled her nose and told him he smelled worse than the boys' locker room at her school.

Somewhere in asking her how she knew what the boys' room smelled like, he'd forgotten to finish reaching for the cigarette. It's still there sometimes, the gesture, the need, sometimes even the cigarette, but it isn't the same as it was. Maybe because of Priya. More likely, because once he saw the impulse manifested in someone else, it didn't bring the same comfort. So still because of Priya.

This time it's Ramirez who kicks him—gently, because the pointed toe of her monstrous heels hurts like a bitch when she puts a swing behind it—and nods. The pen shifts, but doesn't let go of her hair. "No matter how many times they break, they always put each other back together. Deshani's there to catch the pieces if she falls apart."

What was it Vic told him, back in November? Some people stay broken, others put themselves back together with all the sharp bits showing?

He'd meant Inara, but it served just as well.

Taking a deep breath, he pulls his phone out of his windbreaker pocket and opens her message thread. *No Oreos, okay? Try?*

Less than a minute later, he gets back *We smashed all of them up to make truffles. Better/worse? And I'll try.*

It shouldn't even surprise him that his phone buzzes again a minute later, this time from Deshani's number. *I'll keep an ear out; her room is snack-free, so I'll hear her on the stairs if she gets itchy.*

And she will, because she'll probably be sitting on the floor of her bedroom, back against the door, and listening through the night to hear the creak of stairs or shuffle of carpet. Deshani is probably what God had in mind when he made mothers so fiercely protective.

"In Colorado, it's illegal for anyone under the age of eighteen to have or use a stun gun," he says finally, and both partners give him the slightly jaundiced look that comes of really not trusting where this is going. "She's already got pepper spray, so what's the next best thing we can give her?"

"Baseball bat?" suggests Ramirez.

Vic pinches the bridge of his nose and slowly shakes his head.

Her name is Libba Laughran, and the first time you see her, her multi-layered prom dress is hiked up enough to show the shoulders of the boy

94

with his face between her thighs. She's sitting on the hood of a car, one hand holding up her skirts, the other in his hair, throaty cries filling the night as if they're not right out in the open, as if no one could possibly hear and come investigate.

Her dress is so bright a pink it nearly glows in the night, but on the wrist of the hand in his hair, you can see a corsage with a white carnation, the edges of the petals deep red like they've been dipped in blood.

You see her holding his hand at church, their bodies an appropriate distance from each other but their hands always reaching out to the other whenever one steps away. You see them at the movies, walking to and from school.

Fucking each other in the hammock in her backyard and laughing each time they nearly fall out of it.

They love each other, you think, at least as much as they can understand it when they're so young. They whisper to each other, end every phone call and conversation with it. Neither of them even seems to notice anyone else.

There's something to that, maybe, but it's not going to save her. This isn't a thing that good girls do, no matter how in love they might be. It isn't respectful, it isn't right. She's young, so it's understandable, but you can't let it go unremarked. You can't let her friends think this is forgivable, acceptable.

It isn't until they're caught—her mother comes home several hours earlier than expected, when they're still naked and involved with each other in the backyard—that you realize just how young she is.

Fourteen years old, and already a harlot.

Her mother is weeping as she chases the half-dressed boy through the yard and away from their property, ignoring her daughter crying behind her. You lean against the other side of the fence and listen to the mother's lecture, all the ways she and her husband taught their daughter better than this.

You're not surprised when Libba sneaks out of the house that night to go find the boy she loves.

You're not surprised when she fights you, because she's clearly a girl who goes after what she wants, and she wants that boy, she wants to live.

You just can't let that happen.

This boy may treat her gently, but she's too young to know what men will do, so you have to show her.

You have to show her all she'll ever be to men when she stops being a good girl. It's not something she can get back, after all.

You start to leave her there, on the church floor, but she's only fourteen. So you drape her rags back around her, enough to cover the important bits, and lay the carnations over the cloth.

White, tipped in red that bleeds down through the petal veins into the heart.

You remember.

Mum shoos me up to bed around one. I sit on my bed, shadows dancing across the walls from the flickering light of the electric tea candle in front of Chavi's picture. It's the same one we have downstairs, though this frame is made out of chips of colored glass and sweeps of metal. It's the same ring of yellow silk chrysanthemums.

My current journal is in the nightstand drawer, a pen hooked to the front cover. It's decorated with what is, quite frankly, a profoundly disturbing collage of battered stone president heads, all but one pictures from the day trip Mum and I took with Eddison back when we lived in D.C. The exception is tiny, almost invisible in the gap between Kennedy and Taft, a little blue lizard with a placard gripped in its mouth, roman numerals on the little grey square. That lizard appears on all my journals, somewhere. Sometimes on the outside of a cover, sometimes on the inside, sometimes just tucked into a margin on one of the pages.

Chavi's journals would be easy to put in order, because she was more consistent. The bottom left corner of the inside front cover always had a drawing of me, holding a date. It might be a picture of a page-a-day calendar, or a monthly calendar with one box circled, or a representative doodle for holidays. Each notebook started with the next day of the year. All you have to do to put them in order is look inside the front cover at the calendar.

Chavi was almost to August.

I am never going to fall asleep.

I wait until Mum is probably—hopefully—sleeping across the hall, then ease down the stairs. There's one three-quarters of the way down that will creak unless you step just to the left of center, but the next one you have to step all the way to the right or it'll groan. I grab hold of the railing and skip both.

The candle in front of Chavi is dark. The last one to bed blows it out so we don't accidentally burn the house down. I want to—maybe need to—relight it. I don't, though. There's enough light bleeding in through the glass in the front door to make the picture visible, even if not clear. The streetlight, pale and somewhat yellowed, stretches up the walls and along the side of the stairs. It breaks at the hall ceiling, arcing up at strange angles to play along the banister for the landing.

A car drives by outside, shifting the light, and for the second before I can close my eyes, the shadows make it look like something is swaying from the banister.

My heart thumps painfully, and I duck my head as I walk down the hall to the living room. Something brushes my shoulder and I flinch, then call myself ten kinds of idiot when I realize it's just my hair. We checked every inch of the house, then armed the alarm. There's no one here but me and Mum. I can list reasons why it's okay to be this jumpy. I can name them, and naming is supposed to help, but somewhere between wondering who's dead and if someone is watching the house, there's a memory that's a little too present tonight.

When my dad hanged himself from the banister of the house in St. Louis two days before the first anniversary of Chavi's death, his feet didn't brush my shoulder. I didn't get close enough to find out if they would.

I walked home from school, unlocked the front door, and before I could even bend down to kiss Chavi's frame, I saw him. I stopped and looked up at him, but he'd been there a couple of hours maybe. He was definitely dead. I didn't have to touch him to check. He'd bought the rope a few weeks ago so we could put up the hammock, only the hammock had never gone up.

I didn't scream.

I'm still not sure why, but I remember standing there, looking up at my dead father, and just feeling . . . tired. Numb, maybe.

I walked back outside, locked the door, and called Mum, listened to her use her work cell to call the police as she raced home to me. She got there before the cops did, but didn't go inside to look. We just sat together on the front step until the officers got there, followed by the ambulance that was probably protocol but also very unnecessary.

I was still holding the mail, including the brightly colored envelopes that had my birthday cards from the Quantico Three. They'd arrived exactly on time.

We stayed in a hotel that night, and we had just settled into bed, knowing we wouldn't sleep, when there was a knock on the door. It was Vic, holding a bag with long-sleeved FBI shirts and fleecy pajama pants, a CVS bag of nonhotel toiletries, and a half gallon of ice cream.

I'd known Vic almost a year at that point, and already respected him, but what made me love him a little was that he didn't tell me happy birthday. He didn't even mention it, or the cards. Even though it was clearly a suicide, he still came out to Missouri to talk to us, to make sure we would be okay, and he never once asked us how we were feeling.

It was almost three o'clock before he left to go find his own room somewhere, but he pulled one more thing out of the bag and handed it to me. It was ungainly wrapped in a brown paper grocery bag, but when I opened it up after he left, Oreos spilled out onto the bed, twelve zipped sandwich baggies with three cookies each, and a day and date on each bag in Eddison's spiky writing.

Acknowledging the need, rationing the impulse.

It was the day I fell a little in love with Eddison, too, as family, as a friend. Because the Oreos admitted I wasn't okay, and the rationing said I was going to be.

There are no pictures of Dad on display, not the way we have Chavi still with us. That Chavi didn't choose to leave is part of it, but more than that . . . if Dad had needed to leave, even if he thought suicide was the only thing that could give him relief, Mum would have understood. However their marriage did and did not work, it allowed for that, at least.

But Dad killed himself in a way that would guarantee I would be the one to find him. We'd only been in St. Louis a few months, and I'd very purposefully not joined any clubs or anything that would keep me late at school. Mum wouldn't get home from work until the evening, so barring catastrophe, there was never a way I wouldn't be the one to see him first.

Almost anything else Mum could have forgiven and mourned, but she'd never forgive him for making me find him.

I honestly don't think he thought about it. Don't think he *could* have thought about it by that point. Probably the only thing he was capable of thinking about by then was that he couldn't use one of the trees out back, or a neighbor might see and cut him down before he died, save him somehow when he didn't think there was anything to save. In my heart of hearts, I firmly believe he was so focused on making sure he wouldn't be found that it didn't occur to him that at some point, he would be.

That will never matter to Mum.

The pictures of him weren't burned, they're just not out. Carefully packed away, preserved, because someday I'll want them even if Mum never looks at them again.

We called his family, that next day. When we left London, Mum and Dad cut ties with both families. Or maybe they left London because they cut ties. I've never been entirely sure what happened, only that neither of them liked speaking of it, so I have no idea how many cousins I have anymore. They left family, and religion, and maybe faith in its way, and the first time we talked to my grandparents since leaving was to tell them that Chavi had been murdered.

They blamed my parents for taking us away, for taking us to America, the land of guns and violence, and somehow it didn't matter to them that she'd been killed with a knife in a neighborhood a hell of a lot safer than the one we'd lived in in London, it was my parents' fault for leaving.

We didn't talk to them again for a year, and then it was to tell them about Dad, and again somehow it was our fault. If Mum hadn't taken him away from his family, he would have had the support he needed. If Mum wasn't a heathen, he would have had the comfort he needed. Mum hung up before Dad's mother could really get going. They needed to know he'd died, so she told them, and that was as far as she was willing to take things. We have, in theory, this massive family, but in reality it's only me and Mum and the bit of Chavi we keep with us.

Like the little over two hundred notebooks filled with her large, loopy handwriting, stacked off to one side of the living room like a broken mountain.

If I can't sleep, I should be productive and sort through my journals, find the ones from San Diego, but I can't do it without turning the light on. It's too late (or too early) for light that harsh and there isn't an outlet close enough to the pile of notebooks for me to drag the table lamp over.

When I walk into the kitchen and flick on the soft, muted light over the stove, the bags of chocolate chips are still plopped on the counter. In the fridge, fake trays of cardboard covered in parchment paper hold small, lumpy balls of crushed Oreos, cream cheese, and sugar. Grabbing the cartons of heavy cream, I dump them into the one pot we keep out and set the burner to medium-low. Cream heats slowly, and you have to be careful not to boil it or it gets gross. When the little bubbles start flocking along the sides, I stir in some sugar, then drop in the chocolate and cover the mess, turning off the heat to let the cream melt the chips on its own.

The trays line up neatly on the counter, along with the box of toothpicks. I open the box so I can stick a pick into each ball, but my hands are shaking. I stare at them for a minute, trying to figure out if I'm pissed off, scared, or tired.

Or, you know, all three, because fuck.

But the answer really seems to be: *need*. Because I know what happened in San Diego, and what happened after we left; because patterns rarely repeat by accident; because Dad gave up and I'm not as strong as Mum . . . because Chavi's death is a pain that does not, cannot, make sense, and I have trays full of ways to make it feel a little more real.

I pull the cover off the pot and stir it all together. As I use the toothpicks to roll the Oreo balls in the chocolate, my hands are still shaking. My stomach is still cramping with need. It doesn't matter that I know it'll make me sick, that the concrete pain doesn't actually make the emotional pain any better. It doesn't matter that I've learned again and again and again that it doesn't help.

It just matters that it feels like it should.

When all the balls are covered in chocolate, I shove the trays back into the fridge to cool and set. I wish fridge doors could slam. It would feel satisfying, wouldn't it, to know that at least for the moment, I haven't given in to that?

Mum's leaning against the doorway into the hall. The way her weight is slouched against the frame, her throat bared because her temple rests against the wood, tells me she's been watching me for a while. "How much chocolate is left?" she asks, voice husky and a little thick.

"Some. Not a lot."

"We've got a couple of bananas." She shifts slightly, her toes curling away from the cold tile. "Mushier than you like, but not bruised yet."

"Yeah. Yeah, okay."

So that's how we end up sitting on the floor of the living room dipping bananas into the pot of chocolate, a dozen or so fat white candles covering the various tables. I can't magically make more bananas appear when the two and a half bananas are gone, and Mum takes the pot to the sink before I can think of looking for something else to dip in there.

"I was kind of expecting there'd be a dent in the truffles," she says when she comes back, sinking gracefully to the carpet.

"You'd have stopped me after a few."

"Yes. But I didn't have to."

"It doesn't help."

"When has that ever mattered, when you wanted it to help so badly?"

I don't really have an answer for that—it's not like it isn't something I think every goddamn time—so I snag the edges of the bottom notebook and pull the closest stack in front of me. I find the lizard clinging to a leg of the Eiffel Tower and show it to her. "Split out anything from one-forty to one-eighty, just in case. That's at least fewer to page through."

"You came up with this when you were five?" she mutters.

"Nine. I had them covered in gift-wrap before that, but I redid all of the early ones when I decided I liked the lizards."

By the time she goes upstairs to get ready for work, we've got the five and a half months of San Diego split out for me to read through. Mum being Mum, I have a feeling her next project is going to be putting the rest of the notebooks in order so they can be boxed up properly. Keeping them out won't drive her up the wall quite as much as it would Eddison, but she doesn't have much use for looking back.

I spend the rest of the morning logged into my virtual school trying to focus on schoolwork. I don't have much mind for it, but in the Skype session with the instructor, I must look like hell, because she forgives me for it. She tells me not to worry about checking in until Wednesday, and if I need extra time just tell her, and everyday kindness feels so strange after the last twenty-four hours and I'm not even sure if I can put a finger on why.

But by eleven, I've done as much as I'm going to do, so I throw the journals in the backpack I haven't used in months, carefully check over my nice camera and settle it in its case in the bag, and head out to chess. My pepper spray is a comforting weight in my pocket.

I don't really expect anything to happen. Jonquils . . . those are an opening gambit. There's time, as strange as that sounds. In chess, the fastest possible victory with resignation or forfeit is called a Fool's Mate. It takes only two moves per player, but—and here's the thing— it relies on White being extraordinarily stupid.

A reasonably stupid man might avoid detection if every murder is in a different jurisdiction, but this case has been in the hands of the FBI for seven years now; remaining uncaught all this time hints at someone not just patient, but smart.

The most interesting chess games are between opponents who know each other well. They know what the other is likely to do and try to prevent it at the same time they try to advance their own gambit. Every move requires both players to completely reassess the board, like a twelve-by-twelve Rubik's Cube. I don't know who killed my sister, but I know a fair amount about him. His murders tell a story.

He doesn't repeat flowers, and he doesn't taunt.

Whatever the jonquils mean—if they are from the killer—it's only an opening move.

If they're not from the killer . . . whoever it is already knows where I live. Trying to make myself a prisoner in my own house won't make me any safer than continuing to go out.

I remind myself of that during the walk. I even mostly believe it.

Corgi's out in the parking lot when I arrive, walking toward the pavilion with two cups of coffee in his hand. Not the Starbucks kind, just the crappy free shit the grocery store gives out in tiny Styrofoam cups for the seniors. He startles when he sees me, almost spilling the coffee over his gloves. "Jesus wept, Blue Girl, had a night?"

"That's what we're calling it," I agree. "Looks that bad?"

"I wouldn't want to meet you in a dark alley." He gives me a head-to-toe once-over, then nods and sips from one of the cups. "Maybe not a lit one, neither."

"How 'bout a parking lot?"

"I hear us soldiers are brave, or used to be." He grins at me, and he really does have a nose out of a hobbit movie, but his eyes are clear. I've seen him after a bad day, and the week that follows. He's doing okay.

Everyone's there, including a very hungover Happy. Rather than take a seat, I clear my throat. "Does anyone mind if I take some pictures?"

The men look at each other blankly, then back at me.

"I take photos. It's kind of what I want to do for a living. If it's okay with all of you, I'd really like to get some pictures to keep once we move. Not posed or anything, because that's awkward, but just . . . all of you. As you."

Happy stares mournfully into his coffee, as if the answers to the universe are in there somewhere but fucked if he can muster the energy to find them. "You would pick today," he sighs.

"Not just today. Sometimes."

"Take your pictures, Blue Girl," says Pierce, setting up his pieces. "Today you're like to set fire to the board, you stare at it too long."

I watch the games for a while, my camera still in its case in my bag, letting them get back to normal. It's not at all uncommon for someone to not be able to focus on a game, to prowl around the tables and sort of keep an eye on all the matches in progress, or if someone has a doctor's appointment or something and we have an odd number. It doesn't take them long to settle in.

When I pull out the camera and look through the viewer, the world seems to sharpen. Focus. Not that terrible things aren't still out there, or even in here, but there's a glass barrier between all of that and me.

It's like I've forgotten how to breathe, and someone just poked me in the ribs to make me suck in air.

I take shots in both black and white and color, making especially sure to catch some good, clear angles on Landon. The only last name I know is Gunny's, and there's really not a way to ask around without being very weird.

Things seem more obvious behind the camera. Like the way Corgi keeps one eye on the game and the other on Happy. The way Yelp's hands are shaking and his eyes are shadowed, and the way Jorge watches him without seeming to. Jorge usually moves lightning fast, slamming his pieces against the board and pulling his hand back like he's about to get shot, but today he moves slowly, sliding the pieces so the felt bottoms stay in contact with the polished wood. Nothing sudden, nothing sharp. When Phillip reaches out to capture Steven's bishop, his sleeve rides up, showing the monorail track of stitches over a long-ago wound, just a thick, pale line with dots running to either side.

Gunny looks even older, if such a thing is possible. The soft folds of skin look deeper, the scar tissue around his temple more stretched. I get a few shots of Hannah, too, both when she's up to check on her grandfather and when she's back in the car with her knitting. She's got a stack of knit baby blankets on the backseat; when I ask her about it, she says she gives them to the local hospital, for the neonatal ward. So every baby goes home with a good blanket. It's the first time I've ever asked her why she spends so much time knitting, because it's always seemed like a strange question to ask, but I love the thought of it, someone brand new and innocent going home in something made with love.

Eventually I head inside to get a drink. For the first time, I actually take it to a table and sit down. They have a new kind of cookie that smells amazing, and I haven't eaten since the bananas, but I'm not going to, not until Mum is there and I know she'll tell me to stop if I go too far. I'm still a little too fragile from last night (this morning?) to trust myself.

I'm barely seated, the notebooks in a stack at my elbow, when I see Landon walk in and look around. Fuck. He's obnoxious enough when I can just walk past him, but if I'm an easy target?

"Do you mind if I join you?"

I glance up to find Joshua standing almost behind me, his eyes on Landon. He was already at a table when I came in, nose buried in a new hardcover and apparently oblivious to the world. We've chatted, occasionally, when we've crossed paths. He's nice enough, never pushy or inappropriate. I don't really want the company today, but . . . I really don't want Landon's company. "Sure."

He sits down across from me at the four-seater, giving me space, and drops his coat into the chair next to him. I shift mine from the table to the last chair. Oh look, no more room. I eye him warily, not sure if I'm up for casual conversation, but he just opens to his bookmark, wraps his hand around his drink, and goes back to reading.

All right then.

Landon sits down a few tables away, with a battered, coverless paperback that's either the same one he was reading a month ago or one that's been similarly mistreated. I'm constitutionally incapable of trusting people who treat their books that badly. But he opens the pages, and aside from looking over at me a bit too much, he seems to be stationary, so I lay my keys in easy reach on the table, the trigger for the pepper spray nice and accessible, and open the first notebook.

The thing about the journals is that there is nothing consistent about them. I write almost every day, but not *every* day, and the entries could be anything from *all is well, nothing to report* to pages of info-dump. The first time Dad grounded Chavi (for holding hands with a boy in the couples' skate during her eighth-grade field trip to the roller rink) she went off on an epic rant that took her fourteen hours and a little over half the notebook to get down. We both used it for whatever was on our minds, whatever that might be, so there are drawings and photos and maps, phone numbers or addresses or even shopping lists, to-do lists, test review, all mixed in with the actual commentary of what we were doing or how we were feeling on any given day. It's possible to skim the entries, but with how quickly thought can jump without any kind of break or segue or warning, it's not possible to do so quickly.

As I dive into the entries I remember how, against all odds, and entirely in spite of myself, I was actually kind of happy in San Diego. I had friends there.

Well.

I had a friend there, and others I was friendly with.

The flowers started in March, just like now, with a bundle of jonquils, but I had no context for them. No reason to think it wasn't the boy I was tutoring, who blushed every time I looked at him and could never talk above a whisper. They were just flowers; it was just a boy who might have been sweet if he'd given me the flowers directly instead of putting them at my door.

After the jonquils came calla lilies, then a crown of baby's breath, a wreath of honeysuckle, sprays of freesia. The last one was a bouquet of carnations, the white ones with the red tips that look like they're bleeding. There are pictures tucked in there, the pages fluffed around them.

The carnations arrived two days before the movers did, and the next week we were in Washington, D.C.

A week after that, I no longer had a friend in San Diego. The Quantico Three asked me new rounds of questions, looked at me with new shadows in their eyes, and I decided I could research the other deaths myself, rather than ask anything of my agents that would make those shadows deeper. Eddison asked me if I wanted context for their questions, and I said no.

He looked so relieved.

Reading how happy I was in San Diego hurts, because it was an anomaly. It hurts, and it pisses me off, and I've been so angry since Chavi died, and I just . . .

I want . . .

I am so fucking tired.

I close the last notebook, scrub at my face as if I can peel away the layers of rage and grief. Joshua is long gone, but so is Landon, thankfully. There's a little folded note where Joshua was sitting, though, with the same phone number that was on the card he gave me a few weeks ago. His friend's shuttle service.

I toss the note, because I still have the card in my wallet. It's a nice gesture for him to make, and he isn't being pushy about it. I just don't want to use the service.

The walk home is freezing, and gets even colder as the last bits of sunset give way to full dark. Mum will probably arrive not long after I do. To keep my mind on something other than the cold, I go over my to-do list for the night: scan the photos from the journals, upload the ones from chess, and pass them along to the agents.

There's nothing on the front step. I want that to be a good thing.

I'm not sure I know how to recognize a good thing anymore.

He's never really thought about it, Ramirez's teasing being a part of the team dynamic nearly since she joined, but he actually misses it when she's being sensitive.

Because Eddison knows it's ridiculous that he's got his personal cell in or near his hand at all times, that he flinches every time any phone around him rings. He knows he's twitchier than a long-tailed cat on the front porch of a Cracker Barrel, and it would actually be refreshing for his partner to needle him a little for it.

But of course, she knows why he's twitchy. She agrees with it. So she won't mock him for it, even if he sort of needs it (and how fucked up is that?), because it's probably taking all her restraint not to tap her pen straight through her damn desk.

She's off at lunch right now, an apology sort-of date with the gal from Counterterrorism she had to abandon on Sunday, and Vic is being silent support for Danelle as she goes through her newest round of interviews with the DA's office. Danelle is fairly stable, all things considered, practical enough to acknowledge the nightmare she's in, just optimistic enough to wait it out and hope for better.

His work cell goes off, and he flinches, checks his personal phone even though he knows by the ring it's the official one. He frowns at the name on the display. "Hello, Inara."

"Eddison. Vic still with Danelle?"

"Yes. What's up?"

"Bliss and I aren't coming down this weekend like we'd planned." Under her voice, he can hear wind and car horns, the sounds of the city. She must be out on her fire escape, or maybe on the roof. Outside, anyway, and he's not surprised she took the conversation away from her roommates. "I left a voice mail for Hanoverian, but he doesn't immediately check his personal one if there isn't a second call."

"Something came up?"

"Sort of. Bliss is having A Day."

There's a snarled "Fuck you!" in the background, and it's on the tip of his tongue to ask how that's different from any other day, but he's growing. Or something.

"Any particular reason?"

"Some. Her parents are pushing for her to come visit. They don't like that she's not ready."

Bliss was missing for two and a half years. One year into that, her entire family moved when her father was offered a teaching position in Paris. As difficult as it is for the other girls to settle into families that never gave up, how much harder to reforge connections with the family that moved on?

"And they keep calling her Chelsea," she continues after a moment, and he can hear Bliss's swearing getting distant, softer.

"It's her name," he feels obliged to point out.

"It isn't. Call me Maya, I won't even blink. Call me Samira, I'll cut you."

He laughs in spite of himself, not because he thinks she's joking, but because she's absolutely serious. She spent years making sure Samira Grantaire didn't mean anything, the ghost of a little girl left behind long before she was physically abandoned. Inara is the name she chose, Maya the name she accepted because the Gardener gave it to her and she wanted to live, and she's too pragmatic to stumble over a thing like survival. Maya may be a scar, the ink on her back, but Samira is, in some ways, the wound that can only heal if it's never, ever mentioned.

He clears his throat to get rid of the last of the laugh. "But she doesn't want to go by Bliss forever, surely?"

"Not especially. For now she thinks it's funny. She's got a list of possibilities."

"Any contenders?"

"I'm rooting for Victoria, myself," she says blandly. "Think Vic will be flattered?"

Eddison chokes, and then gives up and laughs again. Vic would be flattered, is the thing, but it would never be less than hilarious. "Jesus."

"So Bliss is feeling fragile, which means she shouldn't be around breakable people."

"I know you and your roommates have unique definitions of breakable when it comes to each other, but is it a good idea to stay in?"

"No, which is why we're going to get a hotel for a couple of days. We already had the nights off from work. She can rant and rave, and not have to feel guilty about shredding innocent people."

"I'm not sure we count as innocent. Or breakable."

"Vic's daughters are, and she would never forgive herself for hurting them." Her voice is soft, probably too quiet for Bliss to pick up. "I know his girls are strong. We both know that. But they are innocent, despite his work, and it's . . . it's a bad idea."

"What else is going on?" he asks, and receives a sour noise in response. Not that he's often perceptive, but Inara always seems to hold a grudge when he manages it. "What else is setting her off?"

There's a long silence, made staticky by wind and the distant sound of Bliss's cursing, but that's okay. Eddison may not be the most patient person in the Bureau, but he does know how to wait when he's sure there's an answer on the other end of it.

When Inara finally answers, her voice is pained, the words slow and reluctant. "I got another letter from Desmond."

"A letter from—wait, *another*?"

"This is the fourth one. They come to the restaurant, and the return address is his lawyer's office. I guess that explains how he knows where I work."

"What is he saying?"

"I don't know. I haven't opened them." She sighs. "I have them. I'll give them over. I really did mean to tell you guys at the first one, but that was when Ravenna had her meltdown with her mother, and I forgot. Then the second one, and I meant to, I did."

"But you're used to keeping secrets." He's actually rather proud of himself, how evenly and neutral and nonjudgmental that came out. It might even sound supportive.

"The third one came once Amiko's suicide hit the news."

"Her you call by her birth name."

"Her I saw safely lowered into the ground." It makes more of a difference than it probably should, but he's sure as shit not going to argue with her about it.

"And now a fourth one."

"The envelopes are thick. They don't feel like there's anything but paper, but it feels like a lot of paper."

In the least complicated sense of things—and since when has that been his life?—Desmond MacIntosh shouldn't be contacting Inara because he's a defendant and she's a witness and a victim kidnapped by his father.

"If I give the New York office a heads-up, can you drop off the letters before you hole up in the hotel?"

Anyone who hasn't danced with her in an interrogation room probably wouldn't catch the hesitation before she says yes.

"Get out to a beach, if you don't have a place already," he suggests. "It's not warm enough for tourists yet. Might help."

"Yeah?"

"Wide open, wild. Endless expanse."

She hums thoughtfully, and he knows she's picking up on all the layers in the words: because the Garden was contained, perfectly manicured and maintained, artificial, but the ocean is untamed, big enough to make you feel tiny, and completely itself. There's no façade, no mask, no glitter.

It just is, and he thinks Bliss isn't the only one who'll find it soothing.

Even if neither she nor Inara will admit to it later.

"I'll let Vic know about the change of plans," he tells her, rather than make her commit one way or the other to the idea.

"Text me the name of the agent you talk to," she says. "I'll ask for them."

He hesitates before signing off, because shit, this really isn't his thing. "If you need anything . . ."

"Why, Eddison, are you going soft? What a terrifying thought."

Maybe it shouldn't be comforting, but it is.

She'll be okay. Bliss will be okay.

Someday.

When I'm leaving the house for chess on Thursday and find the bundle of purple-throated calla lilies on the step, I realize that whatever Mum and I are trying to achieve in Huntington, it's going to be more complicated than we'd originally planned for. I take the pictures, check the card—just *Priya* again—and leave them there for the police or the agents or whoever gets sent out in response to my text to Eddison and the email to Agent Finnegan. After giving myself five minutes to wrestle with the decision—mostly to make sure I'll be able to live with it afterward—I send a second text to Eddison.

Tell me the rest.

If the rest of the game is going to play out, there's not a way to avoid it. I have no doubt he'll limit what he tells us, and Mum and I can pretend ignorance to the rest. No one has to give away any secrets yet.

Life did not use to be this complicated.

Ten minutes later, I get a reply with a time and a flight number, which I forward on to Mum. She'll offer to pick him up, he'll refuse because he doesn't do well as a passenger unless it's Vic driving, and he'll probably get to Huntington about an hour before she does.

Which still leaves me with most of a day to fill, and a little too much fury to risk going to chess.

Another few minutes, and my phone dings with an email from Agent Finnegan with the names of the two agents he's sending out to pick up the flowers. It should take about an hour from Denver.

They pull in forty minutes later, lights flashing from their black SUV. I'm in the kitchen, sitting in the little nook at the window and poking a spoon into a bowl of congealed oatmeal. As you do. The agents are young, probably not long out of the academy, one of them a pretty blonde who'll have to fight tooth and nail to ever get respected in her field, the other a broad-shouldered black man with shoulders that suggest he got a football ride through college.

"Priya Sravasti?" the man calls through the front door after knocking. "I'm Agent Archer, this is Agent Sterling. Agent Finnegan sent us."

Through the window, I can see Sterling already crouching by the lilies, blue neoprene gloves on her hands.

I check the email with the names again, then head to the door. "You guys made good time."

Agent Archer smiles, warm and easy but still professional. "Finney—Agent Finnegan—told us he'd consider it a personal favor if we took up as little of your day as possible."

Vic has some good friends, I think.

Archer asks me a few questions—did I touch the flowers, did I see or hear anyone, do I feel safe staying on my own?—all things that I already sent in the email to Finney, but more than most people, I suppose, I understand that this is the job, even when it seems a little redundant. So I answer patiently, even when he purposefully repeats himself to see if my answer changes or if I remember something new.

As we talk, Sterling examines the bouquet carefully, making sure not to dislodge anything in the wrapping. The tissue paper is that same cheerful spring green, the color sharp, and the folds are still visible from the packaging. When she's seen as much as can be seen without unwrapping it, she lowers the bouquet gently into a large plastic bag and tapes it shut. Her writing across the bag and seal is a little rough, awkward where the plastic pleats. It seems like it would be easier to label it before the bag is sealed.

Then again, they probably have to guarantee that what's on the label is what's in the bag, which is harder to do if it's prelabeled.

Sterling takes the bagged bouquet to their car and puts it in a lockbox in the trunk. Then she pulls out a stepladder and a pair of toolboxes.

I look at Archer.

He smiles again and tucks his small notebook into his coat pocket. "Finney said your mother's company approved the cameras; we'll get them set up while we're here."

"Boxes are in there," I tell him, pointing at the coat closet. "They're a brand your Agent Finnegan recommended."

"Front and back, any other doors?"

"No."

I walk Sterling through the house to the back door. Mum and I honestly kind of forgot there was a back door until Finnegan asked to check if any flowers were there. There weren't, and the fence makes that yard a little difficult to get to discreetly, but it makes more sense to have a camera there than not.

Just in case.

From her toolbox, Sterling pulls a rolled-up kit that hooks neatly over the door like a wreath hanger. It has all sorts of pockets on it, so all her tools are in easy reach when she's up on the stepladder. It's kind of genius, really.

Archer, however, does not have one, so I shrug into my coat and join him on the front step, and when he points to a thing, I hand it to him. Our kitchen stepstool is sturdy enough for me and Mum, but it creaks under the agent whenever he shifts his weight.

"I studied your sister's case at the academy," he says after a while, the wires for the camera tangled through his fingers.

I should probably respond, at least make some kind of polite acknowledgment.

I don't.

He doesn't seem put off by that. "They have us go through some open unsolveds, so we know before we get to the field that we can't settle every case. Hand me those pliers, please? The needle-nose?"

I do.

"You must really miss your sister."

"It's not something I like to discuss."

His hands still. "I guess not," he mutters. For a while he works in silence. One of the neighbors across the street waves as she hauls her twin toddlers to her van. I wave back, even though she isn't looking anymore, because one of the boys is. Archer clears his throat. "I'm sorry."

"For?"

"It was inappropriate of me to get personal. I was just trying to make conversation."

"Conversation is the weather, Agent Archer, or traffic. Spring training. I don't really need to know that you've probably seen naked photos of my dead sister." I watch the van pull out of the drive. The other twin presses his face against the window in an unsuccessful raspberry; I give him a little wave all his own. "I'm aware the academy uses the case as a teaching tool; Agent Hanoverian warned us a few years ago."

"But you gave permission, or your mother did."

"We didn't. We weren't asked. The FBI is allowed to use its own cases to train new agents; they don't have to have permission from victims or families. Let me guess: you found the case fascinating and you're grateful for the chance to work on it?"

"Something like that."

"Don't be grateful. That means being glad terrible things are happening."

"Hanoverian lectures at the academy from time to time. He's pretty big on gratitude." He points at an Allen wrench, so I hand it to him.

"Do you listen to what he's grateful for?"

"Finney didn't tell us you were feisty."

I eye the stepstool, then decide there's no way to kick it out from under him without risking injury to myself. Vic would be disappointed if I broke an agent; Eddison would be pissed if I broke myself. "I'm going to check on Sterling."

When I carefully open the back door, Sterling glances at me and shakes her head. "I told him not to bring it up."

"So you studied it too?"

"When I was in middle school, my best friend and I walked home one day to find her father getting arrested for a series of murders. What he did to those women . . . the day we studied him, I went home and spent the rest of the night throwing up, because I used to spend the night at his house once or twice a week. I've never told her."

"Why not?" Would it make a difference, coming from a friend?

"It shaped her life enough; why should I add to it?" Dusting her hands, she unhooks her kit and steps down the ladder. "I'd guess you already live your sister's case every day. Do you need me to talk to him?"

"Not this time. We'll see if it happens again."

I appreciate it, though, that she's willing. She looks young, probably not long out of the academy, and taking a senior partner to task can't be easy.

"Let's make sure your computer can communicate with the cameras, and then we'll be out of your hair." With a small, sideways kind of smile, she hands me a business card. "That has my cell and email, if you need something and Finney's busy."

"We're going to get along just fine, Agent Sterling."

Archer's the one who actually gets everything linked up, but Sterling shows me how to scan through and isolate time stamps, and how to grab a screenshot from the stream and attach it directly to email without having to save it first. Once I show her I'm comfortable with it, they gear up to go.

"You know," Archer says abruptly, as Sterling gets the tools back in the SUV, "if you're going to hide your head in the sand about the other cases, you should be grateful other people have studied them. The Bureau's not up in arms just because someone sent you flowers. They have meaning."

"No one's sending me flowers," I tell him, aware of Sterling's watchful eye. "They're delivering them to my door. If I didn't think that meant something, I would never have mentioned them."

They pull out of the drive a little after noon. Eddison isn't going to be here until six or so, depending on traffic out of Denver, which gives me a lot of time and not enough schoolwork or focus to fill it.

Here's the thing about purple-throated calla lilies: the second known victim, Zoraida Bourret, had them framing her head like the arch in a Mucha print. Her crossed hands kept a single lily clasped to her sternum.

Every victim has a flower, and it has a meaning, something that ties it to the girl in the killer's mind. Two days before she died, Chavi wore a crown of silk chrysanthemums, and when I found her, there were real ones through her hair. Easter morning, when Zoraida helped corral her younger brothers and sisters for a family photo, she wore a single calla lily as a corsage on her white Easter dress.

I don't know what the flowers mean to the bastard, but I do know that Eddison wouldn't be so scared if any other families got deliveries like this. Whether this is a fan or the killer, it's meant for me.

That's something Archer in his I-studied-the-case-so-I-must-be-an-expert arrogance probably doesn't get.

Eddison does; I can't help but wonder if he'll mention it.

I heat up a can of soup for lunch and pour it into a travel mug. A lady in Starbucks last week was telling her phone really loudly about the new stained-glass windows her church just put in and how beautiful they are. At the time, I didn't particularly appreciate having to listen to the conversation; I might be a little good with it now. Investigating the windows sounds like a perfect way to fill these hours.

Jonquils followed by calla lilies. It's hard to call something a sequence with only two entries on the list, but so far it follows the order of the murders, and it follows the order of the deliveries in San Diego. No one starts a pattern with the intent of abandoning it partway through; if something's going to happen to me, it won't be until the flowers run out. I'm safe enough for now, even in churches.

With my camera bag over one shoulder, I pull up the address on my phone and start walking, sipping every so often at the soup. I finish lunch before I reach the church, a yellow-faced monstrosity that cannot possibly be the right place. It's one of those churches that sacrificed character for size, large and looming and more than a bit soulless. I'm not Christian—I'm not really anything—but growing up beside the little grey stone church in Boston gave me certain opinions of what the buildings ought to feel like.

There are windows in the building, tall and narrow and completely colorless. What the hell was that lady talking about then?

I stand for a bit in the parking lot, the temperature fairly comfortable in the midtwenties, and shit, what is wrong with me that I now find that comfortable?

"You lost, honey?" calls a woman leaning against a side door, pale smoke curling upward from the cigarette in one hand.

"Maybe," I answer, walking up to her. "I heard someone talking about new windows, and—"

"Oh, that's over in the chapel." She waves her hand, accidentally trailing the smoke into my face. "Here, I'll show you. One of the church founders got pissy when they put up the new building, so he bequeathed money that could only go into making a traditional chapel. He didn't like the way the church was modernizing."

The woman leads me through what can only be called a complex of buildings, all faced in that ugly yellow stone, but over the curve of the parking lot, and after a grassy stretch, there's a little red-brick building tucked up against the woods, and holy hell, there's probably as much glass as brick, if not more.

The woman smiles at me, or at my awestruck expression, and flaps her hand toward the door. "It's unlocked, honey. Take as much time as you need."

Setting the empty mug down on the front step, I pull out my camera and pace around the outside of the chapel. Most of the windows are bigger than I am, intricate and graceful without being cluttered. I'm used to churches where the pictures are either biblical scenes and figures or complete abstracts, but these are mostly nature based. One has mountains and clouds, stretching out into the distance. Another has swirls of white through a dozen shades of blue and green, the rush of water giving way to tall trees in the next window, and great bunches of flowers in the one after that.

Between the large windows, small rosettes maybe twice the size of my head are stacked vertically in threes, a little more traditional in the kaleidoscopes of color, the leading beautifully detailed. Even when I switch over to black and white, the richness of the colors still manages to shade in.

I'm not sure how many times I circle the building before collecting my mug and heading inside. There, where the sunlight spills colors across the floor, it's a little more chaotic, the colors from the north and west windows all layering over each other and canceling each other in fragments of clean light. There are no chairs, no pews, just a quartet of velvet-cushioned kneelers made of dark wood.

Chavi would have both loved and hated this tiny chapel with its mess of color and light.

I find the strange angles, the ones where the dust glitters and dances and makes the light look tangible, the places where the colors pool on the stone in a way that forms new images recognizable only because we're human and so very strange.

Eventually, I sit down on one of the kneeler-cushions, tilting my head back against the wood, and soak in that feeling that reminds me so much of Chavi's quest to capture the light and color on paper. As much as it frustrated her, she would never have given up pursuing her own version of the Grail, because sometimes it's the quest that holds the meaning, not the reward.

When I lean forward to nestle my camera back into its case, my pocket crinkles.

Oh, right, Inara's letter. From a week ago. Somehow I completely forgot about it in all the fuss.

I should probably apologize for that.

Dear Priya,

Thanks for writing back; I have to admit, I feel a bit less like an idiot now. And less of an imposition.

Still flailing, though.

As much as the general public knows about the Garden, there's so much more that they don't. I have a feeling most of it's going to come out in trial, and I already know some pieces are going to get very problematic reactions. The Gardener's lawyers are trying to insist that I be brought up on charges. Being a runaway isn't a crime, but using a false ID to work is, and if they could prove I stole cash from my grandmother's house after she died, I'm sure they'd be on that, too.

I'm honestly surprised they haven't tried to claim I murdered my Gran, as if a woman who did nothing but smoke and drink in front of the television couldn't possibly drop dead without help.

And I get it, I really do. I'm a powerful witness. I'm articulate and not overtly emotional, and I can go a long way in speaking for the girls who aren't here to do so themselves. Anything the defense can do to discredit me would help cast shadows on all of us.

Do you ever feel like pop culture has lied to you?

When I read articles or watch segments on the Garden and the investigation, Inara always comes off as calm and completely in control of herself. She doesn't make abrupt turns in conversation, never gives interviewers a chance to be confused by what she's saying.

I wonder if this is her being unguarded, giving up some of that control. Or maybe just setting it aside, letting herself rest until she needs it again.

I know what that feels like.

We have all these movies and shows obsessed with the justice system. They give this impression that everything happens immediately, the trial and the investigation happening at the same time, cops desperately getting some new piece of significant evidence to the prosecutor just in time for the big reveal and dramatic closing statements. They make it look like a conviction is something the victims have in hand to help them start the grieving process.

It's bullshit, of course, but until now, I didn't realize just how far it is from the truth.

Thirty years of crimes causes a lot of delays, especially if the asshole is rich and has a really good legal team. The destruction of the Garden—it never occurred to me that could make things harder. It was our way out. It also destroyed the code-locked doors that kept us prisoner, so the defense is trying to claim that we were free to come and go and we chose to stay. The prosecution is trying to put a name (and proof) to every victim, but some of the bodies were destroyed in the explosion and some weren't even in the Garden, but out on the property. You'd think the rest of the bodies on display would be sufficient.

Vic is trying so hard not to let any of us get discouraged, but he told us recently to prepare ourselves for the possibility that we could see the anniversary of our escape before the actual trial starts.

Even if they only sought justice for those of us who've survived, they have so much proof, and it might not even matter. Eddison says the defense has a whole roster of doctors and shrinks ready to delay things further.

Eddison actually scolded me once for wishing the Gardener had died in the explosion. He said a trial was the way for us all to get justice.

Is that what any of this is? Justice? Girls afraid to leave their homes for all the attention they're getting, harassed at school and work and therapy? A boy who swears being in love absolves him of all sin? A man who might escape sentencing to live in an expensive nursing facility the rest of his life?

People keep telling me to be patient, to wait for justice.

Even if he gets convicted, even if he gets sentenced to life without parole or even death, how is it justice? We have to keep opening our wounds for everyone, bleeding again and again and again, knowing full well what he did to us; how is a verdict of guilty going to change any of that?

What kind of justice puts a twelve-year-old girl on the stand before court and cameras and makes her talk about being raped?

If they found the man who killed Chavi, do you think it would help you? Is this just me being cynical?

I really am trying to believe in this justice thing, but I can't help but think how much easier this would be if all three MacIntosh men had died that night.

If there's not enough left of Chavi for her to care about justice, why should the rest of us need it so badly? What can we even do with it?

I don't have an answer for Inara; I don't even have an answer for me.

But I wonder, sometimes, if it had been me that died that night, if it had been Chavi left behind to mourn and change: given how much she loved the idea of grace, would that be enough to preserve her belief in justice?

Eddison pulls into the parking lot, looks up at the stone chapel, and shudders. To his dying day, he will never understand why Priya doesn't hate churches after how she found her sister's body. He knows the no-longer-a-church back in Boston held dear memories for both of them, knows that she looks at the windows and thinks of sunny afternoons with Chavi, but he can't quite wrap his brain around her continued love for little churches with great windows.

Priya walks out in her long winter coat, the one she bought purely because it sweeps dramatically down the stairs like a Disney villain and makes her mother laugh. Those two have a relationship far outside his ability to explain. She ducks into the passenger side, tucking her camera bag and a stainless-steel mug around the base of the seat before she sits. "Welcome to Colorado, population: frozen."

"What makes it worse than D.C.?"

"Mountains."

He watches as she leans her head back against the seat, closing her eyes. "You okay?"

"Tired. Nightmares." She cracks her neck, settles almost sideways against the window so she can see him. "Getting kind of pissed."

He nods. "Oreos?"

"I've been okay, actually." But she's frowning, twisting her gloved hands in her lap. "Tempted, yes, but so far, I'm okay."

"Scared?"

"Yes."

He appreciates that she doesn't feel the need to mask it.

The Sravastis' rental is a blandly nice house on a street of blandly nice houses, none of them particularly distinct. Where some of the neighbors have tried to add personality with flags or statues, the Sravastis' house has a bleakly impersonal façade. He can't say he's surprised by it.

Before following her into the house, he stops at the front step, looking up at the overhang. He can see the camera, the lens aimed where it can take in the widest view possible. There's no light to show whether or not it's on, which he likes. Helps it to be a bit more discreet.

"He doesn't look out of place," she tells him, pulling off her heavy coat and hanging it in the closet.

"What's that?"

"Whoever's leaving the flowers. Both times they've been left in broad daylight, so whoever it is, he doesn't look out of place in this neighborhood. There are people on the street who work from home, or just don't work, and he doesn't stand out as not belonging."

"Tell Finney that?"

"No, but I told Sterling and Archer." She holds a hand out for his coat. He pulls off his gloves and scarf and shoves them into pockets before giving it to her. "Coffee?"

"I'll make it." Because he's had Priya's coffee, and it definitely tastes like it was made by someone who doesn't drink coffee. It's an experience he'd rather not repeat.

"I'll meet you in the living room, then." Leaning down, she reaches into the small drawer of the spindly table and pulls out a box of matches. She strikes a match without looking and lights the squat red candle as she presses a kiss to the worn corner of Chavi's glittery gold frame.

After she heads upstairs, he looks at the picture. Chavi was significantly darker than Deshani and Priya, almost as dark as her father, but Christ, she looks like Priya. Or maybe Priya looks like her. He's seen her put on her makeup with nothing but a tiny compact, never faltering with the heavy black liner or the soft silver, white, and blue shimmers.

How much of that is because she sees her sister looking back at her from the mirror?

Shaking his head, he walks down the hall to drop his computer bag on the couch and turns into the kitchen. Priya may not like coffee but her mother mainlines it, and sure enough the coffeemaker is the most well-loved element of the kitchen. He has to fuss over it a moment, figuring out the settings because Deshani has something against basic coffee, but it doesn't take long for it to start doing its thing. He can hear Priya come back downstairs, settling into the living room.

When he walks back into the living room, he nearly drops the mug. Priya is stretched out on her back on the carpet, dark hair in a puddle around her, her legs crossed at the ankles and propped on the arm of the couch. Her hands are clasped against her stomach. He closes his eyes, takes a deep breath to push back the images from the files he's gone over often enough to memorize.

"Blue," she says.

"What now?"

"Chavi liked red; I'm all blue."

He opens his eyes, looks for the blue in her hair, around her eyes, the blue spark of the crystals at her nose and between her eyes. Her red lipstick is a few shades darker than all the pictures of Chavi, but she's blue and silver, not red and gold, and maybe it shouldn't make as much of a difference as it does, but it helps.

He sits on the couch and reaches for his bag, but she shakes her head. "Wait for Mum. No sense in doing it twice."

So they spend the next hour talking about Ramirez and the woman in Counterterrorism she isn't calling a girlfriend yet, about Vic and his panic about his eldest daughter going off to college in the fall. They talk about spring training, making guesses about who might make the long slog all the way to the World Series, and that's something he was able to give her, that love of baseball and numbers and crazy statistics.

Deshani comes home half past seven, dropping bags on the coffee table and grunting at them before trudging up the stairs.

He glances at Priya.

"She'll be more human once she's changed clothes," she answers, plucking at her striped fleece pajama pants. "Once she gets home, she wants to be in real clothes."

"You two are the only people I know who consider pajamas more real than suits."

"Because you'd rather be in a tie than a Nationals shirt?"

He doesn't have an answer for that. Or rather, he does, but it isn't going to help him any.

Priya rolls to her hands and knees, then levers up to standing so she can get plates and silverware from the kitchen. She also comes back with a bowl, and shrugs at his curious look. "We only have two plates unpacked."

"Heathens."

"Quite literally."

He snorts, but accepts one of the plates. By the time Deshani joins them wearing leggings and a long-sleeve Cambridge T-shirt, Priya's got the food sorted out for all three of them. The routine is comfortable, familiar from those seven-odd months they lived just outside of D.C. Deshani regales them with tales of her misogynist assistant, who can't manage to hide how disgusted he is to be reporting to a woman, and her own delight in offering him a demotion if he'd prefer a male boss. It's sharp and funny, and Eddison gets the feeling that the only reason the idiot hasn't been fired is because Deshani finds him entertaining.

It's a little disturbing.

It's only after the meal is cleared, and Priya's fingers are crumbling the fortune cookie without actually eating any of it, that Deshani sighs and glances over at the battered black case. "All right. What's the bad news?"

Christ.

He leans back into the couch, scrubbing at his face to pull his thoughts into some semblance of order. "When Aimée Browder was murdered in San Diego, we came to the conclusion that it must honestly be a terrible coincidence."

Priya closes her eyes, too deliberately to be called a wince, but it still makes him feel like a heel. There's probably a better way to start this conversation but damned if he knows what it is.

"You didn't notice anything out of place, no one who looked familiar from Boston, and we couldn't find any connections. As strange as it was for you to have ties with a second victim, there wasn't anything to point to it being anything more than a freak chance."

"You suspected, surely?" Deshani asks sharply.

"Yes, but there was nothing to back it up."

"The flower deliveries would have changed that, though."

He nods reluctantly. He doesn't want to make Priya feel bad—worse—but her mother's statement is an obvious one. "There wasn't

any reason for you to attach significance to them. Not without knowing the details of the other cases."

"Why are the flowers significant?" Priya asks quietly. She leans
against Deshani's bent legs, her eyes still closed, and Deshani's fingers
run gently through the blue-streaked hair.

"Just like Chavi was found with chrysanthemums, each victim
has been left with some kind of flower. The first girl had jonquils; the
second had calla lilies."

"And Aimée?"

"Amaranth."

Priya lets out a soft huff. "Her mother grew amaranth. She had
a garden on the roof of their front porch, and she grew amaranth to
cook with. Aimée used to steal some every day to pin around her bun.
Her mother could never keep a straight face when scolding her for it,
and they'd always end up laughing together. You know another name
for amaranth?"

He shakes his head.

"Love-Lies-Bleeding."

Oh, hell.

"So whoever's delivering the flowers is copying the order of the
murders," Deshani says. She frowns down at Priya's hair, using her
thumb to measure growth from roots to the base of the colored
streaks. "We need to fix this."

"I keep meaning to ask."

Eddison clears his throat.

Deshani arches an eyebrow in response.

"There isn't a way to know yet if this is our killer, or a local creep
who figured out who you are and is getting off on terrorizing you. The
presence of the flowers in San Diego, the similarity you remember in
the cards, suggests the former, but we can't back it up yet."

"What would be proof?"

He freezes, and both women shift to look at him more clearly.

"Oh," Priya whispers.

"Oh?" Deshani echoes, tugging lightly on a lock of her daughter's hair. "Meaning what, precisely?"

Eddison nods. "Unless or until he tries to attack, or we catch him in the act of leaving the flowers, there's no way to know. The flowers by themselves don't mean enough."

"Don't mean enough?"

"Aren't by themselves a threat," Priya says. "Without evidence to the contrary, they're both gift and warning."

"Schrödinger's flowers," snorts her mother. "Lovely."

"What does that mean for FBI involvement?"

Why didn't he ask Vic to come with him? Vic is so much better at all of this.

"Eddison?" Deshani's eyebrows are in danger of disappearing into her hair. "Why do you look like we just called an executioner?"

"No matter who's leaving the flowers, it's still an FBI matter," he tells them. "It crossed state lines, which makes it ours."

"But?"

With a sigh, he gives them a carefully edited version of Vic and Finney's history with Section Chief Martha Ward, and her very narrow view of case responsibility. They listen intently, with the kind of focus that can be intimidating if you don't know them and downright terrifying when you do. When he's finished, mother and daughter share a long, inscrutable look.

"Small picture," Deshani says eventually. "How likely is she to prevent the agents coming down here?"

"If it stays intermittent, not very," he admits. "Finney doesn't like politics and he doesn't want to leave the field, but if it comes down to it, he's been in the Bureau almost as long as Vic; if he wants to take a swing at her, he can probably make it hurt. As long as the visits don't take up much time, she likely won't interfere."

"Until they get more frequent?" Priya shakes her head, and there's something shadowed in her eyes, something he's not sure how to ask about. "When the lab reports on the bouquets start showing more time and expense than she'll approve?"

"Priya . . ."

"Are we stuck in the middle of this?"

"Maybe." He ignores Deshani's muttered curses in favor of maintaining eye contact with Priya, trying to be as reassuring as possible. "Vic and Finney aren't going to just roll over and take it. They're going to fight for you. We just have to catch this guy before it comes to that."

"But in the meantime, my daughter is left at the mercy of someone who knows where we live and may have killed her sister."

He can't help but cringe at that.

"So what's being done right now?"

"Finney's looking into Landon," Eddison says. "The lack of a last name is making it difficult."

"So you think he's a possible suspect?"

"Person of interest, at this point. We'll see where it goes."

"Is it always waiting?" Priya asks quietly.

"It is, until it isn't." He gives her a lopsided smile. "But you already know that."

"So we wait."

"Why did you come all the way out here to tell us this?" Deshani's head is cocked to one side, her thumbs tapping the top of her feet in a repetitive but indiscernible rhythm. "There's nothing that couldn't have been delivered over the phone."

"Because I wanted you to see my face when I promise you that I'm not letting this bastard touch you."

Both women study him long enough to make sweat bead along his hairline. They have that effect on people separately; together they can be overwhelming.

Then Priya lets out a huff of air that might be laughter. "He needed to see our faces, Mum. We're family; he wants to make sure we're okay."

Deshani's snickering isn't what brings the blood rushing to his face, but it doesn't help.

He can't say she's wrong.

The next morning, Eddison brings fresh donuts and sits on the couch with a stack of paperwork while I Skype with my tutor in France. Despite everything else going on, I'm actually on top of my assignments, and the tutor is confident I'll be able to fold into a normal classroom without too much difficulty come fall.

Mum and I discussed trying to graduate early, here in the States, and starting university in the fall, but that felt a little like cliff-diving: exhilarating in theory, maybe not the most sensible way to live your life. The school my tutor is partnered with has a lot of international students, so they have a good support system in place for kids struggling with the transition to all French, all the time.

When I've gotten in enough work to feel virtuous—and Eddison has drunk half his body weight in nonhotel coffee—we bundle up to head out to chess.

"You walk this every day?" he asks.

I shake my head, waiting for the light to change at the intersection. "I average out to three times a week. Just whenever I feel like it."

"Any pattern?"

"I tend to skip Tuesdays; they're popular for doctor appointments."

Eddison nods, silently repeating the words, and it's like I can almost see him writing it down in his little mental notebook. As much as he lives out of the Moleskine in his back pocket, he really does try not to whip it out as a part of normal conversation, even when it involves a case.

It's warm enough today that my heavy coat isn't necessary, cold enough that the hoodie over a long-sleeve tee isn't quite doing the trick. I still have my scarf wrapped around my throat and tucked down under the zipper, with gloves and hat and boots in place. But it's mid-March in Colorado, and it's finally starting to feel a little like spring.

He has the photos that I took from chess, but he wants to get a feel for the men themselves. Specifically, though he hasn't said it, he wants to get a feel for Landon.

Happy hails me from halfway across the parking lot. "Blue Girl! Come play me! I've been losing!"

Eddison snorts softly beside me.

Shaking my head, I walk up onto the grassy island and greet everyone. Gunny is asleep, the sides of his face covered by the flaps of a hat I'm pretty sure I saw Hannah knitting last week. Landon is down at the opposite end, where he tends to hover. Gunny doesn't quite trust him, I think, but won't tell him to leave. "This is my friend Eddison," I announce. "He's in town for a couple of days."

Eddison nods, looking a bit menacing in his long tan coat. Somehow, the neon-green scarf isn't quite enough to ruin the look.

Pierce scratches at his nose, looking Eddison up and down. "Cop?" he asks finally.

"More or less."

Several of the men nod, and that's about as far as introductions go. The photos I emailed had captions with names so far as I knew them, and while names like Yelp and Corgi and Happy aren't especially helpful, they were something to start on.

I sit down across from Happy so I can hear the conversations start back up. Eddison prowls around the tables, looking down at the games in progress. I guess cop (more or less) is enough like veteran to establish rapport. No one looks at him twice, really.

Except Landon.

Landon fidgets, more than usual. His eyes dart around as if to see how everyone else is taking the intrusion, and he drops almost every piece as he tries to move it. One of the rooks drops so hard it leaves a dent in the board, despite the felt padding on the bottom.

As Eddison settles onto the very end of the bench next to Landon, he strikes up an easy, comfortable conversation with the other men. It's interesting to see the agent side of Eddison, when he isn't tap-dancing around a child's sensibilities.

They talk about neighborhoods and safety, and I don't think they even realize how much they're telling him about where they live and what's going on around them. He invites introductions from them, garnering last names without any apparent effort, and makes them all laugh with stories from physical training at the FBI academy, which they try to top with boot camp escapades.

Landon is again the exception. He doesn't offer his name—not even his first one, though it's already been said by one of the others—and he doesn't look away from the board the entire time they're talking neighborhoods. Eddison takes note of whenever Landon flinches, and I'm willing to bet he has a map of Huntington ready to mark up with possible areas for Landon's residence.

Without any overt intimidation, Eddison has Landon absolutely terrified.

It's a little worrisome, actually, because yes, Landon is a creep, but he shouldn't be this scared unless he's a creep with something to hide. It's also kind of hilarious, because Eddison and Mum have more in common than I thought. I'm pretty sure he'd be offended if I told him.

I'll save it for a special occasion.

Generally—by which I mean every single time I've been here—Landon doesn't leave the pavilion until I do, so he can follow me into the market. This time, he barely makes it an hour before he mumbles a goodbye and walks very quickly away.

Steven, one of the Desert Storm vets, looks after him, glances at Eddison's thoughtful smirk, then turns to me. "You should have said if he was bothering you."

"Didn't want to disrupt the dynamic."

"Safety's more important."

But they're old soldiers, and sometimes there are different views of what is or is not appropriate behavior between males and females. I like the vets, and their awkward chivalry, but that doesn't mean I'm going to assume we hold the same views.

"Eddison is in town for a work thing," I say instead. "Being able to assess whether or not I'm paranoid was just a perk."

Steven turns back to Eddison, who's settling himself comfortably into the abandoned camp chair. "So is she?"

"Paranoid?" At Steven's nod, he shrugs. "No. Man doesn't run like that unless he knows he's thinking wrong thoughts."

"Going to do anything about it?"

"Can't arrest a man for thinking, but he's less likely to act if he's got the fear of God in him."

And they all nod, because the man took care of business, and if it weren't so entertaining, I'd probably be offended.

Sea level and mountains have very different kinds of cold, even if the temperature is theoretically the same, so Eddison doesn't even make it another hour before his teeth start chattering in spite of the heaters. I kiss Gunny on the cheek, making the others catcall and chortle, and lead Eddison into the store.

He scowls at the Starbucks logo. He has something against fancy coffee, so any place that charges him more than a dollar for a big-ass cup of black coffee has his eternal enmity. When we lived in D.C., Mercedes's favorite form of entertainment was Eddison and Mum getting coffee together.

While he's trying to set the sign on fire with his glare, I see Joshua get up from his table, a peacoat draped over his arm. He seems to like fisherman sweaters; at the least, he seems to have an endless supply of them. This one is a sort of faded heather that works well with his greying auburn hair. He sees me and smiles, lifting his cup of tea in a kind of salute, but doesn't stop to chat on his way out the door.

Drinks in hand, Eddison and I walk back to the house in comfortable silence. We both stop and look at the empty doorstep.

"I'm not sure if I wanted flowers to be there or not," he says after a minute.

"I know that feeling."

Once I'm safely inside, the door locked behind me, he takes off back to Denver, to check in with Finney and then fly back east. I'm not ignorant of how far he's stretched allowable limits for my sake, and maybe for his own. I was only ever supposed to be part of a case, not a part of his life, but here I am, five years later, closer family than blood in many ways, and I don't regret it.

I don't think he does either, even when it forces him into some difficult decisions.

I give a few hours over to getting ahead on schoolwork, because it seems like the responsible thing to do, quibble with Mum via text over what to do for dinner (she wins, but only because we haven't actually had curry since Birmingham), and then pull out Inara's letter.

I'm not sure why I haven't mentioned it to Eddison. He knows her, even if he doesn't know whether or not he likes her (he gives away a lot more than he realizes). It's nice, though, keeping it to myself. Keeping it *for* myself, maybe.

Setting the letter on top of my current journal, I grab the first of the Washington, D.C. journals from the stack on my floor. All the rest are still downstairs, but San Diego is where things changed and D.C. is where I realized how much things changed, and I can't help but read back through them looking for clues.

Two years ago, I made a friend in San Diego. Her name was Aimée Browder, and she was in love with all things French. Despite my intention to keep myself to myself, she was there; just all the time there, without being pushy or nosy. I let her talk me into French Club and movies and hanging out, and some afternoons I'd sit by the door in the ballet studio where she took classes and do my homework to the sounds of classical music, murmured instructions, and the thumps of successfully landed jumps.

In spite of everything, she was my friend, so when Mum and I were about to move to D.C., I asked Aimée if we could keep in touch. And we did, actually, for about a week and a half. I wasn't worried for the first few days of silence; we were both busy. She'd respond when she got the chance.

Then I got a call from her mother, who was sobbing so hard she had to hand the phone to her husband so he could tell me Aimée was dead. Their daughter, my friend, had been murdered, and as soon as he said church and flowers, I knew it was connected to Chavi in some way. It didn't seem possible that it could be coincidence.

That night wasn't the first time I ate myself sick. Far from, really; it had been almost three years by that point. I think it was the worst, though. I stuffed myself so overfull I couldn't even cry it hurt so badly, gasping for breath and feeling like I was about to split down my sides. Mum was two seconds from hauling me to the hospital to get my stomach pumped, but somehow that was the thing that tipped me into full-blown hysterics.

I didn't want Eddison to know it was that bad. Didn't want Vic and Mercedes to know at all.

They called from San Diego with questions about Aimée, things they had to ask for the investigation even if they really didn't want to. I could hear how worried they were, and though I was still sick as shit, I *craved* more, just because it hurt so badly.

It took days before I could eat again. Even then, Mum had to make me. I couldn't look at food without my stomach cramping painfully.

To distract myself, I started researching the other murders, because I couldn't shake the feeling that my ignorance had gotten Aimée killed. Mum pretended she wasn't clinging as she looked over my shoulder. She was the one to notice that the flowers surrounding the murdered girls matched the bouquets that had shown up on our doorstep in San Diego.

Yellow and white jonquils for Darla Jean Carmichael, dead as long as I'd been alive.

Purple-throated calla lilies for Zoraida Bourret, found in her family's Methodist church on Easter Sunday.

Clumps of baby's breath for Leigh Clark, a preacher's daughter in Eugene, Oregon.

A crown of honeysuckle for Sasha Wolfson, whose cousin told stories of a girl who plucked blossoms out of her hair to touch their sweetness to her tongue.

Colorful sprays of freesia for Mandy Perkins, who built fairy villages in nursing home gardens around Jacksonville, Florida.

White carnations for Libba Laughran, veined and tipped and red so they looked like they were bleeding. She was only fourteen when she was raped and killed outside of Phoenix.

No flowers came to D.C., though, nor to Atlanta after we moved that November. There were none in Omaha or Birmingham, aside from the ones sent by the idiot coworker in Nebraska. No mystery flowers, then, so it never seemed worth telling my agents.

If we hadn't left San Diego when we did, it would have been columbines at our door next, for Emily Adams, seventeen years old, from St. Paul, Minnesota, and no relation to later victim Meaghan Adams. She was a musician, according to the articles and tribute pages we read. She sang like an angel, especially with folk songs, and played every instrument she could get her hands on. A few days before she was murdered, she organized a rally in response to a school shooting in Connecticut; she clipped a couple blue columbines to the end of her guitar, to honor decades of victims as she played.

When the bastard killed Emily, he draped a ribbon of flowers over her throat, to hide the gaping wound. It was mentioned in a couple of articles about the killing, but there were pictures, too, on true crime websites that somehow managed to get crime scene photos from most of the murders.

Impressive, considering the FBI wasn't brought in until the tenth victim, Kiersten Knowles.

Even with all the research Mum and I did, we don't have half the information the FBI does, but I'd guess we're no further from the answer. All these facts to be found but nothing that leads anywhere. If I get a name someday, the identity of the man who murdered Chavi and the others, will that bring peace? If he goes to trial and is found guilty, is that justice?

I look at the folded pages of Inara's letter, then reach for a pen and loose paper.

Dear Inara,

My mum has said on occasion that it's a shame people can only die once; one of her dearest wishes is to find our nightmare and kill him again and again and again, once for each person he killed and once again just for us.

I don't know that it's any more or less just than imprisonment or formal execution.

I used to think it would mean something. I'd dream about being in a courtroom when a jury foreman read out guilty, and the unknown man with the blurred-out face behind the defense table would start weeping. Noisily, messily, the kind of crying that leaves you mortified because there are just globs of snot dripping everywhere. He'd be broken, and Mum and I would laugh, giddy and bright, and fall into each other's arms.

We'd be happy.

We wouldn't hurt anymore.

At some point, I realized that it wouldn't bring Chavi back. Nothing would.

Suddenly I couldn't stand the thought of any resolution that left the asshole alive, weeping or not.

I have no answers.

I have no wisdom.

What I have is a healthy sense of spite and a determination that someday I'm going to learn how to do this thing called living. Maybe that's as far as justice can stretch.

There's no actual reason to switch his destination from D.C. to New York, but Eddison does it anyway, thumb rubbing against the dark screen of his phone where the message from Vic sleeps. At the moment, still a little raw from worry and frustration, he doesn't want to look into his motivations all that deeply. Not when there's something itching at him about how the Sravastis took the news about the stalker, and he can't put his finger on what it is or why it's bothering him.

So he makes the switch, knowing he can take the train between cities and get a few hours of paperwork in, and maybe he'll even call it virtuous. The train is a hell of a lot more comfortable than the plane, anyway.

He hates the subway, isn't particularly fond of the metro back home, but it still seems a better option than dropping fifty bucks on a taxi just to get into the city. He stands against one of the poles, a safe distance from heaped shopping bags, luggage, and sprawled limbs, counting stops and listening to the familiar mix of phone calls, conversations in a dozen languages, and the fuzzy music that seeps too loud out of headphones and earbuds.

A little girl perched on her grandfather's lap catches his eye and giggles, her hands fisted in a hand-knit scarf almost the same obnoxiously bright green as his. He smiles slightly, and she giggles again before burying her face in her grandfather's shoulder. She's still laughing, though; he can see the two puffs of ponytail high on her head shake.

He knows, in a purely theoretical sort of way, that Inara lives in a shit neighborhood. She was straightforward about that much the first time they questioned her. When she was released from the hospital, she moved right back in. The agents in the New York office prefer to visit the restaurant if they need to see her or Bliss for something.

Knowing it is very different from seeing it.

Standing outside the stairs to the subway, he takes a deep breath and promptly gags on an unexpected lungful of garbage and urine from the alley. He adjusts to the smell after a minute or two—he's breathed worse, in his line of work—and carefully buttons his suit coat and trench to cover the gun at his hip. He'd feel better if he could access it quickly, but that's not the kind of attention he wants to bring to himself, especially not when he's technically on his own time.

He finds the building, a faded brick monstrosity with the remains of a wrought-iron gate hanging around the front steps. There's an intercom to the left of the door so guests can be buzzed in, but that seems more like wishful thinking. He's not sure if the sledgehammer hit it before or after the bullets but either way, it's not working. In the tiny lobby, half the mailboxes are cracked open, envelopes and circulars strewn over the floor. He can see official letterhead on some of the stomped-on envelopes.

The girls' mailbox is just fine, though, freshly painted in dull silver that almost matches the tarnished metal beneath, and covered in flower stickers. Above it, a note on cheerful pink paper is pinned to the wall. He recognizes Bliss's handwriting, large and round, almost bubbly, really only missing the cute shapes above the lowercase *i*'s. *If you take our mail, I take your balls. Or lady-balls, I'm not particular.*

Jesus.

It's signed with a fucking smiley face.

Both paper and ink are a little faded, and their mailbox is intact, so clearly it struck the right tone for the building. Adjusting the weight of his bags on his back, he heads into the stairwell. There's an elevator shaft, but it seems to be lacking the rather necessary elevator.

And doors. Doors would be important.

He's a little winded by the time he reaches their floor, second from the top, and is contemplating adding stadiums to his exercise regimen. He can run for miles across level surface, but stairs are surprisingly problematic.

Fortunately—or not—he doesn't even have to remember the apartment number. All he has to do is look for the drunk passed out on the floor. The man's been sleeping outside their door for years, apparently, and none of the girls have the heart to chase him off or tell the cops, so they just go up to the roof and down the fire escape to come in through their very large window.

Eddison isn't that kind.

He kicks the drunk's feet, just hard enough to jolt him without risking energy. "Find someplace else, buddy."

"'Sa free country," the man slurs, curling tighter around his bottle.

Leaning over, Eddison grabs the man's ankle and starts walking backward, hauling the swearing and wailing drunk along with him until he can plant him halfway between doors.

Inara's door opens and a head pops out, red-gold hair fluffing out around it in an enormous halo. "Hey, are you harassing our drunk?"

"Just moving him," Eddison replies. He drops the man's ankle. The drunk promptly sprawls along the floor, messily gulping from his bottle. "Are you Whitney?"

"And you are?"

He's unaccountably relieved by her blatant suspicion. "Special Agent Brandon Eddison, here to see Inara if she's in."

The woman's face lights up in recognition. She's probably in her mid or late twenties, one eye discolored and the pupil blown in a way that looks permanent. "Hang on. I'll get her."

After a short wait, a sleepy-eyed Inara walks out into the hall, still shrugging into a hoodie. Her hair is mussed around her, her feet shoved in Eeyore slippers. "Eddison?"

"If we go to the roof, will you be warm enough?"

She nods and fumbles with the hoodie's zipper. She has to stop halfway up to wrestle her hair out of the way before she can close it the rest of the way. Her hands, curled into the sleeves, rub at her eyes as she leads the way up to the roof. The roof is strewn with furniture, from basic lawn chairs to a plastic-wrapped couch under a makeshift awning that may have started life as a pair of hammocks.

She walks all the way across the roof until they can sit in a cluster of canvas camp chairs against the front ledge. If he leans over just a little, he can see their landing of the fire escape, two of Inara's roommates smoking and laughing.

"You realize it's three in the afternoon?" he asks eventually.

She scowls sleepily, and it's a little bit adorable in a way she generally isn't, soft and growling and a bit like a grumpy kitten. "Kegs had a party after closing," she mumbles around a yawn. "We didn't get back till eight this morning. And then we were helping Noémie practice her presentation for her eleven-o'clock class."

"And you go to work . . ."

"We have to leave around four-thirty." She pulls her feet up onto the chair. "What's up?" "Judge Merrill granted the no-contact order," he tells her without preamble. "Any further attempts to contact you, and Desmond can be charged."

Well, that wakes her up. She stares at him for a moment, her pale, almost amber eyes wide and fixed on him. Then she blinks, thinking her way through it, and finally nods. "That was fast."

"There wasn't really a way for the defense to argue against it. While it wasn't illegal for Desmond to write you, it was inappropriate, and the judge wasn't happy with the content of the letters."

"The cont—shit. Of course you had to read them."

He clears his throat. "Vic read them. And the judge and lawyers, but Vic. Vic read them."

She rests her chin on her knees, and he has the uncomfortable feeling she's stripping the words far past what he wanted them to mean. Christ, his mental health and well-being are suddenly very dependent on her never meeting the Sravastis. Priya and Deshani understand him far too well as it is; he does not need them teaching Inara anything. A man needs to preserve some capacity for self-delusion, after all. All she says, though, is "I guess you wouldn't find the letters of a lovesick twat very interesting."

He snorts and leans back in the chair. "From what I understand, that part of it wasn't the problem."

"Problem?"

"From what Vic tells me, somewhere in the midst of begging your forgiveness, Desmond slipped in a few pleas for you not to testify against him or his father. To, ah . . . *understand*."

She blinks at him.

"Asking forgiveness is one thing, even if he still doesn't seem to have a full grasp of his part in things. Asking you not to testify, putting that kind of pressure on you with the weight of your history . . . that's attempting to influence a witness, and that crosses into bad territory."

"Still claims to love me?"

"Yes. Do you believe him?"

"No?"

He looks out over the roof, noting scorch marks where there used to be a flourishing crop of marijuana, from her stories. There are baskets of toys here and there, and it looks like someone tried to make a swing set out of piping at one point or another. He wouldn't ever trust a child on it, but it probably makes parties a little more interesting.

She sighs, and it takes more than he expected not to look back at her. Some truths are easier when no one's watching. "I know he believes he loves me," she says slowly. "Whether or not I believe he actually does . . . I don't know. Maybe he's like his father, it's love as he knows it, but I don't . . . I don't think I want to believe that love can be that out of touch with reality."

"Maybe he needs to believe it's love," he offers. From the corner of his eye, he can see her nod.

"I'll buy that. If it's real, maybe it absolves him in some way. Everyone's fascinated by the things people do for love."

"But you think it's a little more than that."

"If it wasn't love, what was it?"

"Rape," he says bluntly.

"Exactly. Boy like Desmond, he doesn't want to think of himself as a rapist."

"Why didn't you read the letters?"

She's silent for long enough that this time he does look back at her. She's staring down at her slippers, fingers stroking the tufts of black along the Eeyore heads. The slippers are ridiculous and not something he'd expect her to love or even really to wear, but that's probably exactly why someone gave them to her.

"Surviving the Garden," she says finally, voice barely more than a whisper, "*thriving* in the Garden, relied on understanding the Gardener. Understanding his sons. I'm out of the Garden now, and I don't *want* to understand anymore. I don't want to live in that anymore. I get that he needs to explain, but I need to not listen. I need to not bear that weight. I need . . ." She swallows, her eyes bright with tears, but he suspects she's pissed more than sad. "I need to not hear him swear he loves me."

There's something there, something Vic would probably recognize and know how to gracefully address.

"His feelings aren't your fault, you know."

Eddison is not graceful.

She snorts, blinking away the tears and the rage, back to more comfortable ground with mockery and sniping. "I learned a long time ago not to claim responsibility for men's *feelings* about me."

"Then you already know that whatever his feelings for you, whatever he thinks those feelings are, you don't have to feel guilty about the pain they're causing him."

"Okay, Yoda."

A squeal of metal gives them half a moment's notice before a head pops up over the ladder to the fire escape. "Inara! Come introduce your agent!"

He glances at Inara, mouths *Your agent?*

She just shrugs. "It's better than pet agent."

Thank fucking God.

"Come on," she tells him, sliding to her feet. "You can meet the ones here and then come with us. Now you've seen the apartment, you're going to twitch until you check out our route to work."

"You always take the same route?"

She just rolls her eyes and starts down the ladder.

Most of the young women are familiar from Inara's stories of them. After introductions, four of them get dressed and head out, their uniforms already at the restaurant. They chatter and laugh on the subway, doing hair and makeup without mirrors or mistakes despite the swaying of the train and the constant stops and starts. They exchange greetings with a few people who seem to be regulars on the route.

Eddison has shared a hotel room with Ramirez enough to have a slightly befuddled awe for the process of full makeup, but that was seeing her tools spread out across the entire top of the dresser with multiple mirrors. Watching this quartet makes him fervently glad to be male, where getting his face ready for work may or may not mean shaving.

The Evening Star is much nicer than he expects, given where the girls choose to live. Even in his suit, he feels a little underdressed.

"Come meet Guilian," Inara says, pushing him into the restaurant. "Besides, Bliss will pout if she knows you were here and didn't say hello."

"Pout? Or cheer?"

"I don't see why she can't do both."

Guilian is a large, heavyset redhead whose thinning hair is retreating from his scalp and finding refuge in the bristling moustache that hides most of the lower half of his face. He clasps Eddison's hand in a firm grip, his other hand on the agent's shoulder. "Thank you for helping Inara get home safely," he says solemnly.

If Eddison looks half as uncomfortable as he feels, he can completely understand why Inara is snickering beside him.

Bliss is hardly five feet of snarls and attitude and a mouth bigger than the world, but when she bares her teeth at him, it's a hell of a lot closer to a smile than he usually sees from her. "I thought I felt the tone of the place lower." Her curly black hair is pinned back in an intricate twist, safely away from the food, and it's only seeing her stand next to one of the other waitresses that he realizes her uniform is slightly different.

The waiters all wear tuxedos, the waitresses strapless black evening gowns with stand-alone collars and cuffs in crisp white, black bow-ties at their throats. But Bliss—and, he's willing to bet, Inara—has a style that comes up over her back, the collar stitched to the neck. It covers the wings.

He looks over at Guilian, standing in the door to the kitchen, and the restaurant owner and chef nods.

Small wonder Inara came back to work at the same restaurant.

Bliss kicks him in the ankle, more annoying than painful, and it isn't hard to imagine a yappy little ankle-biter dog with her curly hair. "Please tell me he can't write her anymore," she says quietly.

"Not without consequence."

"He doesn't understand consequence as well as he should."

"Perhaps not."

"Is your other pet okay?" Her smile gets wider at his groan, almost friendly. Almost. "Vic mentioned you were gone for a case. Seemed a little strange he and Mercedes wouldn't be there."

"We do individual consults, you know."

"Is she okay?"

"She's fine for now," he sighs. He's starting to think he did something terrible in a previous life to be surrounded by such dangerous women in this one.

He'd do it again in a heartbeat.

"If Guilian offers you the chef's table, take it," she advises him. "He doesn't do it often."

"Isn't that in the kitchen?"

"Yep."

"Don't you all hang out in the kitchen when you're not checking on patrons?"

Her wicked laugh answers that. A wiser man would make his excuses, maybe. Make his escape, definitely.

But Guilian holds the kitchen door open in invitation, and Eddison finds himself nodding, and what the hell, how often is he going to get to eat in a restaurant this nice?

The baby's breath looks different this time. The tissue paper wrapping is sky blue, not green, and there are thin blue ribbons twined through the stiff clusters. The card is the same, though, and I dutifully send pictures along to Finney and Eddison before heading back inside to make sure we have a couple of clean mugs.

When my new agents arrive, Archer accepts the offer of coffee with a startled smile, while Sterling sheepishly asks if we have any tea.

Lord, do we ever.

Archer keeps giving me strange looks as they check over the bundle and ask me questions, like he expects me to still be bitchy about last Thursday. I don't generally have the energy for grudges, but if it makes him sweat, I'm content to leave the impression uncorrected. Sterling keeps an eye on him, in a very subtle, understated way. Archer probably doesn't even notice. I don't know that I would have picked up on it if she hadn't deliberately caught my eye before turning back to him.

It's weirdly comforting.

I have the security footage pulled up on my laptop, cued to about half an hour after Mum left for work. It's too dark to get a good picture of whoever left the flowers and I'm not sure if that's purposeful or not. There's maybe an impression of height (average) but even when Archer fiddles with filters to bring out more detail, the person is too bundled up against the cold to get anything useful. Only their eyes and a bit of the nose are visible.

"Do you recognize him?" Archer asks, as Sterling scans back earlier than the time stamp.

"How are you so sure it's a he?"

"Way he walks, stands," Sterling answers absently. Her eyes are glued to the screen, looking for anything that jumps out before the mystery man approached.

Archer leans against the back of the couch. "So that's a no on the recognition, then."

"I can see why they gave you the shiny, shiny badge."

Sterling turns her aborted laugh into a throat-clearing cough. "We'll ask your neighbors, find out if anyone saw where he came from or went. Maybe someone will know who he is."

"Did your section chief give approval for that?"

"We're not going to stop doing our jobs in anticipation of being told to back off," she says easily.

"And when the neighbors ask what's going on?"

"You really think they don't already know who you are?" Archer shakes his head at his partner's glare. "Every spring, every city with a victim starts plastering photos all over the place with if-you-have-new-information-call banners. Your mother was profiled in the *Economist* and said you were moving to Huntington. People know who you are, Priya. It's inescapable."

"Just because you've studied a case obsessively doesn't mean everyone else is familiar with it," I retort. "Most people don't pay that much attention to something that doesn't directly affect them."

"When the new neighbors bring a serial killer trailing along after them, it tends to affect people."

It affected Aimée, but of course, none of us knew that was a possibility until it was too late. He's still an asshole for pointing it out.

"You don't even know if this is the killer," I say, and Sterling nods.

"Who else could it possibly be?"

"You should have seen some of the letters and gifts we got from the crime fans and amateur grief counselors. You'd be amazed how many people thought it was appropriate to send us chrysanthemums."

A tinkling piano theme rings out during the appalled silence, and Sterling glances at it with a frown. "Finney. I'll be right back." Answering the call with a perfunctory "Sir," she heads into the kitchen.

"When do you move to Paris?" asks Archer.

"May."

"Hm." He fidgets with the cuff of his coat, fingers running along the nearly invisible line of stitches. "You know . . ."

"I'm assuming I'm about to."

"Finney really didn't warn us about your mouth."

"How would Finney know?" I give him a sweet, innocent smile and swallow the last of my tea.

Archer stares at me, then visibly collects himself. "You know that if this is the killer, this could be our only chance to catch him? We may never again know what city he's in *before* he kills."

"Looking for a career boost, Agent Archer?"

"Trying to bring to justice a man who's killed sixteen girls," he snaps. "Seeing as one of them is your sister, I'd think you'd be a bit more appreciative."

"You'd think."

I can actually hear his teeth grinding.

"Finney said you live here in Huntington," I say after a while. Warmth seeps into my fingers where they're wrapped around my empty mug. "From what I understand, you're supposed to be doing drive-bys before and after work?"

"I *am* driving by, yes."

"Then it seems to me the person in the best position to learn anything would be you. After all, if he wanted me or Mum to see him, he'd just knock on the door or ring the bell." I shrug at his nasty look. "The problem with making me bait—as I assume you were going to propose—is that it's of limited value if the target doesn't know he's on a deadline. Why should he hurry?"

"But if you leave before the flowers finish—"

"Did any of his victims get flowers before their deaths?"

"Not that we've been able to determine," Sterling answers, standing in the kitchen doorway and watching us thoughtfully. She flips her phone in her hand, catching it easily. "What are you thinking?"

"I'm thinking we don't know enough to guess at the intentions of the person sending these," I say honestly. "If it's the killer, he's breaking pattern. If it's not the killer, we can't trust him to follow a pattern he didn't create. There's no way to know if he'll go all the way down the line." I know what I'm willing to trust, but they're federal agents; they're not supposed to make assumptions based on gut feelings. "Bait is only useful if you know what the reaction is going to be."

"No one is going to suggest using you as bait," Sterling says, her voice sharp.

We both look at Archer, who at least has the grace to look uncomfortable.

"Finney needs us up in Denver," Sterling continues after a moment. "We'll be back this evening, though, to talk to the neighbors. Hopefully we'll catch them home from work. I'll check in with you when we call it a night."

"Bring a travel mug. We'll hook you up with tea for the drive home."

She actually smiles, a bright flash of a thing here and gone that lights up her whole face.

The agents head out into the grey Monday, sleet drizzling down unpleasantly. I don't have any intention of walking through that to go to chess. Checking the porch has become a habit, though, even when I have no plans to leave the house.

I text the Quantico Three to give them an update, then knuckle down to schoolwork for a few hours. After a lunch of leftover pizza, I plant myself in the living room with the empty journal boxes. For the past week, the journals have just sat there in heaps except when I'm reading them.

Neatly ordered heaps, thanks to Mum, but heaps nonetheless. It's time to put them away for now. I even bring down the journals I have in my room.

Still, when I get to the San Diego books, I take them to the couch and curl up with them. I only skimmed through before, looking for the entries about the flower deliveries, and Mum was the one to make scans for the agents. This time, I want to actually read them.

It feels like sitting with Aimée for a while, and I owe her that much. I'm not naïve enough to think her death is my fault, but it is my burden. I owe it to her to remember her not just as a victim, but as my friend.

Aimée was the effortless kind of pretty, and genuinely didn't seem to recognize that she was. Not that she thought she was ugly, she just didn't seem to pay attention to what was in the mirror short of making sure her hair was in order. When the amaranth was in bloom, she'd pin pink-red clusters around her ribbon-wrapped bun, and her mother would tease her about stealing food. She was in ballet and ran the French Club. Her love for all things French came from her mother, I'm sure, who moved from Mexico to France for school and then fell in love with an American.

We were in French class together, the only two with the intent of actually using the language, not just because we needed it to graduate or get scholarships. I'm still not entirely sure how she talked me into French Club, except that she promised it wouldn't ask anything of me, and maybe I was lonely by that point. I used to be a social creature. I remember that. I just can't remember what it was that made me work that way.

Aimée was sweet, and kind, and she never asked me why I was hurting, and I never explained. It was such a relief to have one person in my life who didn't know about Chavi. One person who didn't know the old Priya, and so couldn't compare me to who I'd been and find me lacking or discomfiting now. Aimée saw my thorns and never tried to tell me I shouldn't have them.

Asking her if we could stay in touch may have been the bravest thing I'd ever done. I couldn't decide how I wanted her to answer. Keeping a friend seemed just as terrifying as losing one.

She was there with me the day I found baby's breath on the doorstep. She'd laughed and said someone forgot to add the flowers, and I pinned it all around her bun until she had a bristling crown like a fairy.

And when I told Chavi about it, the ink all glittery pink for a good mood, I said how much it reminded me of that last birthday party, all the flower crowns and the wreath of white silk roses I still had in my dresser.

Still have in my dresser.

Thoughts of Aimée keep running through my head as I pack my journals back into the boxes, this time keeping them carefully in order. Chavi and I used the journals to settle any number of arguments or faulty memories, or just reminiscing for the hell of it, and they always ended up repacked however we happened to shove them in, hers and mine all mixed together. This time, though, it's just mine in each box, until the last three finished books sit atop the taped boxes.

Over dinner, Mum points at the stacks of Chavi's journals, the sushi roll nearly falling from her chopsticks as she waves them around. "Have you thought about what to do with those?"

"What to do with them?"

"Are we taking them with us?"

The whole house is a mess, as we're finally going through boxes and deciding what we are definitely taking with us to France, what we need to think about more, and what we're either throwing out or donating. It hadn't occurred to me to think about the journals.

"I'm not suggesting throwing them out," she continues after a moment. She eyes me carefully, like she's afraid I'm about to explode. "I'm saying maybe you should read back through them, decide what you want to do."

"Will you mind if I keep them?"

She twirls her chopsticks to flick me on the nose with the clean ends. "I don't like holding on to the past, you know that, but this is

154

not something for me to decide. As much as those are Chavi's diaries, they're also letters to you. If you want to keep them, keep them. Whatever you decide . . ." She blows out a sharp breath, tongue flicking over her lip to catch a grain of rice clinging to the gold hoop. "France can be a fresh start for us, but I will never, ever suggest leaving Chavi behind. I just want to make sure we're keeping them because you want them, not because you feel like you should."

Okay, I can see that.

So while Mum rattles around the kitchen swearing at the boxes of pots and plates and all, I settle back into the couch with the first stack of love letters from my sister. I've only ever seen the pieces Chavi chose to show me.

The early ones are written in crayon, the letters huge and sometimes oddly formed, the spelling absolutely atrocious in a way that's only cute when the writer is in a single-digit age. She was so excited about me, promising to be the best-ever big sister, to love me always, even swearing up and down to share her favorite toys. The one about two days after I was born is freaking adorable, mainly because she was so sulky it practically oozes off the paper.

Somehow five-year-old Chavi hadn't quite understood that a baby sister would be, you know, *a baby*, and therefore not able to play with her right away.

It sets a comfortable pattern. I get up in the morning, check the front step, do my schoolwork, sometimes head to chess or the store, come back in the afternoon to go through my stuff and the linens, more schoolwork, dinner, help Mum with downstairs boxes, and then spend half the night reading Chavi's journals.

On Friday, there's a wreath of honeysuckle nestled on a bed of blue tissue paper, sitting in what looks to be a cake box on the porch.

On Monday, there's a bouquet of freesia in a violent explosion of color, pink and yellow and white and purple and rusty orange, the stems curling out past the large blooms to show the partially unfurled buds.

The carnations come on Wednesday, the burgundy tips bleeding down through the veins of the white petals. That's where they stopped last time. Instead of Agents Sterling and Archer, the latter of whom I've seen only in passing as he drives down our street, Agent Finnegan comes to check on those.

"Are you doing okay?" he asks, not looking away from the rectangle of card stock in his gloved hands.

"Sure." I lean against the doorframe, holding my cup of cocoa close to my face so the steam can offset the breeze. It is warming up outside, hovering in the high fifties the past couple of days, and the meteorologist is cheerfully predicting low seventies next week. It's just that I'm in pajamas meant for inside only, without the urge to reach for the coat only a few feet away. "Just wish I knew what to expect next."

"Columbines," he answers absently, tucking the card into a separate plastic bag. "You know what those look like?"

"Blue? There's a song about them, I think." I didn't actually mean the flowers, but his response is weirdly reassuring, like it didn't occur to him not to tell me.

He stays in his crouch, forearms draped over his knees as he looks up at me. "Your friendly neighborhood creep is hard to learn about."

"Landon?"

"Eddison narrowed down his possible neighborhoods, but no one in those areas claims to recognize him and we're having trouble finding any paperwork on him. No lease, no mortgage. Neither the DMV nor post office has any records of a Landon in the area. We're expanding the search, but it's slow going."

"It isn't Landon on the security camera," I remind him. "The eyes are the wrong shape."

He frowns and glances up at me. "Archer was supposed to tell you: we found the one on the camera."

"What?"

"Student down at Hunt U; he makes extra cash doing deliveries. One of your neighbors identified him in the picture with the freesia. When we talked to him, he said the flowers were dropped off in his car with an envelope containing the address and his delivery fee, and a requested time of delivery."

"He leaves his car unlocked so people can anonymously deliver things through him?" I ask incredulously. "That sounds . . . that's . . ."

"Idiotic in the extreme," he agrees. "Also a good way to land in prison if he assists with illegal goods. He said he'd contact us if anything else showed up."

"So either he chose not to, or these were delivered a different way."

"Exactly. And something off the grid like this could match your paperless friend Landon. He's not at the chess pavilion this morning—I checked on my way here—and we're in court the rest of the week; next week, either Archer or I will accompany you to chess, and hopefully we can talk to him, or even follow him home."

"I haven't seen him since Eddison was out here. So, week and a half?"

"Not at all?"

"Nope."

"Have your vets?"

"Haven't asked." I watch his frown deepen, his gloved fingers rubbing against each other in thought. "You're worried."

He reaches for his hair, catching himself just in time. He's an odd mix of parentage, delicate of face but burly of body, his skin Irish pale and densely spattered with very light brown freckles, but his hair silky and dark. "Victor Hanoverian trained me. We were partners until I got my own team and he pulled Eddison and Ramirez. I've seen him walk into hostage situations and crossfire without so much as twitching. So the fact that he emails me every day to ask if there's any new information? Yes, I'm worried, because him being twitchy scares the shit out of me."

It's an honesty I don't expect out of someone who's practically a stranger, but I'm grateful for it. "He's scared about what happens when the flowers catch up to last year's victim, isn't he?"

"Or what happens if you leave before they're cycled through," he admits. "If you move, what if he does too? That puts the case out of FBI hands."

"Could you give the case file to Interpol?"

"Yes, and if it comes to it, we will. But will they give it any attention?"

"Thank you."

"For what?"

"For not downplaying," I say with a shrug. "If I hadn't hidden my head in the sand after Chavi died, maybe I would have known to report the flowers in San Diego. We wouldn't be doing all this, and you wouldn't have to sneak around your section chief. Maybe Aimée would still be alive, and the girl after her."

"Hey, now, no." He straightens out of his crouch, one knee cracking painfully, but aside from a wince he doesn't seem to care. He's a little shorter than I am, but he holds himself taller, a presence even when he isn't putting effort into it. "You can't think that way."

"It's the truth, isn't it?"

"We have absolutely no way to know that. Priya, look at me."

His eyes are dark, iris almost impossible to discern from pupil, but he has the most ridiculously long lashes I've ever seen on a man.

"You cannot think that way," he repeats firmly. "None of this is your fault. We have no way to know what would have happened if things had been different in San Diego. What we've got is right now. You are doing everything you can."

"Okay."

He looks frustrated, and I wonder if I'm going to be getting a call from Eddison or Vic. Agent Finnegan, while very kind, doesn't know me well enough to successfully argue a point. "Let's see what the camera caught."

The footage shows a woman this time, a heavy sweater open over the black, red, and yellow polo shirt worn by the employees at the gas station a few blocks down. I don't recognize the woman herself, but that's no surprise; I only go into the store when the cold makes me have to pee too badly to get all the way home from chess. When that happens, I'll buy a drink or a candy bar so I'm not the asshole who uses the bathroom without being a customer, but it's not so often that I know anyone who works there.

"I'll go down and see if they can identify her," Finney says as he heads out. "And, Priya . . . the sum of what you can do is what you're already doing. Don't suffer weight that isn't yours to carry."

Columbine comes in a variety of colors, and looks like two different flowers stacked together with a white broad-petaled heart, throats dark to match the thinner, longer petals underneath. The ones that arrive on Friday, delivered by a very confused postal worker who found them in his passenger seat, are blue and purple.

Emily Adams sang about blue columbines, just a few days before she died.

Which is probably why, for the first time, the ribbon on the bouquet isn't curled plastic. It's white satin, printed with black music notes. Not just the flowers of her death, but something of her life, as well.

Ramirez is in Delaware, doing a follow-up consultation to a case they closed in February, but apparently she didn't tell the sort-of girlfriend this, because there is an enormous bouquet of sunflowers on her desk.

The deliveryman had to hold them while Eddison shoved aside enough paper to make room for it. Ramirez loves sunflowers. He knows this.

But he also knows that he's got flowers of an entirely different sort on his mind, so he can't find the delivery anything less than disturbing.

He's a decent partner, though, so he takes a picture and sends it to her so she can make the appropriate noises of appreciation to the gal from Counterterrorism.

Then Vic walks into the bullpen, half a chicken salad sandwich in his hand and a pinched look on his face. "Get your coat," he snaps out. "We're going to Sharpsburg."

"Sharps—Keely?"

"Got attacked. Inara's with Keely and her parents at the hospital."

"Inara's in Maryland?" But he's already got his coat and Vic's, as well as their guns and badges, and they can sort those out once Vic's swallowed down the rest of his lunch. He grabs the small bags under their desks just in case. They shouldn't need to spend the night, not so close to home, but it doesn't cost him more than a second so he might as well.

"Keely's on spring break; she asked Inara to visit for a couple of days."

It's probably for the best that Inara works at such a ridiculously upscale restaurant, given how much time she's having to take off in all of this.

Vic finishes the sandwich in the elevator and takes his gun and badge, getting them hooked on his belt. "We'll get an update on the way."

Except for the update—which really only tells them which hospital Keely was taken to, and that the attacker is in custody—it's a silent two hours to Sharpsburg. It's hard not to imagine the worst.

Keely has been dealing . . . as well as she could possibly be expected to. She was kidnapped on her twelfth birthday, brutally raped and beaten, only to wake up in the Garden. She was only there a few days, staunchly protected by Inara and the other girls, but to hear Inara and even Bliss tell it, those few days stank of more fear than any other time. Then the explosion, and the rescue, and the publicity . . . Keely has already dealt with more than any child her age should have to.

The local police told the hospital they were coming; they've barely held up their badges before they're being directed to a private room near the ER.

They find Keely's father pacing anxiously up and down the hallway, scrubbing at his face. Inara stands beside the doorway, watching him, her arms crossed over her belly. Eddison's not sure if it's to ward off vulnerability or cold; the air-conditioning is blowing a little too cold for her tank top to be comfortable. He can see the edges of one tattooed wing over the curve of her shoulder.

"Her mother is in with her, and one of the female officers," Inara tells them instead of hello.

"Our update was terse," Vic replies. "What happened?"

"We were in the mall, and decided to stop for lunch. Her parents were in another part of the food court. Keely picked a table for us, I went up to get the food. Heard a fuss and turned around, a woman was going after her with a knife. Called her a whore, said rape was a punishment from God."

"And then?"

"It caught everyone by surprise. They were just sort of frozen. So I pushed through and decked the bitch. May have broken her nose. She dropped the knife, and by then one of the security guards had approached, so he cuffed her and I got to Keely."

"How bad?"

After shrugging out of his coat and handing it to Vic, Eddison pulls off his thick black sweater. It had seemed more comfortable over his shirt and tie than a blazer that morning, when they were supposed to be at their desks all day. Now he's glad for it, because Inara actually smiles at him when he holds it out to her.

"Thanks. I gave my hoodie to Keely, to help her hide a bit. People were staring." The sweater is big on her, the neck wide enough to show her collarbones, but she shoves her hands in her pockets rather than crossing them again. "The cuts are shallow, mostly on her arms because Keely was holding her arms up to defend herself. There's one on her cheek, but they called in a plastic surgeon to come take a look at it."

"Is this the same mall where she was kidnapped?"

"Yes. It's not her first time back there. Her therapist encourages her to go."

"So her attacker knew who Keely was."

"Hard not to," Inara says dryly. "Not like our faces haven't been plastered all over the news or anything. And Keely lives here."

Keely's father acknowledges them when he paces close enough, but spins on his heel to keep pacing the other way.

"They've been trying really hard not to be clingy," Inara tells the agents. "There, but not hovering. It was their idea to let the two of us eat alone."

"Are we about to have a conversation about where guilt belongs?" Vic asks in a mild voice.

Inara snorts. "No. I've had enough of those for a while, thank you. He's just trying to pace himself exhausted before he goes in to see her, I think."

Vic gives Eddison a look, then knocks on the door. "Keely? This is Agent Hanoverian. Is it okay if I come in?" He waits for her muffled assent before he pushes the door open, and gently closes it behind him.

Eddison leans against the wall next to Inara, both of them watching Keely's father pace. "You only hit her the once?"

"Yes."

"I'm impressed at your restraint."

"If the security guard hadn't been there by that point, I might have done more. Maybe not. Guess it would have depended on whether or not she came at Keely again."

Mr. Rudolph finishes another lap and spins to start the next.

"They've been talking about moving to Baltimore. He can transfer, and her mom has family there. They think it might be better for Keely to get out of Sharpsburg."

"What do you think?"

"I think Baltimore gets basically the same news," she sighs. "I don't know. Maybe I'm not the best judge. I went back to the same apartment, the same job."

"Eighteen is different from twelve."

"Is it really? I never would have guessed."

He smirks, and because they're side by side, he can even pretend she doesn't see it. "You injured at all?"

She holds up her left hand, which has a bandage wrapped around the palm. It's not the same as when he first met her, but it's close enough to make him wince. "I was an idiot. Went to grab her hand, grabbed the knife instead. But it gave me the leverage I needed for the punch. It's a couple of stitches. Shouldn't scar too badly."

The burns from the explosion in the Garden scarred, and she has a set of stretches to do whenever she thinks of them so she doesn't lose flexibility with the hand.

"I'm surprised you're not in there with her."

"I was for a while, but she kept looking over to me when the officer was trying to take her statement. I offered to come out here so the officer could be confident the statement was Keely's alone."

"And you stayed out because?"

She mutters a curse and pulls her phone out of her pocket, awkwardly because it's on her left and her grip isn't as strong. But as she thumbs the screen on, ignoring a fresh stream of texts with names he can recognize as other Butterflies, she pulls up a message from Bliss that makes his heart skip.

It's a screenshot from an article online, time-stamped less than an hour ago, and under an obnoxious click-bait headline, there's a picture of Inara. He can't see much of Keely, hidden behind Inara's body with the older girl's too-large hoodie wrapped completely around her, arms holding it in place in a tight embrace. But he can see where Inara's tank top rode up her back and hasn't been fixed yet, showing the lower wings of a Western Pine Elfin, can see the fierce protectiveness on her face as she looks off to one side.

"They call me by name. The restaurant, too. Bliss is warning Guilian; he'll remind the staff that no one answers questions about anything that isn't connected to the food."

"Do they mention her?"

"Keely Rudolph of Sharpsburg, Maryland. They even say her school. Her fucking middle school."

"Maybe Baltimore wouldn't be a bad idea. They could register her under her mother's name."

"We survived. We shouldn't have to keep hiding."

"No, you shouldn't."

"Some of her classmates have been giving her a hard time. Keep covering her locker in butterfly stickers. Leaving craft-shop butterflies on her desk. Even one of her teachers asked if the Gardener had a butterfly picked out for her."

"Inara."

"I'm used to a shit life. It means I'm grateful for my friends at every moment, but it also means I'm used to being deluged with terrible things. She's not. She shouldn't have to be. She's a good kid, with parents who would do anything for her, and . . ."

He clears his throat uncomfortably. "It isn't fair?"

"What is? This is just wrong." She puts her phone away and knocks her head gently against the wall behind them, closing her eyes.

"Scars fade," she says quietly. "They don't disappear. It isn't right. We live with the memories; why do we have to live with the scars as well?"

He doesn't have an answer for her.

She wouldn't accept one if he tried.

So they watch Keely's father pace the hospital hallway, listen to the indistinct murmurs that come through from the room, and wait.

Her name is Laini Testerman, and the silk hibiscus she wears tucked behind one ear every day may be the most concealing piece of clothing she willingly wears.

You've really never seen anything like it, but the hotter-than-usual Mississippi spring has this girl stripping down at every opportunity, even when she really shouldn't. You've never seen shorts so short, so high up her ass you can see the curves of her cheeks. If she's not at school, she's in a bikini top, each one smaller than the last.

When she babysits, she brings the children out of doors to run through sprinklers and hoses, or to play in pools, and never urges them to change into swimsuits first. Right out in the open where anyone can see, she tells little girls to just strip down to their underwear and jump in, often with boys there in the yard or pool with them. Right out facing the street.

You were contemplating killing her for her own lack of modesty, but this seals it. You can't let her corrupt other girls like this.

You don't want the children to see, though, and she spends most of her time when she's not at school babysitting. She's saving up for a car, you learn, listening as she waxes eloquent to a friend about the freedoms she'll have with her own car. It's hard to get her alone given how busy she is.

But late one night, she leaves her house and rides her bike to the community pool, climbing over the fence despite the lock on the gate. She drops her bag and towel on a chair, but follows it with her swimsuit, until she's diving gracefully into the water naked as the day she was born.

The clip is still in her hair, bright and bold even in the distant glow of the streetlights.

Then you hear the fence rattle again, and a boy drops down to the deck. He drops his towel and trunks next to her things, but he doesn't jump in. Instead, he sits down on the side, his legs in the water, and watches her swim laps. She's swift in the water, her strokes strong and clean, and you know she swims competitively for school.

Would they still want her on the team if they knew about this?

She laughs when she notices the boy, and swims over to brace her elbows over his spread knees.

It's tempting to get it over with that night, but you don't have any flowers. You know where you can find them—you've been watching her, after all, you've known it would have to be her—but it takes another day to drive a few hours out. It's more effort than you'd normally go to, but the town's having a Hibiscus Festival. It feels appropriate.

And it feels appropriate to place a bloom over each nipple, where her tops should cover, a cluster of them over her too-often revealed crotch, and one more, the brightest bloom you could find, right in her whore mouth.

After seeing Agents Sterling and Archer off with the Tuesday delivery of marigolds, I head to chess, needing an escape from the house and the boxes and journals. Mum loves marigolds. Dad was allergic to them, or said he was. Really he just hated them, and said he was allergic so Mum wouldn't bring them into the house or plant them outside. It meant that she planted a border of marigolds along an entire wall of the old church, and he always had to go around to the other door in order to maintain the fiction.

But just as we're coming up on the anniversary of Chavi's death, we're also coming up on the anniversary of his, so marigolds are a little more painful today, the wound a little more jagged.

It's warm enough for jeans and a fleece, with a scarf draped around my neck just in case. The fleece is bright red and used to be Chavi's, and it's so much louder than anything I usually like to wear. There's something comforting about it, though. It's as red as my lipstick, and the scarf is a deep, cool emerald like Mum favors, and it's like wearing pieces of them.

Only not in a creepy Ed Gein sort of way, because no.

I'm aware of the looks the vets are giving each other long before they finally designate someone to ask about it. It's Pierce who clears his throat, looking steadily down at the board between us. "You all right, Blue Girl?"

"Coming up on a couple of painful dates," I answer, because it's true and that's about as far as I want to get into it right now. Gunny knows I have a murdered sister. They all know I've mentioned a mother, but never a father. We wear our scars, and sometimes the pain is as much fact as memory.

"Landon hasn't been back."

I drop my hands to my lap. "Is this something I should be apologizing for?"

"No!" he squawks, and Jorge and Steven both shake their heads at him. "No," he says again, more calmly. "We just wanted to check if he was bothering you elsewhere."

"I haven't seen him." But that makes me remember Finney's concern. "Have any of you?"

They all shake their heads.

Tapping my queen across a three-square diagonal to where she can be easily captured, I put my hands back in my lap. Pierce gives me a flat look, but accepts the sacrifice. It's as good a way to change the subject as any.

"How much longer you with us, Blue Girl?" asks Corgi.

"Not quite six weeks. We're neck deep in the Sorting of Things, getting rid of a lot of things we've been hauling move to move for no apparent reason."

"Women are so sentimental," Happy sighs.

Yelp elbows him.

"More lazy than sentimental," I tell him with a small smile. "We just move so often it never seemed worth unpacking everything, and if we weren't unpacking, why go through the boxes?"

"But if you're not using it, why keep it?"

"Because the important things were mixed in with the other stuff; we couldn't just throw out the whole box."

"Don't argue with a woman, Hap," urges Corgi. "Not even a younger one. Their logic ain't like ours."

Gunny wakes to a pavilion full of laughter, and smiles at me even as he blinks sleep from his eyes. "You're good for these weary old souls, Miss Priya."

"You're all good for me," I murmur, and it's true. With the exception of Landon, this is a safe place, full of people who make me feel not just accepted but welcome, scars and scary smiles and all.

After losing spectacularly to Pierce—and isn't he disgruntled about that—I play a quiet game with Gunny, then wander around with my camera in hand. The FBI has the pictures they can use; I want more for me, for when I'm gone.

My camera's still up around my neck when I walk up to Kroger. I can see Joshua walking out, in yet another fisherman sweater and no coat. I take a couple of pictures, because he's been kind without being pushy. When he notices me, he smiles, but doesn't stop. There's no sign of Landon, so I get my drink and head home. I still pay attention as I walk, but I don't feel the lingering discomfort of anyone's eyes on me.

I shoot Finney and Sterling texts to let them know that the vets haven't seen Landon, then scroll down to Eddison's contact and press "call." I read about the attack on Keely, saw the picture of Inara; I haven't decided yet if I'm going to write her about it or let her take the lead on whether or not to mention it. Given that Eddison spent half the weekend texting me rants about the Nationals' spring training roster, he's still too pissed to be finished processing.

"I'm not sure if that's good news or not," he says when I tell him about Landon. "I'm glad he's not bothering you, but this makes it a hell of a lot harder to find him."

"Why are you so sure it's him?"

"Why are you so sure it's not?" he counters.

"Did he strike you as being smart enough?"

"Socially incompetent doesn't mean unintelligent."

"It does mean he'd be noticed. If you were a teenage girl, would you be inclined to meet him at night?"

"If I were a teenage girl," he echoes. "I think I've had nightmares that started out that way."

"Well, here's another nightmare for you," I mutter, coming up to the doorstep. "There's been another delivery in the past couple of hours."

He swears softly, a solid string of sharp syllables, sounding stressed and stretched too thin. "What is it?"

"I don't know." There are three flowers on the list with *h* names, and honeysuckle is the only one I can keep straight. "Something tropical? Looks like it belongs on a sunscreen bottle." The individual blossoms are big, with a handful of large, frilled petals overlapping slightly on the edges and a long, long stamen sticking out like a pollen-beaded erection. The petals are dark purple at the heart, brightening quickly into a bold, orange-tinted scarlet, then to a cheerful yellow on the edges. From above, they look like they belong on *Fantasia*. I switch him to speakerphone so I can snap pictures and text them.

"Hibiscus," he says after a minute, husky with resignation. "Do you feel safe, Priya?"

"Nothing's gone inside the house so far."

"Priya."

"Vic's rubbing off on you."

"Do. You. Feel. Safe."

"Safe enough," I tell him. "I promise. I'll lock the door, I'll stay away from the windows, I'll keep one of the good knives in hand."

"Do you even know where your good knives are?"

"Sure, Mum found them yesterday. They're sitting on the counter until we get enough stuff for a full box."

There's a soft slap of flesh audible through the phone; I suspect he just smacked himself in the forehead. "All right. Finney will stay with you until your mother is home. Or Sterling and Archer, whoever comes out. Don't argue on this. They will stay."

"Wasn't going to argue." With the way all three agents drive, it takes less than an hour from the Denver office. Mum won't be home for three. At some point, it feels like they should be able to hand things off to the local police, get the lab reports from them, but I don't know the rules for that.

"I'm going to call Finney. You call me back if you need to, okay? Let me know you're still doing okay?"

"I'll check the feed, get the delivery cued up for them."

"Good."

I settle into the couch with one knife on the padded arm and another on the coffee table, my computer open on my lap. I was only gone two, maybe two and a half hours, so the delivery footage should be easy to isolate.

Should be.

The only person I see on the camera after the departure of the agents is me, leaving and coming back. The delivery doesn't seem to exist. I scan back through, more slowly, and find ten minutes where the feed is frozen. Just stuck on a single frame. The cameras are hooked to our Wi-Fi, which is supposed to be a secured network. It shouldn't be hackable.

I check the time stamps around the freeze. Oh God. The flowers were left right before I got home.

I don't remember reaching for one of the knives but there it is, my fingers white-knuckled around the handle. I didn't pass any pedestrians or cyclists, so whoever left these had to be in one of the cars that went by me.

Don't ask me why this is more frightening than being home alone when they get delivered. Maybe because when I'm out walking, I'm more vulnerable. In here I have weapons—knives, blunt objects, Chavi's bat from softball—but out there I only have pepper spray.

I should be safe until the flowers finish.

If I keep repeating it, maybe I'll believe it again.

APRIL

Geoffrey MacIntosh lives in the infirmary of his prison, his health still too tenuous to remove him to a cell. He's on constant oxygen, his lungs permanently seared by the explosion of the greenhouse complex, the plastic tubing for the cannula actually locked behind his head so he can't loosen it enough to harm himself with it. Or, Eddison would suspect, for anyone else to harm him with it. The attack on Keely has made national news.

He used to be a handsome man, the Gardener. There are pictures in the file, and all over the Internet. A charming, charismatic fifty-something with sea-green eyes and dark blond hair, always impeccably dressed. Filthy rich, both inherited and earned, and willing to spend small fortunes on charities and other philanthropic endeavors.

And his greenhouse, of course. His Garden.

But the man in the hospital bed has bubbling scars running down the right side of his body, the flesh twisted and stretched. His fingers are thick and stiff with rippling tissue. His throat is pocked and sagging, the scars climbing up to tear at his face. His mouth is pulled down on one side nearly to his chin, teeth and bone showing in places, and his eye is simply gone, too damaged to leave in place. The healed burns wrap back around his scalp. His left side is better, but not unscathed. Pain has gouged deep lines around his mouth and eye. Some of the burns are still resistant to healing, seeping infection around fresh grafts.

He looks nothing like the man who spent thirty years kidnapping, killing, and keeping teenage girls as human Butterflies.

Perhaps perversely, Eddison really wishes he could take a picture to show the survivors. To reassure them.

And because Bliss is Bliss, to really enjoy the sense of vindictive glee that will surely arise.

MacIntosh's lawyer—or one of them, anyway; he's hired an entire team to defend him—sits to his client's left, where he can be seen by the remaining eye. He's a tall, thin man in an expensive suit that isn't tailored quite right, like he was too impatient to get it done. It leaves him looking a little swallowed by it, and his clear discomfort with the infirmary doesn't help.

"Is there a reason you needed to see my client in person, Agents?" the lawyer—Redling? Reed?—asks sharply.

Vic leans against the foot of the bed, hands curled around the sturdy plastic rail. His expression is hard to read, even for Eddison. It's almost like he doesn't trust himself to show anything, for fear of what might show.

Eddison can understand that.

"Call it a kindness," Vic says too mildly. "Mr. MacIntosh. An hour and a half ago, your son Desmond was discovered dead in his cell. He shredded his pants to braid together a noose, and tried to hang himself from the end of his bunk. He was unsuccessful in breaking his neck, but he did cut off his air supply. He was pronounced dead at five forty-two."

Despite the suddenly shrieking heart monitor, MacIntosh looks frozen, unable to react. His eye darts around, landing on the agents, on his lawyer, at the space near the foot of the bed where the nurse says Desmond sat on occasion.

"Suicide?" says the lawyer, fingers twitching toward his phone. "Are they sure?"

"Biometrics on the cell; no one went through the door after he was accounted for last night. Not until they saw him this morning. He left a note."

"May we see it?"

It's already in an evidence bag, Vic's initials the third in the chain, but he holds it out so it can be seen. There's not much to see, really—just a single line in black ink, the letters slanting forward with the speed of the writing: *Tell Maya I'm sorry.*

The lawyer glances at his client, but MacIntosh displays no awareness of the note.

One of the nurses bustles over to hush the monitor, her hand on the inmate's good shoulder. "Sir, you need to breathe."

"His son just died," murmurs the lawyer.

"Well, unless he wants to join him, he needs to breathe," the nurse answers pragmatically.

Vic watches in silence, finally turning to the lawyer. "We don't need anything from him. We have no questions."

"This is your kindness?"

"He heard it in person, from someone who isn't gloating. He heard it from another father. That's the kindness."

Eddison gives the man in the bed one last look before following Vic out. He didn't say anything. He never intended to. He's there for Vic, and maybe for the survivors.

For Inara, who understood the fraught relationship between father and son perhaps better than the MacIntoshes themselves. Inara, who'll know this was Desmond giving up as surely as him finally calling the police was. Not bravery, not what's right. Just giving up.

Vic is silent through the process of leaving the prison, getting their guns back, retrieving the car. He lets his partner do the talking, but Eddison knows how to talk to guards. It's nothing like the discomfort of talking to victims. They hit the road back to Quantico, Vic still absorbed in thought.

Eddison pulls out his phone, double-checks a few things before firing off some texts. They're almost to the garage before he gets the response he's waiting for. He dials, letting the car's Bluetooth pick up the call. At the sound of the ringtone, Vic gives him a sideways look.

"You're a bastard for calling before noon," comes Inara's sleepy mumble over the line.

Another day, he might tease her. Not today. "I wanted to make sure we were the ones to tell you." He glances over at Vic, who nods. "Everyone else still asleep?"

"It's barely after eight; of course they're asleep."

"There's a box just outside your door; take it and your phone and head up to the roof."

"Is that supposed to make sense?"

"Please, Inara." There's something to Vic's voice, a weight, a grief, that makes Eddison shift in his seat. From the rustle of fabric, he can tell it works on Inara as well.

"Bliss, let go," she mutters. "Have to get up."

"'S'early," they can hear Bliss groan. "Why?"

"You can sleep."

"Oh, it's . . . shit. That means it's important. Where are we going?"

"Roof."

The agents in the car listen to the rustles and thumps of the girls getting out of bed, and Eddison wonders which of them had the bad night, that they were sharing. The girls did that in the Garden, curled around each other like puppies whenever they needed the comfort. There are snores in the background, one set soft and whuffling, another putting a chainsaw to shame, and a tinkling bit of piano music. A door closes, and the next thing they hear is another heartfelt groan from Bliss.

"Jesus fuck, this box is fucking heavy, Eddison, what the fuck?"

"Your morning eloquence is astounding," he says dryly.

"Fuck you."

Eddison grins. Vic just shakes his head.

"Take the phone; I'll take the box," Inara says, and there's a sharp thump before the line disconnects.

Eddison hits the "call" button again.

"Shut up," Bliss answers. "No one's fucking coordinated in the fucking morning."

There's something solid and reassuring about Bliss's habitual profanity. It's like counting on the tide.

"All right, we're up on the roof and it's fucking freezing," she announces at a normal volume. "What's going on?"

"You're on speaker?"

"Duh."

"Inara?"

"Yeah, I'm here," she says, the words garbled by a yawn.

"We've got some news for you."

"Good or bad?"

"Just news, I think. I'll leave it to you to decide." He takes a breath, wonders why he's the one doing this instead of Vic. "Desmond was discovered dead in his cell this morning."

A long silence crackles over the line. He can hear the whistling of the wind, and even the faint blast of car horns.

"He killed himself," Inara says eventually.

Bliss snorts directly into the phone. "Someone could have shanked the fucker."

"No, he did it himself. Didn't he?"

"He did," Eddison confirms, and Bliss mutters soft curses. "The box is for if you need to break shit. I had a friend drop it off."

"If we need to . . . Eddison." But he can hear the almost-laugh in Inara's voice, and he knows she's opened it.

And he knows, because it's his cousin's specialty, that the box is full of the most god-awful ugly mugs in existence, cheap things so badly painted you wonder that anyone would pay even a quarter for them. She buys them up by the gross, using them in therapy at the women's shelter she runs, because there's just something about smashing the damn things that feels so good.

"If you need more, let me know. I can hook you up."

Vic flinches at the sound of shattering ceramic.

"That one was Bliss," Inara informs them wryly. "How did he do it?"

And that's the thing about conversations with Inara; they circle. Even when she doesn't mean to, even when she's not doing it to purposefully confuse people, she has a way of sidling around a thing until she comes back at a more comfortable angle. You just have to wait for it.

"He tried to hang himself," Vic replies. "He ended up strangling himself."

"Fucker couldn't even do that right," snarls Bliss.

"Inara . . ."

"It's okay, Vic," Inara says softly. Weirdly enough, Eddison believes her. "The Gardener can try and brazen through a trial, trusting the faults in the system and his own sense of superiority. That kind of confidence was never going to be Desmond's."

One of Vic's hands leaves the wheel, touches the pocket with Desmond's last note. Eddison shakes his head.

"The Gardener? Was he told?"

"We just came from the infirmary."

"You told him in person?"

"Vic's a father."

That earns him a sharp look from his partner, but a soft sound of understanding from the speakers. "The prosecutor's office called about the contents of the letters," she says. "They said he seemed to get more unstable after Amiko died."

"You said he bonded with her over music."

"Finding out I turned the letters over without reading them, the no-contact order . . . well, it's not really a surprise, is it?"

"That doesn't mean it makes less of an impact," Vic tells her.

"True. But this . . . this isn't as bad as I thought it would be."

"Finding out he's dead?"

"I thought you were calling to tell me another of the girls was dead."

Shit. Eddison definitely hadn't thought of that.

From the slightly sick look on Vic's face, neither had he.

Well, it's been a hell of a morning.

They can hear another mug shatter.

"Yeah, so we'll need that hookup to get more of these."

"Inara? It's okay to grieve for him, if you want."

"I don't know what I want to do, Vic," she replies, then laughs bitterly. "I guess I don't want him to be worth any more of my time and attention. But that's hardly fair, is it?"

"What is?" Eddison asks before he can think better of it.

She gives a soft huff of amusement, an unconscious echo of a hospital hallway and a pacing father and a terrified, traumatized little girl. "We'll get some of the others to take our shifts tonight. Maybe go back out to that beach."

"Did it help?"

"We can run forever and there's no glass wall to stop us."

So yes, it helped.

"Try not to tell anyone else just yet. They want to control how it hits the news."

"Thank you for telling us. And for the fucktastic mugs."

They can hear another one shatter.

Eddison gives up and laughs into his hand. "I'll give you my contact's name; she can tell you where she gets them."

"No, Bliss, not off the roof!" The call ends abruptly.

But Vic is smiling a little, that terrible grimness fading. "They'll be okay, won't they?"

"I think Inara will have some bad days, but for the most part, yes. I think this takes some of the burden away from her."

A cell phone goes off, making them both flinch. Eddison can feel the vibrations against his belt. He pulls it up, his stomach sinking as he sees Priya's name on the display. "Priya? Are you okay?"

"There are petunias on the doorstep," she says, her voice sharp and fragile. "Mum forgot something and came back before she even got out of town, and they were there. The camera didn't see a goddamn thing."

Friday's camera footage shows a half hour of static instead of a delivery of petunias. It isn't frozen in place like before—the time stamp is continuous—but it's just snow. Just half an hour, though; it comes back on after that. Between that and all the clocks in the front half of the house being reset, Archer's theory is a short-range EMP. They're not that hard to find, he says; it's even easy to make them at home.

Oh, the joys of technology.

Archer does . . . something . . . to the cameras, as Sterling argues urgently into her phone, trying to get permission from the section chief to take Landon's picture and go out canvassing in the neighborhoods Eddison thought were most likely. The conversation does not go well, and is immediately followed by a call to Finney. He can't countermand his boss's restrictions, though, and his garbled voice sounds as frustrated as Sterling does.

Archer does not look optimistic about the camera. "Hopefully the shielding will protect it through another pulse," he says, screwing in the cover.

"Hopefully?" Mum asks dangerously, still in her work clothes.

"It's a basic home-security camera; it's not really meant to be indestructible."

Mum glowers at the camera, swearing under her breath in Hindi.

On Sunday we drive up to Denver, ostensibly for shopping. Really it's just to get me out of Huntington for a while. She points out the building where she works in LoDo; she doesn't suggest going in. Even if I were in any mood to meet colleagues putting in extra time, Mum hasn't personalized her offices since Boston.

The first two years of moving around, her company was sending her to clean up HR departments in struggling branches. She was there to get things back to where they should be. Right after we got to San Diego, they offered her Director of Human Resources in their Paris branch; the current director was looking to retire within the next few years, but the woman he'd been grooming for his position had just been poached by a German industrial firm. They wanted Mum to keep putting out fires in different offices here in the States, but also start learning all the international aspects of the business, the French and EU laws that required different compliance.

I think that may have been what let me bond with Aimée, actually, when I'd spent the other moves avoiding friendships. She was so damn excited when she found out I'd eventually be living in Paris; that was her dream. So, while everyone else in the class learned enough to meet graduation and scholarship requirements, Aimée and I drove the teacher crazy needing more.

We eat someplace a bit nicer than usual because why not, and the whole time we're there, I can feel the anger curling and crawling and clawing up my gut, hungry for far more than what's on my plate, because I can't get the petunias out of my head.

Everyone who knew Kiersten Knowles talked about her laugh. She was always laughing, and had one of those laughs that could fill a room, make you join in before you'd even finished turning around to see what was funny. Kiersten Knowles was a creature of joy. That is, until her aunt—her best friend in the world—was killed by a drunk driver.

Kiersten stopped laughing.

She was murdered after her aunt's funeral. She stayed in the church while everyone else headed to the reception; she told her father she needed a little time alone to say goodbye. When he got worried and came back to check on her, he found her dead on the floor, parallel to her aunt's coffin, her body dotted with little nosegays of petunias.

It makes a hell of a picture. I've seen it online, along with one that was never meant to be included in the case file much less leaked to the world at large: her father, finally allowed near her, caught as he was falling to his knees, one hand braced against his sister's casket, the other hovering over the petunias in his daughter's hair.

There's a picture of Aimée's mother, weeping as she tears all the amaranth out of the garden on the roof of their porch. They're powerful, emotional photographs, the kind of expressive, one-in-a-million shots any photographer is lucky to get, like the one of me reaching back for my sister as the paramedic carried me away.

Those pictures get plastered everywhere because we're a culture fascinated with crime, because we think the families' private pain is for public consumption.

Kiersten's was the first case the FBI worked. One of the officers was friends with Mandy Perkins's brother and mentioned the similarities to his captain, according to the articles I read. Mandy Perkins was victim number five—five years and five murders before Kiersten—the one who liked to make fairy villages in gardens. Mercedes was still in her last year of college, not even to the academy yet when Kiersten was murdered, but there's a picture of Eddison and Vic standing outside the church, talking to a uniformed police-woman. Vic looks calm, competent, completely in control of every-one around him.

Eddison looks pissed.

When we get home, there's a wreath of clover over the doorknob, stiff wire holding the shape, and wires dangling from the overhang where the camera should be.

Mum and I just stand there for a few minutes, looking between the two points.

Clover is for Rachel Ortiz, who was killed at the Renaissance Faire where she was in the cast. Clover was her character name, a silly shep-herdess who danced everywhere and carried a basket of pink and white clover blossoms to give to children. On her bodice, she wore a pewter pin that said *gaolbait* so people would know she was a minor and there-fore not to be harassed.

She was raped, the bodice with its pin beside her when she was found in the tiny wooden chapel the Faire used for weddings.

Mum offers to call Finney and Eddison, so I stomp up the stairs to change back into pajamas. Archer will be over in a few minutes, she calls up, because he's local; Sterling and Finney will drive down from Denver and bring a new camera with them. We saw Archer on his drive-by this morning, before we left for Denver. Patrolling might make Finney and Vic feel better, but it's sure as shit not doing anything for my peace of mind.

I don't come downstairs. There's nothing I can give them. Finney calls up the staircase when he gets here, but I don't answer, and a moment later I hear Mum's soft murmur. I know he's hoping to see me, to check on me so he can tell the Quantico Three he saw for himself that I'm doing okay.

Instead, I go into my closet, find the shoe box on the top that used to hold my photography ribbons back when I entered contests, and pull it down. I switched the ribbons to another box a few moves back, in theory consolidating. To be honest, I'd kept the ribbons in this one so long that it just became the ribbon box, so Mum never thinks to check for an Oreo stash there.

My hands are shaking, making the cellophane rattle. I drop the first Oreo twice before I can actually get a hold of it, dark crumbs flaking off on my thumb and index finger from the strength of my grip.

It tastes like ash.

But I swallow it, and shove the next in my mouth, chewing only as much as I have to before I can swallow that one too.

I should never have researched the other cases. I told myself I needed to, that I owed it to Aimée to hold their names in my heart, but I should never have done it, because I can *see* them so clearly, because I know what friends and family have said about them, because I feel like I know them.

Because now it's not just Chavi I see when I close my eyes, butter-yellow chrysanthemums spread around her, the tips of the petal fringe dipping into blood. It's Aimée, her hands folded to clutch a spray of amaranth to her ballerina-flat chest, her entire body surrounded by the flowers. It's Darla Jean Carmichael, the first girl, her throat destroyed amidst a fall of white and yellow jonquils. It's Leigh Clark, raped so viciously the medical examiner had doubts she would have survived even if her throat hadn't been slashed. It's Natalie Root, her head pillowed on thick stalks of hyacinth, all shades of pink and purple and white like a patchwork quilt.

The Oreos sit heavy on top of an already larger-than-usual dinner, but I can't stop, because I can see the numb look on Dad's face when he met us at the hospital, the shock that never entirely left his eyes. I can still hear Frank's weeping as he tries to pull me away from Chavi, still feel the blood, cold and tacky on my hands, my cheek, my chest, my clothing soaked through in a way Chavi's wasn't, safely set aside, because my sister was naked on the floor of the church.

I can see that picture of Inara, the fierce and protective rage on her face as she tried to shield a child from yet another senseless attack.

My stomach is rolling, protesting, but when I finish the first package, I open a second, forcing the damn cookies past the cramping nausea. This is a pain that makes sense, this is a pain that will stop as soon as I stop, and I can't stop, because none of this makes sense.

None of this makes any fucking sense at all, and I can't think how they choose this, my Quantico Three, and Agent Finnegan, too, and Sterling and Archer, I don't understand how they can face this day in and day out. It doesn't matter that it happens to strangers.

Kiersten Knowles, Julie McCarthy, Mandy Perkins, they were all strangers to me.

But I can see them, petunias and dahlias and freesia, bloody skin and church floors and it doesn't—

"Priya! No, sweetheart, no."

My hands close around the package of Oreos before Mum can yank them away. She grabs the ribbon box, sees two more packages there, and ducks out the door to throw the whole damn thing down the stairs. She kneels down in front of me, hands spread over mine, thumbs covering the ragged opening in the plastic so I can't pull any out.

"Priya, no."

She's crying.

Mum's crying.

But she's the strong one, the one who's always okay even when she isn't (especially when she isn't) and how can she be crying? It shocks me enough that I let go, and she throws the package back, heedless of the crumbs that spill over the grey carpet. Her arms wrap around me like a vise.

The back of my throat is burning, and now that I'm not shoving more Oreos in my mouth, I can feel the nausea rising.

"Come on, sweetheart. Up you get."

She hauls me up with her, always stronger than she looks, and together we stumble across the hall to her bathroom, because I still can't look at my bathroom without expecting to see all Chavi's things strewn about. But Mum's is neat and tidy, everything stacked or in little containers or cups or tucked away behind the side mirror. As she rummages through the cabinet, I drop down onto the soft, thick rug between the toilet and tub. It's soft, a pale, glittering kind of gold like candlelight.

Sweat beads and drips along my hairline, down the sides of my face, and I can feel the tremors move up from my hands to the rest of my body.

"Two glasses," says Mum, folding down next to me. She holds out the first cup of salt water. It's disgusting and hard to drink, and I'm gagging more often than I can swallow, but when I've choked it down, she hands me the second one. Vomiting is always painful and nasty, purposefully triggering it even more so, but if I can do it now before it has a chance to build up, it won't be quite as bad.

Still really bad, though.

Mum pulls my hair back and knots it into a messy bun, one of her terry-cloth headbands keeping the stray bits from my clammy forehead. Her manicure bowl sits at her knee, a washcloth folded into the cool water.

It's been months since I've done this—I swear to God I was getting better—but it's still a routine.

With one spectacularly vicious cramp, I start puking into the toilet. Between rounds of heaving, Mum flushes the bowl, wringing out the cloth to wipe sweat and sick from my face. Even when the puking is (probably) done, that nasty feeling remains, the will-it-won't-it hesitation that makes me reluctant to leave the bathroom.

The vomiting hurts, strong and acidic and tearing at my throat, and I start crying, which only makes it worse. My chest aches with the force of the heaves, with the effort it takes just to try to breathe.

Mum curls around me, stroking my hair, the sides of my throat, her fingers cool and moist from changing out the cloth. "It all adds up," she whispers against my ear. "We're going to get through this."

"I just want it to stop," I croak, "but then . . ."

"What?"

"We told him where to find us. We told him where we were going next and we dared him to come."

"Dared? No. Begged," Mum says firmly. "But if you are having even the slightest doubt, we stop now."

It seemed simple when Mum proposed the idea back in Birmingham. If the killer really is watching us, if him being in San Diego, killing Aimée, wasn't a coincidence, he'd almost certainly notice the profile in the *Economist*. Tell him where we'll be, she said, and he'll be there. It'll be the best chance for him to be caught.

Which might be fine, except we still can't fucking find him.

There was no way to anticipate the Denver FBI office having the section chief from hell. We *should* have anticipated he'd get around the cameras; he hasn't been getting away with this for so long by being careless. It just seemed like such a brilliant plan when Mum told me about it, even if we had very different reasons for liking it. She wants to find him and kill him.

I want to hand his ass over to our agents.

Wanted.

Now I want . . . I don't know. It's hard to think through the cramping pain in my belly and the feeling of being marooned. I'm far from abandoned, I know that, but logic doesn't help much against the *fear* at realizing the FBI is hamstringing its own agents, that we'll suffer for that.

"We're not giving up," I mumble.

"Sweetheart—"

"He'll kill until he's stopped. Isn't that what they always say? That if they're getting away with it, they have no reason to stop?"

"Priya—"

"Other mothers will lose their daughters."

"Other sisters," she sighs. "You know, I am this close to sending you off somewhere to vacation for a month. Should send you ahead to Paris to decorate the house."

"He'll keep killing."

"Stopping him is not worth destroying you."

I watch her get up and walk away, knowing she won't go far. To my room, maybe, to clean up the cookies before they attract bugs. The mini-vac whirrs, and a moment later she comes back with my toothbrush in hand.

My mouth is currently a kind of nasty I'm not sure a toothbrush can touch, but I brush and rinse and spit obediently, and when there isn't imminent danger of more hurling, Mum helps me wash my face. It's early yet, especially for us, but we curl up in her bed that's been too big since Dad died. She clicks the TV on, skipping through channels until she can put on a nature documentary narrated by a man with a deep, soothing British voice.

Mum says BBC is the only thing she really misses about London.

I'm not sure either of us ever really sleep; we just sort of drift on exhaustion and emotion-numbed minds. When her alarm goes off, she throws it across the room.

It keeps going off.

I bury my face in her shoulder. "There's nothing to unplug."

"I know."

"It's not going to stop until you make it."

"Shush."

It's another five minutes before either of us feels like making the effort, and even then we just haul her comforter downstairs to curl up together on the couch. She has her phone in hand, and I can hear her fingernail tapping against the screen as her thumb flies, typing out a message. I'm assuming it's to her boss.

It could also be to Eddison.

I should probably let him know I had an Oreo incident, but I really don't want to. Not because he'll be disappointed—he understands—but because he'll be worried.

More worried.

Shit.

Eventually Mum's stomach starts growling enough she has to leave our nest of warmth. I'm hungry, but the thought of eating anything makes me queasy. She brings back a bowl of oatmeal and bananas for herself, and hands me a smoothie. It's a good compromise. Substance, which my body still kind of needs, but not heavy. And it's a drink. I'm not sure why that makes a difference, being able to drink it instead of bite and chew, but it does, and it might just be purely in my head.

"Will going to chess make you feel better?"

Brotherhood isn't the only reason struggling vets cluster. Seeing your own demons reflected back at you, it creates a safe place to just be wounded. It gives permission, in a way, to not be okay. You go to your brothers (and sisters) and not only will they watch over you when you are clearly incapable of doing so yourself, they will never tell you to be anything other than what you are, even if on that particular day what you are is a collapsing wreck of a human being.

"Maybe," I say eventually.

"Then go get showered and dressed; I'll go with you."

"To shower and get dressed?"

She shoves me off the couch.

When I come back downstairs, still slicking on violently red gloss over the lip stain, she's standing at the base of the stairs dressed to go out. As I lock the door behind us, she checks to make sure the new camera is on and positioned.

Given the casual way he disarmed and ripped out the last one, I don't think the camera is really going to help.

But it's like locking the door, the sense of safety more than the fact of it, so I wait until she's finished fussing with it before I lead the way down the sidewalk. At the end of the street, she stops, looks back over her shoulder at the house, and shakes her head.

When we walk up the grass—slowly brightening as spring settles in—half the vets stumble awkwardly to their feet at the sight of my mother.

Happy and Corgi let out wolf whistles.

Mum gives them one of her sharp-edged, charming smiles.

They gulp, and Pierce starts laughing. "You must be where Blue Girl learned it," he wheezes, one hand clutching his chest.

Settling comfortably across from the slumbering Gunny, Mum shoots me a look. "Blue Girl?"

"Speaking of, we should really pick up some dye. My roots are nearing voting age."

The weird thing about Mum coming to chess—one of many weird things, really, given that it's the middle of a workday—is that she hates chess. She hates playing it, hates watching it, hates even hearing about it. She once canceled our cable subscription for a week so Dad couldn't try to make her watch any more documentaries about famous games or players. So the fact that she's sitting at the end of the table, watching all the games with barely concealed bemusement, isn't about chess, it's about me.

Because Mum isn't clingy, doesn't hover, but sometimes you just need that visceral affirmation that the people you love are all right, that they're just there in front of you. Close enough to touch.

Sometime after Gunny's woken up and introduced himself, a navy-banded police car pulls up next to the island and parks. All the vets straighten, the ones with their backs to the lot twisting around to try to see. A pair of officers climb out, puffy black jackets over dark blue uniforms with mustard trim down the pant legs.

A handful of the men relax, recognizing them.

"Pierce, Jorge," greets the older of the pair, his thick hair entirely white and silver. "How you doin'?"

"Nice and warm today, Lou," answers Jorge. "What brings you out here?"

Lou pulls a hand-size notebook out of his back pocket. "We heard from some neighbors that Landon Burnside plays with you sometimes."

Burnside?

Mum pokes me hard in the thigh.

Corgi scratches at his bulbous nose. "We've got a Landon, sure enough. Don't know his last name, though. Average sort of guy?"

A bland, little nothing of a man.

Lou's partner holds up a photo, and yes, it's Landon, not that there was really any expectation otherwise.

Corgi nods along with some of the others. "That's him. What's he done?" His eyes don't go to me when he says it, but Yelp's do, and Steven's.

"He was found dead last night in his room." White light flares in my vision, but doesn't clear with frantic blinking. It just hangs there, blinding me, until Mum's finger pokes between my ribs hard enough to make me choke. Spots dance as the world flickers back into view.

"How was he killed?" Mum asks calmly. "Can you say?"

The officers exchange a look and a shrug. "Hard to say; he's been dead awhile. Examiner's working to figure out what was done to him."

"Done to him," Mum echoes. "So you do suspect foul play."

"Yes, ma'am."

Tapping the back of my hand to pull my attention to her face, Mum nods toward the parking lot. "I'll tell them. You call."

"Ma'am? You have any information on Mr. Burnside?"

"I can tell you that the FBI considers him a person of interest in an ongoing investigation," she says, and her voice is smooth and strong the way it is at work.

I pull away from the table, careful to keep within sight of the officers as I take a few steps from the island. My hands shake, and the phone nearly drops twice before I can get a good grip on it.

"Hey, Priya," comes Eddison's hoarse voice in my ear a minute later. "Checking in?"

"Landon's last name is Burnside."

"A last name? Excellent, that will—Priya, how in the hell do you know his last name?"

I choke on a bewildered laugh. "He was murdered a while ago. He was found yesterday."

"Local cops?"

"Who else?"

"Hand over the phone, will you?"

The cops are both looking at me, though Lou is listening attentively to Mum. I walk back up and hold out the phone. "This is Special Agent Brandon Eddison; he'd like to talk to you."

Lou's partner looks at me intently, then takes the phone from my hand, gently, like he's afraid if he touches me I'll shatter, and steps to the far end of the island before speaking. He must introduce himself, but I can't really hear. Before I can sit back down, Mum hands me her phone.

"Agent Finnegan. Just in case."

I nod, walk away again, and pull up the number Agent Finnegan gave us. I usually email him, though lately I've fallen to texting whenever there's a new flower delivery. I count the rings until he picks up.

"Agent Finnegan," he says crisply, half a bite away from brusque.

"Sir, this is Priya Sravasti, and Landon the creep was found dead yesterday."

He mutters a handful of curses in Japanese. "I'm going to ask this, understanding that it's a rude question—"

"They don't know when he was killed, so I can't try to tell you where we were."

"Have you informed Hanoverian?"

"Eddison's on the phone with one of the local cops right now."

"All right, I'll get the contact info from him so we can request a visit to the body and scene. Are you safe?"

"Mum and I are out at the chess park." Which, come to think of it, isn't exactly an answer. It's all I've got, though.

"Once the officers let you go, head home and stay there. If you don't feel safe there, come up to Denver and get a hotel, just let me know which one."

"Yes, sir."

"Priya?"

"Yes, sir?"

"We're going to get you through this." His voice is warm and firm, and under other circumstances I'd probably find it reassuring, perhaps even comforting.

But his hands are tied.

I sit back down and give the phone to Mum. God, the smoothie feels so heavy in my stomach, and I keep swallowing against the need to vomit.

"So this man was stalking you?" asks the older officer.

"Maybe," I mumble. "He was definitely a little too focused on me for comfort." I glance at Mum, who nods. It's not like they aren't going to learn all this anyway. "I've been getting flowers that correspond to a series of unsolved murders; given Landon's attention on me, the agents thought he might be connected. They wanted to talk to him but he stopped coming to chess, and they weren't finding any trace of him on paper."

"He didn't have ID; his landlord told us his name."

His partner returns to the table and offers me my phone. "You seem to have Murphy's own luck, Miss Priya."

"Excuse me?"

"Well, only that I was on the force in Boston when your sister died," he explains in a thick Texas drawl. Oh God, no wonder he looked at me so intently. He recognized me. "My wife and I moved here when her pop got sick, but I'm not like to forget your family. What a tragedy. Tell you what, though, you've grown just as pretty as your sister."

I gape at him. I don't think I'm even capable of more than that.

Mum gets to her feet and slides around until she's mostly blocking me. "If that's how you feel is appropriate to speak to my daughter, you won't be speaking to her at all," she informs him frostily. "Your partner can deal with us, while you back the hell away."

As the officer stumbles through an apology, Corgi leans over to tap my knee. "Keep learning from your mama, Blue Girl," he whispers. "Together you two could scare the world into behaving right."

I squeeze his hand because I can't even attempt a smile.

"Go call the captain," Lou tells his partner, and watches him walk away. "My apologies, ma'am, miss. I'll speak to him about it."

"Remind me of his name," Mum says, in a tone that's far less question than command.

"Officer Michael Clare," he replies. "I'm Officer Lou Hamilton, and I'm sorry to be doing this, I know it's a stressful time, but I do have to ask you both some questions in light of this new information. I promise, I will be the one asking." He gestures up to the Krogers. "You might be more comfortable inside. Gentlemen," he adds to the concerned vets, "Clare will have some questions for you, too, about Mr. Burnside, if you don't mind."

Gunny nods gravely. "We'll wait for him. Be safe, Miss Priya."

Inside the café, Lou settles us at a table and goes to get us drinks. I can see Joshua a couple of tables away, buried in a book, and behind the counter, the sparrow-barista greets the officer with cheerful familiarity.

I don't remember Officer Clare. To be fair, I don't remember any of the uniformed people I met the night of Chavi's murder, or the couple of days after. Really the first strangers to make an impression were the Quantico Three. Five years later, though, Officer Clare remembers me.

Even though I never really thought Landon was behind the deliveries, there's something terrifying about learning for sure that he isn't.

If it isn't him, then who?

"All right, Finney, you've been digging for a week now; tell us something good."

The helpless laugh from the speaker in the middle of the conference table is less than reassuring. "I really wish I could, Vic, but we lost the only person remotely on our radar."

"Now that we know more about him, was he likely for the previous murders?" asks Vic, sprawled in one of the high-back rolling chairs. One elbow is braced on the plastic arm to prop himself up, two fingers digging into his temple to hold off what looks like a hell of a headache. Ramirez's pen is tapping a mile a minute against the table, which can't be helping.

It's most of why Eddison is being careful to pace *behind* Vic.

"Landon Burnside lived off the grid. No state-issued ID, no car, no credit cards, no bank accounts, no property. Worked odd jobs for cash, rented the mother-in-law suite for cash in a friend's house."

"But?"

"But the friend was a cousin, and our guy's name was actually Landon Cooper. Did two and a half years of a seven-year sentence for statutory rape and assorted charges. Was supposed to register when he got out, instead he skipped state and turned up in Colorado. DNA came back this morning to confirm his identity."

"Any chance he detoured through San Diego two years ago?"

"No; he was still locked up. He just got out fourteen months ago. He only served time the once, but he went to trial a couple other times, and had complaints that never made it that far. Garden-variety creep"— all three agents cringe—"who likes teen girls a hell of a lot more than teen girls like him. He was in prison in Michigan when Aimée Browder was killed."

"What if he was killed to protect Priya?"

Ramirez and Vic both swivel in their chairs to look at Eddison, and even Finney is silent on the phone.

Eddison shrugs. "Asking seriously: what if the bastard killed Landon because he was bothering Priya?"

Ramirez is still staring, looking somewhat sick, but Vic's clearly had the thought already. "Walk us through it," he suggests.

"I could buy the flowers being taunts, if anyone else got them. Any other family member, any other victim. But it's just Priya. The deliveries are about her, not the murders. If we look at the flowers as gifts . . ."

"He was courting her, and when she moved away, he killed Aimée because it was as close as he could get to Priya," Ramirez says.

"Whatever motivates him to kill, it isn't sex; only half of his victims are raped, and even that seems more about punishment than sex. He sees something else in them, and whatever that thing is, he sees Priya as being better. He wants Priya for something the others were never even considered for. She means enough to him that he actively looks for her not once, but twice. And he finds her."

"So he starts courting her again," Ramirez picks up, the flow familiar from a thousand other conversations, when the teasing falls away for the sake of work, and they're so close to being on the same page on a case. "Flowers, cards. But then there's Landon. If he's watching her, he knows Landon is bothering her."

"How?" asks Finney.

"Because he's watching, too. He knows when the Sravastis are out of the house, knows when to make the deliveries or have them made. Deshani's schedule is fairly fixed, but Priya's changes based on her mood. And we know the psychology of these kinds of gifts: he'll want to see the reaction to them."

"He sees Landon because he's already following Priya."

"And that's where Landon crosses the line this guy has drawn. He thinks of Priya as his, and Landon was encroaching."

"It'll be a few days before the official autopsy results are in," adds Finney, his voice crackling through the speaker, "but the Huntington ME feels pretty comfortable loosely mapping out the events. Landon had been dead roughly three weeks when he was found, probably since just after Eddison's visit. He didn't have heat, so the cold slowed decay, but eventually the smell started filtering into the rest of the house and the cousin went to investigate. First came a couple of subduing blows, and there's evidence of some kind of restraint. Rope, probably. Once he was tied up, he was castrated."

Eddison knows that, the local lieutenant told him that, but it still makes him wince.

"Guy wasn't neat about it, either," Finny continues. "He wanted it to hurt. There was a hell of a beating after, just to let it really sink in, before he went at Landon's throat. It's messy, strong, full of rage. This guy was pissed."

"Same knife?"

"Impossible to know. They'll make casts, but the decay will make it hard to be definitive. It's similar, at the very least."

"And nothing left behind."

"Just Landon. Took the rope with him, even."

"So why hasn't he tried to go inside Priya's house?" Ramirez asks. "Clearly he can take care of the cameras, but there's no sign that he's tried to go in, even when Priya has been home alone. Why not?"

Scrubbing at his face, Eddison bites off a growl. He jerks his chin at the bright stack of case folders. "The answer's in there somewhere. Something we haven't connected because he's seeing something we're not."

"Finney?" says Vic. "You have the freshest eyes when it comes to these cases. Anything jump?"

They can hear the click of keys and the shuffle of papers, Finney going through his copies of the case reports and his own notes on them. "Maybe."

The agents at Quantico wait, but he doesn't immediately continue. When the silence stretches into discomfort, Ramirez throws her pen at the speaker. "Well?"

"What makes him decide whether or not to rape?"

"We've never known," Eddison answers automatically.

"Look at Leigh Clark," Vic says. Neither of his partners reaches for that folder; they don't need to see those pictures. "Of the girls, hers was the most vicious attack. If she'd somehow survived, she would have almost certainly had permanent damage from the rape alone. What was it about her that made him lose control like that?"

"Her parents held back in their statements. They didn't want to say anything bad about their daughter, but most of the other interviews mentioned that Leigh was a wild child. Sex, smoking, drugs . . . so the extra viciousness was a punishment?"

"Zoraida Bourret was treated gently, her throat was slit while she was unconscious, and unconscious not from a blow to the head but from partial asphyxiation." Vic's thick fingers drum on the table. "Every statement in that folder says she was a good girl, family first, never went out with anyone because she was needed at home."

"But Natalie Root wasn't a virgin," Eddison points out. "She was only a few months out from a pregnancy scare, and she was left unmolested."

"And Rachel Ortiz," adds Ramirez. "She was raped, but the ME said she was almost definitely a virgin before the attack."

"But we're looking at facts; he's deciding based on his perception of them."

"I'm starting to see why none of the bosses want to split you three up," Finney observes dryly. "But let's play: if he was watching the girls to pass judgment on them, then he watched Priya five years ago. She and her sister were incredibly close, so for him to make any meaningful evaluation of Chavi, he saw a lot of Priya, too."

"And he fell in love with her."

"Isn't that a jump? Especially if we're saying this isn't about sex?"

Ramirez shakes her head. "I said love, not lust. Like courtly love: it's supposed to be chaste, pure. And think about it, Priya doesn't date. She isn't friends with boys. She does her schoolwork, she plays chess with a bunch of veterans, she stays in with her mother. If it's perceived purity he's hung up on, you can't really do better than Priya."

"Then wouldn't he have attacked her after I was there?" Eddison points out, an ache gripping his chest.

"You didn't spend the night."

"No, but we were alone in the house for a few hours before Deshani came home. And we walked to and from chess together the next morning."

They all absorb that in silence, then Finney clears his throat. "You were protecting her. In nosing around Landon, you were protecting Priya. He probably saw you as an ally."

Ramirez glances to Eddison, the corner of her mouth jumping slightly. "And anyone who's seen you and Priya spend time together wouldn't see you as anything other than family."

He flips her off rather than answer, though she's not wrong.

"So when he gets up to date on the flowers, what happens then?" Finney asks. "Do we think he's going to approach somehow? Attack her?"

"She's moving in a month."

"Chavi's girlfriend, Josephine," Ramirez says, skimming through the yellow folder. "She mentioned an unfamiliar man at the neighborhood spring festival a couple weeks before the murder. Said he wasn't creepy, just attentive, especially to Chavi and Priya."

"To both of them?"

"She said he mentioned having a sister. He seemed to find it charming how close they were." She closes the folder and taps her thumbs against it, not in any discernible rhythm. "Chavi and Josephine weren't out except to their mothers and Priya. Deshani said her husband would have gone through the roof, but the girls had been best friends since the Sravastis moved to Boston, so no one ever suspected they were dating."

"So as far as he knew, Chavi was a good friend and a great sister."

"Josephine is . . ." After a flurry of clicking keys, Finney makes a soft sound of triumph. "She's in New York. Columbia Law."

"I could take the train up," Eddison offers. "Take the pictures Priya gave us, see if anyone looks familiar. It's been five years, but something might ring a bell."

"Get more mugs from your friend," Vic tells him. "Inara says they're almost out."

"In a week and a half? The box had three dozen!"

Smacking her forehead against the table, Ramirez dissolves into soft, semi-hysterical laughter.

"Priya called this afternoon," Finney says once they've settled somewhat. "There were yellow chrysanthemums on the doorstep when she got home from a field trip; the oldest vet and his granddaughter took her to their church to see the windows. First flowers in just over a week."

Chavi had a sunburst of yellow chrysanthemums around her head, a few blossoms placed in her dark hair.

"Did Priya . . ." But Eddison doesn't know how to ask that question, not of Finney. Not in front of Ramirez and Vic.

"She asked me for Ward's phone number so she could give it to her mother," he replies. "Speaking of which . . ."

"Don't say it," groans Vic.

"Ward rejected the request for a protection detail on the house, then chewed me out for wasting Bureau resources on a community service murder that has no connection to any active case."

Eddison sputters. "No connection?"

But Vic gives a resigned sigh. "Let me guess: can't be our killer because the profile says he doesn't kill men, can't be the stalker because he's shown no signs of being violent. Pure coincidence."

"Pretty much, and her boss is backing her up. Huntington PD is being remarkably polite over us not telling them about the stalking investigation—I suspect we can thank Deshani for that, after she eviscerated the captain for the behavior of Officer Clare—and they've agreed to keep me updated on the progress of their investigation."

"Is Ward pushing against Sterling and Archer yet?"

"So far she's focused on me and I'm trying to keep it that way. I've got to be honest, Vic, if she gets me much more against the wall, I'm doing my best, but . . ."

"Understood. I've got a meeting with one of the assistant directors tomorrow. He doesn't like Ward, but he also doesn't like interfering in other agents' cases. I'm not sure how that's going to go."

"Both Sravastis mapped out their movements in the days around Landon's estimated date of death," Finney says after a minute. "No holes large enough for the locals to accuse them of anything. That's something."

"Oh?" Vic's voice is far too mild for the complicated expression. "I thought we were all politely ignoring the fact that Deshani is one hundred percent capable of killing a man who threatens her daughter."

"She wouldn't have been messy," Eddison and Ramirez say together.

Finney groans. "Terrifying woman. Let me know what you get from Josephine."

It's Ramirez who reaches across to shut off the speaker, ending the call. "Priya and Deshani are careful," she whispers. "They're smart, and observant, and they pay attention. When their gut tells them something is off, they listen. How do we find someone they don't notice?"

Neither of the men tries to answer her.

Neither of them points out there are only four flowers left to be delivered.

The fourth mega-crash of the morning has Mum swearing in an accent she mostly left in London, with a few Hindi curses slipped in for good measure. A glance outside says the shipping container is once again in the middle of the driveway, not off to the right as it needs to be so Mum can still pull the car out of the garage. I could almost feel bad for the deliverymen—Mum started out displeased about having to take the day off work so she could sign for the delivery, some bullshit about my signature not being acceptable because I'm a minor, but four times? Really?

And because she's in a bad mood, and because we woke up to hyacinths on the doorstep, I am safely sequestered in my room with one of Chavi's journals, staying the hell out of the way.

I haven't read straight through the journals—there's too many to manage it quickly—but I've jumped around, picking them up at random and skimming through. Where mine have photographs slipped in all over the place like bizarre bookmarks, hers are full of sketches, many on the pages themselves, as she either lost track of what she wanted to say or couldn't make the words she had say it. Even after she died, it never felt right to read them. They were still private.

The Chavi of five springs ago was excited and scared in pretty equal measure. She was so happy with Josephine, almost giddy to be dating her best friend, but she was scared of Dad's reaction when he eventually found out. Not just for herself and Josephine, but for me, too—would Dad have insisted on cutting off contact between us once she left for school? And school, too. She'd been accepted to Sarah Lawrence and Josephine was going to NYU, so they'd even be in the same metropolitan area, but it was college and new, and as much as she was looking forward to it, she worried.

I squirm through her entry about her and Mum giving me my bindi, mainly because it segued into a discussion on tampons and pads and other period things, and on the second day of my first period, I was still a bit squicky about it all. I'd known the theory, and obviously I'd been around Chavi and Mum for many, many periods, but still. Not even twelve, at that point. There really isn't a way for a lesson in using tampons to not be mortifying at that age.

Toward the end, there are drawings tucked in between the memories from the spring festival. We held all sorts of neighborhood parties and festivals at the old church, sometimes to raise money for repairs and to augment Frank's salary without him knowing, sometimes for charity. Sometimes just for fun. Chavi had spent both days painting faces and drawing caricatures, and I'd helped younger kids make flower crowns and run a maze made of old bedsheets.

It was what gave me the idea for my birthday party, seeing all the munchkins running around with flowers and trailing ribbons.

Leaving the notebook open on the bed, I slide off and open the top middle drawer of my dresser. I think it's meant for socks or something, but I have it lined in velvet to hold the flower crowns from my birthday. Chavi's was made of silk chrysanthemums, like a fringed headband, and Mum's was a bristling, angular wreath of lavender that made her look like a brown-skinned Demeter. Mine was white roses, big bloomed and heavy, with five different shades of blue ribbon weaving through and trailing down the back.

It's still heavy, but a little too small now.

When we were on a break during the festival, Chavi had chased me through the maze, both of us laughing our heads off, and when I made it through to the exit, Josephine had caught and twirled me in great circles until Chavi crashed into us both. We couldn't even get up we were giggling so hard, breathless and full of life.

I didn't mean to lose contact with Josephine, but I think we both knew it was going to happen. As much as I loved her as another sister, there was a Chavi-shaped space between us, and the edges of it hurt.

With the too-small crown of roses still on my head, perched at a somewhat precarious angle, I plop back onto the bed and start reading again.

She's talking about the second day, when Dad gave Mum so much shit about eating a burger that she went and got two beef hot dogs just to be spiteful, and the tone shifts. I remember us sitting a little apart from everyone, sprawled over a blanket with Josephine in the shade rather than at the picnic tables or the pavilions. Chavi and I always made a point of scarfing our burgers down first so Dad wouldn't see them.

He wasn't any more religious or observant than Mum, but he felt guiltier about it.

Or just guilty, I suppose. Mum seemed to embrace plainspoken agnosticism with a sense of relief.

Reading Chavi's words, I can sort of remember the man who came up to us, because he asked us if we were sisters. I was sitting in her lap, and even back then, when I was a too-skinny almost-twelve-year-old waiting for my weight to catch up with my growth spurt, it was just a stupid question. Sure, Chavi was darker than me, but I was still spectrums browner than any of our very white neighbors.

He seemed sad. I couldn't put my finger on why I thought that, not even when Chavi asked me later, but I remember that. He just seemed sad, even though he was smiling at us.

Chavi mentions him again a week later, after our monthly Sister Day breakfast at the diner. We went to the cinema after that—Saturday mornings, they'd play black-and-white classics on the big screens—and she went to get candy while I was in the restroom. She seemed flustered, but when I asked her about it, she said a jerk from one of her classes asked for her number.

That isn't what she wrote, though. She'd noticed what I hadn't, that someone had followed us from the diner. When I was in the bathroom, she lit into him for being creepy, told him she'd call the manager and the cops if he didn't leave us the hell alone.

He thanked her.

She writes that she was confused as shit by it, but he thanked her for being such a good sister and then left the cinema.

She doesn't mention him again.

A week later, she was dead.

Dammit. I can't remember anything else about him. Just that he was sad and had a sister. I know I didn't write about him; for a while after Chavi died, I escaped into compulsively reading my last weeks with her. I still reread that journal more than any other.

"Priya!" Mum yells up the stairs. "Archer's here!"

He'd probably just gotten to Denver when we texted Finney, and he had to turn around and drive all the way back.

When I get downstairs, he's on the step with the tissue-wrapped stalks of hyacinth. He glances up at me with a grimace. "Sterling says to let her know if I make you uncomfortable, and she'll do something painful to me the next time we spar in the gym."

"I like Sterling."

"I'm sorry I made that kind of protection necessary."

"Why did you?"

He doesn't answer immediately, still crouching down to take pictures of the untouched flowers. "The FBI uses cold cases in academy training to teach us that we can't solve every case," he says finally. "It's supposed to teach us pragmatism."

"What did it teach you instead?"

"You know, I honestly used to think that cases only went unsolved because investigators got lazy." He transfers the flowers to an evidence bag, then seals and signs it. When he straightens, he leans against the wall like he's settling in for conversation. "I was an idiot, and arrogant. My academy friends and I used to brag that we'd have flawless case records."

"Then you learned that life is messy?"

"I grew up black in small-town South Carolina, where my high school mascot was a Confederate general; I thought I knew all there was about life being messy. People look at me now with a suit and a badge and think I don't belong."

"And you want to prove them wrong."

"I do. But . . . I can't use other people to do it. And seeing the strain you're under . . . I was incredibly stupid to suggest you should make yourself bait. I was ignorant and out of line, and I sincerely apologize."

"Accepted."

He blinks at me.

"If you really want to grovel, I can hand you over to Mum; she's much better at demanding that sort of thing."

Chuckling, Archer peels off the neoprene gloves and shoves them in his pocket. "You really are something."

After he leaves, I text Sterling. *No need for unmanning; he even made a very good apology.*

Good, I get back, *but I'll probably try anyway. Really make the lesson stick.*

When the shipping container is finally in place, Mum heads up to Denver to put a few hours into the office. The move is less than three weeks away, so they're piling a lot of work on her to make sure she's ready. To do my part in making sure *I'm* ready for the move, I settle in with the schoolwork that it was too loud to do this morning.

Around four, there's a knock on the door.

I freeze, staring down the hall at the door like if I just look hard enough, I can see through it. I almost call out "Who is it?" but don't.

Easing off the couch, I reach for Chavi's softball bat, which now lives in whatever room I'm spending time in. We had to pack the knives. The bat is heavy and solid, the grip comfortingly rough in my hands.

"Miss Priya?" a male voice calls. "Miss Priya, you home?"

Is that . . . is that Officer Clare?

I switch my screen over to the camera feed, and yes, that's Officer Clare standing on the porch, his hat in hand. His voice is unmistakably Texas. With absolutely no intention of answering him, I take the time to study him. He's probably in his forties, his face worn but otherwise unremarkable. I try to place it against my admittedly spotty memory of the cops around Chavi's murder.

He looks vaguely familiar, but not in any meaningful way. He's not overwhelmingly bland like Landon is—was—he just doesn't spark specific recognition.

"If you're home, Miss Priya," he calls through the door, "I just swung by to apologize for the other day. I'll try you another time."

It seems to be the day for apologies.

Mum has the contact info for Officer Hamilton; I text her with the news of Clare's visit so she can let Hamilton know.

Why would Clare come, without his partner, to a residence where he expects a minor to be home on her own? It's different when Eddison does it; he's family, and it was years before he'd hang out just the two of us. Maybe I'm paranoid, given everything else going on, but I don't like Clare showing up here.

Mum texts back three rows of flame emojis.

Her name is Chavi Sravasti, and she's extraordinary.

She's painting faces at a spring festival when you first see her, and rage fills you. It's been years, but you still remember Leigh Clark's duplicity, her evil. How sweet and demure the preacher's daughter appeared at the same tasks, but it was only a mask for her true behavior.

But there's something different about Chavi. She laughs and jokes with the children, chivvying the adults into getting their faces painted as well. She's talented, too, branching out beyond the school carnival symbols into masks and detailed works. Like most of the girls—and many of the boys—she wears a ribbon crown of tiny fabric roses over her dark hair.

You're not sure what to make of her. She's friendly without flirting, even when the oldest boys and younger men try their best to get more of her attention. Her behavior suggests a good girl, but her appearance . . . bright red streaks spill through her hair, her makeup bright white and gold and heavy black liner, her lips bold and red. Gold and crystal glitters at her nose and between her eyes.

Then her sister comes up, a gawky, too-thin child with a bright smile and a brighter laugh, and despite her youth, she also has streaks in her hair, royal blue, and her makeup is softer, her lips a delicate shade of pink. Appropriate for someone the age she looks. Curious, you look around for their parents. They aren't hard to find; their brown skin makes them stand out in this neighborhood. The mother's hair is unadorned, but even from a distance you can see her dark red lips, the loop of gold through the center of the lower lip, and the spark of crystal at her nose and between her eyes.

Family tradition, then.

A boy comes up to take Chavi's place with the paints, and the girls run off hand in hand, laughing and dancing into each other, never tangling, never tripping. You follow them from a distance, charmed at the sight. Even when their breaks are over and they return to their booths, they're aware of each other, frequently looking up to exchange smiles.

Chavi is such a good sister. You watch them for two weeks, the way Priya—you've finally learned the younger girl's name—takes pictures of everything, the way Chavi draws constantly. They each have their own circles of friends, but you've never seen sisters who delight in spending time together the way these two do.

Priya never sees you, but Chavi . . .

Chavi does, and you're not sure what to do with that. You're used to not being noticed, but she glares at you whenever she sees your attention on her or her sister. And that's really quite extraordinary. Chavi truly has an artist's soul, able to see what others overlook.

So you make it a habit to let her see you at the small stone building that used to be a church, or will be again. Church in limbo, and there's something rather entertaining about that, isn't there?

You're there for the birthday party that includes most of the neighborhood, a less formal repetition of the spring festival only two weeks ago. There are flowers everywhere, real ones blooming around the little grey church and in lovingly tended beds, silk and plastic versions on the heads of most. You see the Sravasti ladies, all in sundresses and open sweaters, bare feet running through the spring grass.

Sweet Priya, with white roses against her dark hair.

Fierce Chavi, with yellow chrysanthemums almost as bright as her smile.

The party is on the Saturday, but you watch them on the Sunday, too, as the family celebrates together. They go out and come back, Priya touching the new piercing at her nose, and normally you would never approve, but her family went with her, this means something to them, and that changes it somehow.

On Monday, as you're following them to school, you hear Chavi remind her sister of a study group, that she won't be there to walk her home. So you're there, following at a discreet distance, making sure Priya gets there safely. They live in a safe neighborhood, an affluent suburb where people know each other well enough to look out for each other, but still. You know better than anyone how evil can hide in plain sight. Priya goes straight home after her club meeting, stopping now and then to talk to neighbors but not leaving her path.

You're proud of her. She's such a good daughter.

Such a good little sister.

Chavi comes to the church that night, full of fire and fury and love, so much love for her sister. You almost don't want to kill her, don't want to take that away from Priya, but Chavi will be leaving for college in the fall, and you've seen what that can do to people, how it can devour good girls and leave husks behind.

But you believe in angels, and guardians, and you know this is for the best. Chavi will always be good, and she'll always be there to watch over her sister.

And Priya will listen, because Priya is a good girl.

When you place the chrysanthemums in her hair, they look like suns in space, and that's fitting, you think. Chavi does burn so bright.

"Eat."

Starting violently at the unexpected sound, Eddison's reflexive grip on the table is the only thing that keeps his ass on the chair, rather than falling to the floor. "Jesus, Ramirez, wear a bell."

"Or you could practice some situational awareness." She pushes a large white paper sack closer to him, then sits a few chairs away where she can see him without being all the way on the other side of the conference table. "Now, eat."

With a grumble, Eddison opens the bag and pulls out a warm container of beef and broccoli. "What time is it?"

"Almost three."

"Jesus. What are you even doing here?"

"Bringing you food from the only Chinese place in Quantico open past midnight."

He always seems to forget how the off-duty Ramirez is simultaneously softer and fiercer than her on-duty persona. Softer, because the sharp suits and heels and I-dare-you makeup is swapped for jeans, an overlarge sweater, and a bushy ponytail, making her altogether more approachable. But the fierceness is still there, or maybe even more present, because when the makeup comes off, there's nothing hiding her scars, the long, pale lines tracking from her left eye down her cheek to under her jaw. Those scars are a reminder that she's a survivor in her own right, one with a badge and a gun and an absolute willingness to fuck shit up if it will save a child.

He couldn't ask for any more in a partner.

"So you're not even going to pretend to be surprised I'm here?"

She flaps a hand dismissively. "Priya got camellias yesterday and amaranth today; there's only one flower left. Given that there's nothing productive you can do there, where else would you be but here?"

"I hate you a little."

"Keep telling yourself that, *mijo*; one day you'll believe it. Now. What are you looking at?"

"Postal records," he answers around a mouthful of vegetables. "If he's watching his victims, it's unlikely he's just passing through, so I'm running forwarding addresses."

She starts to nod, then frowns. "I can see at least two problems with that."

"What if he doesn't bother forwarding his mail?"

"Okay, three."

He laughs and shrugs. "So what are your other two?"

"What if he doesn't live in the cities? If he lives in a town nearby and drives in . . ."

"Smaller towns notice short-term tenants; the communities are more familiar with each other, which would make it risky for him. Besides, I'm looking at states, not cities."

"That is a lot to sort through."

"Yvonne showed me how to let the computer do most of it."

"Showed you?"

He points at the whiteboard wall, most of which is covered in step-by-step instructions on how to set and refine search parameters in the Bureau intranet. As the team's preferred technical analyst, Yvonne is well aware of their individual strengths and weaknesses when it comes to computers.

Turn computer on is taking it rather too far, in his opinion, but to be fair, he did catch her on her way out the door.

"What's the second problem?" he asks.

"What if he's not going directly from point A to point B? Priya and Deshani were only in Birmingham for four months. They were in Chicago for less than three. They're not the only people who live that way."

Eddison drops the takeout container on the table with a wet plop. "How do we find him, then? How do we find him if he's a fucking ghost?"

"If I knew that, would we still be sitting here?"

Fury claws under his skin, making his muscles clench and twitch. Fury, and fear. Deshani called Vic this afternoon, asking if there was anything Priya should do if the bastard approaches her. Vic didn't know what to tell her beyond stay calm, try to keep him talking, and try to call for help. They know this bastard wants Priya, but for what?

He killed to keep her safe, but he's her biggest threat.

"Come on," Ramirez says abruptly, getting to her feet.

"I have to—"

"The computer does not need you staring at it while it does its thing. I will let you come back, I promise, but for now, come on." When he doesn't move fast enough to suit her, she grabs his chair and pushes him at the door. He stumbles up just in time to avoid crashing into the frame.

"I'm up and I'm coming, now will you stop?" he demands.

In response, she grabs his elbow and hauls him after her to the elevator.

They end up in one of the sparring gyms, thick mats covering the floor around raised rings. One wall has lines of rhythm bags and heavy bags. Ramirez points to the heavy bags. "Go."

"Ramirez."

"Eddison." She drops his elbow so she can cross her arms under her chest. "You are exhausted. You are so angry, so afraid, so tangled up in your own head that you're not able to think straight. You're missing the obvious, and digging yourself in deeper is not going to help. Now. Keyed up as you are, you're not going to sleep, so go punch the shit out of the bag."

"Ramirez—"

"Go. Punch. The bag."

Muttering about bossy, interfering women only makes her snicker, so he gives in and walks to the bags. He rolls up his sleeves, sets his feet . . . and stares.

"For shit's sake, Eddison, punch the bag!"

So he does, and with the first thump of impact, that taut coil twisting his gut snaps. He rains blows on the bag, heedless of form or efficiency, messy and powerful and relentless in his rage. His muscles protest the sudden activity but he ignores the pain, focused on nothing but the movement of the hanging bag and where his fist needs to be to meet it.

Eventually he slows, then stops, leaning against the bag and panting. His arms throb, and he's a little afraid to check his untaped fists. He does feel more centered, though.

Ramirez gently takes his left hand and inspects his knuckles. "Nothing looks broken," she tells him softly. "You'll have some lovely bruises and swelling, and I think you left most of your skin on the bag."

"Why didn't you tell me to tape up?"

She reaches for his other hand, looking up at him from under her lashes. It's not something she does to be coy, but rather, when she's not sure if her face is showing what she's thinking. "You seemed like you needed the pain."

He doesn't have an answer for that.

"Come on. Let's get these cleaned and bandaged. Do you have things at home to change dressings tomorrow?"

"Mostly. I'll have to stop and buy . . ." He trails off, almost too tired to chase the fragment of an idea. Ramirez just waits, watching him thoughtfully. "How many places in a reasonable distance of Huntington do you suppose sell dahlias?"

"Say what?"

"Dahlias. They're not exactly easy to find. When Julie McCarthy was murdered last year, it took us over a week to find where her dahlias came from, but we did find the specific store, which we usually don't. A lot of florists don't stock dahlias."

"Okay . . ."

"We've been trying to play catch-up this entire time; why not try to get ahead of him? If he wants to finish out the list, he has to find dahlias somewhere. If we can get word to all the florists—"

"In the state? Eddison, that's—"

"A big list, yes, so we create a master list and borrow techs or agents or, hell, academy trainees, and get them calling. The flowers are always fresh when they're delivered, so even if he has them already, it would only be in the past day or two. The sale of a less-common flower would be memorable. We might even be able to get a photo or sketch from whoever sold or sells the dahlias to him."

"That's . . . actually not a bad idea," she admits. "It's going to have to be Yvonne, though."

"What?"

"Even with her instructions, that kind of search is not something we know how to do. Not on this big a scale."

"Okay, so we—"

"We are not calling her in at four in the morning," she says firmly. "We are going to take care of your hands. Then we will go upstairs and write all of this down, so at a reasonable hour, we can update Vic and get approval to send Yvonne into overtime. Then we will call in Yvonne. Do you know what you're going to do between taking notes and calling Vic?"

"Whatever you tell me to do or you'll make me regret it?"

"You see, *mijo*?" She hooks her arm through his and pulls him toward the door. "You're thinking better already."

Her name is Aimée Browder, and she just might be a gift from God.

You've been worried about Priya. You'd already left Boston—you never spend more than six months in one place—but when you went back to visit, Priya wasn't there. It took a long time to find her; finally you saw her name and city listed in a magazine as a finalist for a photo contest. You moved to San Diego immediately. You needed to make sure she was okay.

And she isn't, you realize. She's still the good girl you remember, but her brightness is gone, her warmth. She's brittle and fragile and so very lonely.

And then she finds Aimée.

You watch, entranced, as Aimée patiently lures Priya out of her pain, chattering in French and dancing around her as they walk. Sometimes literally—she's so graceful, Aimée, and spends so much time at lessons and practice; even when she walks out of the studio late at night looking weary down to the bone, she still looks so in love with her dancing you can't look away. And you see Priya start to bloom, smiling, sometimes laughing even, and talking about French cinema and opera and ballet houses.

It's Aimée who introduces Priya to the boy she tutors, and you see right away that the boy is falling for her. You don't blame him, but you watch, carefully, in case you have to step in. You never do, though. Priya knows her worth, knows what it means to be good, and she never encourages the boy, never sits closer to him than she has to, never accepts any of his invitations out.

Aimée's mother cooks with the amaranth that grows on their porch roof. You've never really thought about it, that flowers can have more of a purpose than to look pretty and feed bees or whatever it is they do, but you can hear the Browders teasing each other about the plants in the kitchen and the blooms around Aimée's bun, the women in a lazy, easy mix of French and Spanish, the father in the occasional booming German no one else understands but that always makes the women laugh.

They take to Priya nearly as well as Aimée does, and you're grateful for that, grateful she has people to give her back that brightness.

You send Priya flowers, trying to show your appreciation for her goodness, your love for her, and your heart warms when you see her laughing over the baby's breath, pinning it in place around her friend's hair like a bristling fairy crown for the stage.

And then one day, Priya is gone. You were away for a few days, tracking down the flowers you needed from nearby towns so no one would link the bouquets to each other, or to you. You haven't done this for so many years by being careless. Just a few days, but you missed the moving truck and the goodbyes and the departure. It took you too long to find her this time, and now . . .

Aimée misses Priya too, you can see it even before she mentions it to her mother. You see it in the way she twirls a cluster of amaranth in her hand, looking at it with a sad little smile, before she reaches up to pin it in place around her hair.

So you gather the amaranth, as much of it as you can find without completely denuding her mother's garden, and you wait, because you've *watched her long enough to know that when she can't sleep, she doesn't bother her parents, or her brother and sister. She slips out of the house and down three streets to the church with a door that's always open, and she dances. She used to go two streets the other direction first, to see if Priya wanted to join her, and they'd pass the dark hours in a church, Aimée dancing, Priya taking photos of stained glass and grace in moonlight.*

You make it painless for Aimée, as much as you can. You do it for her sake as much as for Priya's. She really is such a good girl, a good friend when Priya needed one most. You surround her with the dark pink bunches of amaranth, and you sit with her for a while, looking up at the windows, thinking of Priya.

She was such a good little sister, so worthy of protection. She isn't anything like Darla Jean; she'll stay good. She'll be grateful, when she knows how much you love her.

You'll find her again, and this time you won't stop until she knows how you feel. You can't wait to hear her say she loves you.

The dahlias arrive on Tuesday, three blossoms each as big as my hand, so deep a purple they're just shy of black. It was not quite a year ago that fourteen-year-old Julie McCarthy was found raped and murdered in a church in Charlotte, North Carolina, three dahlias in a line over her mouth, chest, and crotch like a demented chakra map.

My first call isn't to Eddison, or to Mum or Finney; it's to Hannah Randolph, Gunny's granddaughter. Since we learned about Landon's murder—or rather, since the men learned about all the circumstances surrounding his murder—the vets have very emphatically requested that I not walk to and from chess on my own. Hannah offered to give me rides, considering that she waits in the car the entire time anyway.

With all the other vets there to watch Gunny, she can easily swing the mile and a half to my house.

They were clearly prepared to argue with me about it, or so I gathered from their shock when I said yes and thank you. It makes sense, though, and I am grateful for it. Around the time I would normally leave for chess, I call Hannah to let her know if I'm coming.

Or in the case of this morning, not coming.

"Do you mind if I come sit with you?" she asks immediately. "At least until the agents arrive? I don't like the thought of you being alone right now."

"Gunny—"

"Will be just fine with Pierce. If something happens, I am less than five minutes away."

"It would make me feel better," I admit. "Thank you."

"I'm on my way. Call your agents."

I text Eddison, then make some hot chocolate as I call Finney. When Hannah arrives, she steps carefully around the flowers to avoid disturbing anything and accepts the mug with a smile, nodding to the phone at my ear. As I pull up the camera feed, she settles into the armchair with her knitting.

I should learn how to knit. It seems very calming.

"What's the camera show?" Finney asks wearily.

"It blanks out at nine thirty-eight," I answer. "After that there's nothing."

"Snow?"

"Nothing. Like it's not getting a signal but the network is fine."

"Back camera?"

"Happily recording the movements of the fattest squirrel I have ever seen."

"Do you feel safe enough till we get there? I can ask the local PD to send someone out."

I think of Officer Clare and shudder. "Hannah is here with me."

"All right. We'll be there as soon as we can."

For about ten minutes, Hannah and I sit in a silence as comfortable as it can be, given the circumstances. Her needles clack sedately, and there's a soothing, almost meditative quality to it.

Then there's a knock on the door.

It's definitely not my agents, not this quickly. Not even with the way they drive.

Oh, God, it's probably—

"Miss Priya? The boys said you had a mite of trouble?"

Officer Clare. He's taken to swinging by the chess pavilion without his partner, checking up on me, he says. He's been told not to, by both Lou and their captain, but it hasn't stopped him. He just claims it's on his way to the store, or to lunch, and we happen to run into each other.

"Miss Priya, I know you're home. I can see Miss Randolph's car. I just want to make sure you're all right till the feds get here."

Hannah carefully sets her knitting aside. "I'll send him off, shall I?"

"Please," I whisper.

She heads down the hall to the door and opens it just enough to be seen, her body blocking me from view. "We're just fine, Officer," she tells him politely. "If you don't mind stepping away from the evidence?"

"I can stay with y'all—"

"The thought is appreciated, but it isn't necessary."

"I was there, you know, when she lost her sister. Poor kid. When I think of my own sister . . . little sisters need protecting."

"Officer Clare. Your assistance is not needed at this time. Please leave."

He raises his voice. "Now, Miss Priya—"

Pulling up my call log, I find the number for his captain and tap on it. The man answers with his last name and no greeting. "Captain, this is Priya Sravasti, and—"

"Please tell me Clare is not bothering you again," he growls.

"He's at my door and refusing to leave."

"My apologies, Miss Sravasti. I'll take care of it." As he hangs up, I catch a grumble that sounds a bit like "fire his sorry ass" and wonder if that's what will happen.

Hannah eventually shuts the door in Clare's face, twisting both locks. After a moment, she hooks in the chain for good measure. "That man is not quite right," she says, taking her knitting back up. "There's no reason for him to be so focused on you."

"Apparently it's something about this type of case," I sigh. "Mercedes explained the psychology of it once. Sometimes, an emergency responder can get a little stuck on a case that disturbs them, especially if something else is going on in their lives. Some get obsessed with solving the crime, but others latch on to checking up on the family."

"Did he do that in Boston?"

"Not that I recall, but if he was back in Boston, he could have been a lot more subtle about it."

"If?" she echoes.

"It wouldn't be the weirdest way a fan has pushed into a case, according to Mercedes. She's doing a full background check on him."

Hannah shakes her head. "I know humans are complicated creatures, but this seems a bit excessive."

Finney and Sterling arrive not very long after. Finney looks a little green as he steps out of the car. On the driver's side, Sterling manages to look both sheepish and proud.

"Having fun with the lights and sirens?" I ask dryly.

Sterling grins at me before tucking it back behind a more professional expression. "We lost time behind an accident; I didn't want to leave you waiting."

Rolling his eyes, Finney turns to Hannah and offers his hand. "Thank you for staying with her, Miss Randolph."

She shakes his hand. "Do you need me to stay? For after you go, I mean."

"Actually . . ." He glances up at me. "Your mother asked us to bring you up to Denver, if you don't mind. I think she'll feel better if she can keep sight of you."

"That's fine. Thank you so much, Hannah."

"Anytime," she says, giving me a brief hug. "Be safe, Priya." It's the same thing her grandfather tells me instead of goodbye, only he calls me Miss Priya, and somehow Officer Clare hasn't ruined that.

Speaking of whom . . . I tell Finney about Officer Clare, then head upstairs to change and toss some things in a bag to take with me. I don't know if Mum's office has general Wi-Fi, so schoolwork might not be an option.

"Knocked out the camera with the EMP, then cut the wires again," Sterling announces once I'm back downstairs.

"So what now?"

"Now we get you to your mother," answers Finney. "Then we'll discuss your protection detail."

Protection detail, in this case, means Archer is going to stay with me during the day, Sterling is going to stay at the house each night, and everyone is going to pray that Section Chief Ward doesn't find out. It's technically off the books—a personal favor—which is its own can of worms. If anything does happen, the agents could face hell for it. We move in a little over a week but it feels like forever, especially with that rotation in place. Mum arranges a rendezvous time with Sterling, because we're probably safe enough at her office, and the agents head out.

I settle into a corner of Mum's rather sterile office with my laptop. I should do homework—she gave me the network key—but instead I pull up the photos from Gunny and Hannah's church. It was a lovely afternoon with them, and interesting windows were a definite bonus. The scenes were painted onto clear panes, rather than being a mosaic of stained glass, and even with the semi-translucent paint, it changed the way the light filtered through.

Beneath a portrait of the women and the empty tomb, Gunny ran his gnarled fingers over a tiny brass plaque with his wife's name on it. The church secretary was even older than Gunny, and she knew the history of each window and who had sponsored it. When I mentioned my love of windows, she gave me an info card for a small chapel about an hour away. "Some say God gave us the ability to create art so we could glorify Him," she said with a smile. "The windows at Shiloh Chapel make that easy to believe."

I very much doubt I'll get to find out.

I snap the laptop shut with a frustrated sigh. I'd hoped looking at the pictures would cheer me up, but they just depressed me. Reaching down into my bag, I pull out the envelope that was sitting in our mailbox, Inara's neat handwriting across the front.

Dear Priya,

Desmond MacIntosh is dead, has been dead almost a month now, and I'm still not sure how to feel about it. Everyone expects me to be sad, because we were "star-crossed lovers" or whatever bullshit gets spouted by people with insufficient understanding of what star-crossed actually means. Or they think I should be happy, because hey, look, one of my tormentors killed himself, as if seeing suicide among the girls should make me glad to see it in him.

Mostly, though, I'm just relieved, and what the hell kind of reaction is that?

I'm relieved that I don't have to see him across the courtroom, that I don't have to feel his eyes on me as I testify against him and his father. I'm relieved that I won't have to spend hours upon hours seeing his kicked-puppy expression. I'm relieved that his fate is resolved, so I don't have to stress about it anymore.

I've always known I was a generally terrible person, but this drives it home in a way I didn't expect.

Especially when I consider this: I would be so grateful if the Gardener would get his shit together and die of his injuries, or something of that nature. I don't feel the need to kill him, or even for him to kill himself. I just really want him to be dead.

The trial probably won't start until the fall, and while I'm not pessimistic enough to think he'll be found innocent, there are still a lot of suboptimal outcomes. I don't want him taken care of in a psychiatric hospital or nursing home. I want him caged, stripped to nothing like we were and forcibly remade into something horribly fragile.

But even more than that, I just want him dead. The cage is appealing, but he still has enough money to make it comfortable, or as comfortable as it can be given his injuries. I don't want him comfortable.

I want him dead, but people keep looking at me like I should be better than that, like I should rise above, and goddamn it, I don't want to rise above. He hasn't earned that kind of grace.

If you ever get the chance, Priya, just kill him if you can. Self-defense, and then it's done.

Well.

Now I'm all kinds of cheered up, thank you, Inara.

As long as I'm going to wallow, though, I might as well do it right, so I open my computer back up. All of my bastard's victims have memorial Facebook pages, even the ones who didn't have Facebook when they were alive. They're most active in the spring, people posting memories or prayers as the anniversaries roll around, though birthday messages pop up too. The various mods are pretty quick to remove comments by assholes.

I start with Julie McCarthy and work backward, reading the new stories. There are new photos, too, put up by friends and family and classmates reminiscing. I skip Chavi's.

I've never looked at Chavi's since she died. I don't begrudge the people who post there, many of them genuinely her friends. Josephine moderates it, so I know it's respectful. If it helps them mourn and move on, more blessings to them. I just don't want to let other people's memories of Chavi intrude on my own.

When I get to Darla Jean's—the first victim—there's a post from her mother, Eudora Carmichael, dated on this year's anniversary of Darla Jean's death. Eudora talks about missing her daughter's light and laughter, how Darla Jean was all the joy in the family. She talks about missing her son, who never got over his sister's death. After a prayer for justice, she concludes with a picture, a family portrait from that last Easter.

Darla Jean is all blonde prettiness in white lace, and beside her, Eudora is plump and pleasant with the kind eyes she gave to her daughter. Her son stands behind them, and holy shit, seventeen years later I know that face.

I *know* that face.

"Mum!" I croak.

She looks up sharply from her computer. "Priya? Are you okay?"

"Come look at this."

"Priya?"

"Mum, please. Come look at this."

She slowly gets up and crosses the room, sitting next to me on the rock-hard couch. She glances from me to the screen. "Your face says this is important, but I don't follow."

I pull up one of the folders of pictures I've taken this spring, clicking through until I find the one I want. I crop the window so I can place it next to the picture of the Carmichaels.

She stares at the picture for a moment, a muscle jumping in her jaw. This is him, she knows it, too, this is the man who killed Chavi, almost certainly the one who's been leaving me gifts.

She swallows hard, blinking away the sheen of unshed tears, then looks back at me. "You don't have your phone in hand. Are you just in shock, or are you hesitating?"

My mother knows me entirely too well. "I'm hesitating."

"Why?" She sounds curious, not accusing. She's also not reaching for a phone to report it herself.

I hand her Inara's letter and watch her eyes scan back and forth over the page.

"I think I might like Inara," she notes when she's done.

"I think you've just described Eddison's personal hell."

"This is Inara's view, though; what's yours?"

I take a deep breath, give myself the time to truly think it through. There are moments I realize just how unconventional my relationship with Mum is. Moments I have to admit that she probably has sociopathic tendencies and simply chooses not to use her powers for excessive evil.

And I am my mother's daughter.

"How much proof do you suppose there is?" I ask eventually. "Seventeen years without getting caught, he's clearly not an idiot. We give this name to the FBI, how much do you think they'll find that isn't circumstantial? If he had any interest in confessing, he'd have done it years ago."

"You think if there's enough to go to trial, there won't be enough to convict."

"If they try him for it and he gets acquitted, that's it. They can't try him for the same murders again. No justice for Darla Jean straight through Julie McCarthy. No justice for Chavi."

"Landon," she murmurs thoughtfully.

"Landon was a pedophile; I'm not interested in justice for Landon."

Her lips twitch in a proud smile.

"What stops him from following us to France?" I ask.

"So you want to what? Trap him into confessing his past sins so you can record it? Make a conviction more likely?"

"No."

It takes a moment for it to sink in. I've never really been the savage one. "You're serious," she says.

"I want this done," I tell her softly, little more than a whisper. "I don't want to spend the rest of my life looking over my shoulder or wondering who else he's killed. I don't want to move with this still hanging over us. I just want all of this to be over."

She takes a deep breath, clasping her hands in her lap. Her knuckles are white with the strength of her grip. "So how do we do it?"

The laptop slides to the floor with a thunk as I wrap my arms around my mother. "I love you."

"But?"

"But that part has to be me, not we."

One eyebrow tilts dangerously. "You are going to explain that."

"If I do it, it's self-defense. If you do it, you're a vigilante, Mum. Maybe you get a sympathy acquittal, but not without losing your job and rendering yourself basically unhireable. If you're there, the Quantico Three will never believe it's accidental."

"You think they'll believe you?"

"If I'm completely alone? No, that's an obvious trap." From my bag, I pull out the postcard for Shiloh Chapel. "But if Agent Archer is with me and happens to leave me alone?"

"You're going to let him use you as bait after all."

"Yes."

"You trust him not to tell the others?"

"Shit no, that's why I'm not telling him." I smile in spite of myself at her laugh. "His apology was sincere; that means he feels guilty."

"And when a good man feels guilty, he wants to make up for it, not just apologize."

"So I'll ask Archer to take me to the chapel. If you're still playing paperwork catch-up from the days you took off for me, you can't drive me down. And Saturday's my birthday. This bastard has run through all the flowers now, which means whatever he's got planned for me is next; he just needs an opportunity. We can give him that."

"Good Lord, I have taught you well, haven't I?"

"You're up here, safely away from suspicion, and if he is watching me as closely as we think he is, he'll follow."

"And our young, enthusiastic Archer will see a chance to catch a serial killer making the attempt, solve the case, and prove himself. He'll leave you alone, but he won't go far."

"Which gives me backup if I chicken out or something goes wrong. It minimizes the risk."

We sit in silence, both digesting the possibilities.

"You know if anything happens to you, it will shatter Brandon."

I give her an incredulous look. "You never call him Brandon. No one calls him Brandon."

"It would destroy him. You have to know that, Priya."

"I do. That's why I think Archer is a good idea."

It wouldn't destroy Mum, though neither of us says it. It would shred her, maybe even shatter her, but the pieces would come back together sharper and stronger, made of purer steel, because if there's one thing Deshani Sravasti will never be, it's defeated. No matter what happens, she will never let the world break her permanently.

Brandon Eddison, though, has something Mum does not: a gaping, bleeding wound named Faith. He may look for her in the face of every blonde almost-thirty he comes across, but he still thinks of her as that little girl with pigtails and a gap-toothed grin, the adorable little geek who never saw a difference between princesses and superheroes. Until—unless—they find her, that wound will never heal.

That's where I live, I think, all the bits of me wrapped around that terribly fragile heart. I protect the rest of him from that ulcer, but

I make it bleed, too, close and not close enough. A hard enough hit against me will shatter what's left of Faith.

I wouldn't hurt Eddison for anything, but I can't live the life Inara's showing me. I need justice, not the hope of it, but more than that, I need all of this to just finally be done.

"So you'll talk to Archer in the morning?"

I nod.

"Be sure about this, Priya-love," Mum says gravely. "If at any point you're unsure, back away. We can still give him to the FBI."

"I know."

Late the next morning, when I come downstairs after getting the day's schoolwork out of the way, Archer is sitting on the couch with the components of one of the cameras spread over the coffee table. "Morning, sleepyhead," he greets.

"School, not sleep." I head into the kitchen to throw together a smoothie for a belated breakfast.

He follows me in. "You have any plans for the day?"

I pretend to consider it. "Is it okay to go to chess?"

"As long as you don't go off without me."

Pouring the smoothie into a pair of travel mugs, I hand him one and toast him with the other. "I'll get my purse."

His eyes move constantly as we walk. His car is in the driveway, but I miss the walk and he gives in. The extra time to gather my thoughts certainly doesn't hurt. It's interesting to see Archer note and catalogue everything around us.

"How much freedom of movement is implied in this protection thing?" I ask once we pass the gas station. "Like, as long as I have you or Sterling with me, are field trips okay?"

He gives me a sideways look, reassuringly curious. "Got something in mind?"

I pull the Shiloh Chapel postcard from my purse and hold it out for him. "I have a thing for windows. Or, more accurately, my sister had a thing for windows, and I have a thing for Chavi having a thing for windows."

"Convoluted much?"

"Eh. Anyway, Saturday is my birthday, and Mum and I were going to go."

"Were?"

"She has to work. Now that the transition is finally approaching, the branch HR director in Paris is getting nervous. I really want to get pictures of the chapel before we leave, and under normal circumstances I'd just take Mum to work and drive down on my own."

"Yeah, that's not happening."

"That's why I said the under-normal-circumstances bit. Keep up, Archer."

He barks a laugh, his shoulders relaxing a bit. "So you want me to drive you an hour away so you can take pictures of windows."

Reaching back into my purse, I bring out my secret weapon: my favorite photos from the box under my bed labeled simply *Chavi at Church*. On top is the one I love more than anything. It was taken in one of the bigger Catholic churches in Boston, with soaring ceilings that gave the impression of weightlessness, like everything inside it was just floating in the vastness of space. Chavi had already been sitting for a couple of hours in the main aisle, sketching intently, and I'd taken dozens of pictures of her and the interior and the windows from nearly every angle.

But I went up to the choir loft, leaning over the edge of the front protrusion where the choir leader was supposed to stand, and got her standing in silhouette in front of the blazing window, dust sparking gold like a halo around her. If the senior picture was Chavi's personality, this one was her soul, bright and full of wonder.

"Chavi was always trying to capture it on paper," I say quietly, a little pained at using her memory to manipulate. Soldier on, Priya.

"That sense of color, you know, the saturation and the way the light filtered through. Sometimes I feel like if I keep taking pictures of amazing windows, she gets to see them too."

He flips through the rest of the photos, a wonderfully complicated look on his face. Complicated is good. Complicated means his thoughts are going exactly where I'd hoped they'd go. We're in sight of the chess pavilion before he finally answers. "Sure, we can go. I mean, it's your birthday."

"Really?"

"Well, that is what you just told me," he deflects, and laughs when I swat his arm. "It's for your sister."

"Thank you so, so much." I take the stack of photos back and put them away in the outer pocket of the purse. "I promise to stay at chess if you'd rather wait in the café." At his hesitation, I cock an eyebrow. "Whoever this bastard is, he's not about to jump out at me in the middle of a group."

"Fine, but you have one of them walk you inside to meet me when you're done."

"Deal."

He is going to get in so much trouble when he leaves me alone at the chapel. I hope he learns from it, that he lets it make him a better agent. Maybe then I won't have to feel so guilty.

Gunny's awake when I step onto the chess island, smiling at me across his game with Jorge. I smile back, something soft and warm that may only be for Gunny, really, because it doesn't feel like there are any sharp edges to it.

If there's anything I've learned from the work functions Mum occasionally takes me to, it's how to look for the transitions in conversations and gently nudge them in a direction I want them to go. Mum is disgustingly brilliant at it. So while I play a shaky-eyed Yelp, letting him take as much time as he needs to make a decision about each move because his ghosts make him second- and third- and fourth-guess himself, I listen to the idle chatter about doctor appointments and movies and goddamn idiots who don't know how to fucking drive, and then Pierce mentions that his sister wants him to come celebrate May Day with the family.

"One of her grandkids hoards these stupid little fireworks, those poppers, you know? Make a lot of noise but not a lot of flash? Even when I go in expecting it, I just . . ." He trails off, staring morosely at his board with Corgi.

"Take this one with you," Happy suggests, nudging Corgi with an elbow. Liquid splashes up against the side of his foam cup, and I think we're all politely pretending we don't know there's almost as much whiskey as coffee in there. "His ugly mug will give you more nightmares than the noise."

"You don't even know how ugly you are, you stupid bastard, you can't keep a mirror whole," Corgi replies contentedly.

Male friendship is so strange.

"Anyone else have plans for the weekend?" I ask, moving my rook out of immediate danger.

Yelp has a visit with his daughters. He only gets to see them once a month, because the custody agreement was made when he was having a very difficult time and he doesn't feel he's at the point to safely change it yet. His face softens when he talks about them, and the trembling in his hand eases a little. They could help him a great deal, I think, but he won't ever put the burden on them of seeing his bad days.

Steven, it turns out, has a date, and most of the table starts ribbing him about it. He accepts it all with a goofy smile. "She's a Marine widow," he explains. "She knows what it's like."

Gunny is going up to Denver for a great-grandson's ballet recital, with Hannah driving him as always. "Just hope I can stay awake through it," he sighs. "Harder and harder these days."

"Just have Hannah wake you up before the boy's songs," Phillip tells him. "Don't much matter that you sleep through the rest, long as you see him up there."

Gunny nods, takes Jorge's queen with a pawn, and looks across to me. "And you, Miss Priya? Do you have plans?"

"Mum has to go into work on Saturday to take care of some things." Yelp takes one of my bishops. He's going to whomp me solidly in a few moves. "Agent Archer agreed to take me down to Rosemont."

"What's in Rosemont?" asks Jorge.

"A really pretty little chapel with amazing windows. The secretary at Gunny's church told me about it. I like to take pictures of stained glass."

"That's almost an hour's drive," Steven points out. "For windows?"

"My sister was the one to really love the glass," I say quietly. The men all shift and settle, like birds on a power line. "Maybe it's a way of saying goodbye, before we leave."

"Lots of pretty windows in Paris, last I heard." Corgi scratches at his nose, tiny red dots blooming around a broken vein from the pressure. "That's where Notre Dame is, ain't it?"

I stifle a grin at the way he says it: No-tree. "It is," I agree. "It's hard to put into words. I guess it's more like . . . well, Chavi's seen those windows. We went to Paris a few times when we were younger, back when we still lived in London."

"You lived in London?"

"Till I was five. I was born there." I shrug at their startled looks. "Mum got a really great job offer in Boston." And she really, really wanted to put an ocean between us and the families, but I can't say that to men who miss their families more than anything but are a little too broken to be with them day to day. Not all of them, but enough of them.

"You don't sound it."

"You've never seen me after a BBC marathon." And there goes my rook. "I lost most of the accent in elementary school because kids made fun of me, and Mum helped me smooth the rest out. It comes across more when I'm tired."

"My daughter-in-law's like that with Minnesota," Jorge laughs. "She gets so pink about it, too."

Happy takes the conversation into a diatribe about customer-service lines, and I let it go. It's a beautiful day, clear and breezy and nearly warm, and it's tempting to stay all afternoon, but Archer's waiting, and I really do feel safer at home. I can see Officer Clare across the parking lot near the deli, dressed in civvies. Watching. I have no doubt he'll be by the tables to ask after me.

Hannah walks me up to the grocery store, staying with me until Archer looks up from his tablet and sees us. She heads back outside with a kiss on my cheek.

"What'll you have?" I ask the agent. "My treat."

"Black coffee with a triple shot, and thanks."

"Not planning to sleep for the next week, are you?" I step back so I can turn and join the line, and slam into someone. My purse drops to the floor, the postcard, photos, and my wallet spilling out. "Aww, purse, no." I crouch down to pick them up, but another set of hands beats me to it.

I look up to see Joshua kneeling in front of me, my photos and the postcard held out. His tea and a hardcover book sit next to his knee. There's a pair of slim reading glasses hooked onto the neck of his light sweater, the fisherman sweaters probably put away until the fall.

"Thanks. Sorry for running into you."

"That's quite all right. I'm just glad your photos weren't ruined." He nods at Archer, a vague sort of acknowledgment the agent returns.

I drop the pics and card to the table. "Seems safer that way. Oh, and Archer? As thank-you for the ride, I'll get your caffeine fix on Saturday. I want to be down in Rosemont before the sun rises."

His startled cursing follows me to the line.

When I get back with my hot chocolate and his nervous twitch in a cup, Archer's alone at the table. "Before dawn?" he asks sourly.

"Or as close to it as possible. Have you ever seen the sunrise through stained glass, Agent Archer?"

"No," he says morosely. "I'm okay with that not changing."

"But it's my birthday."

He sighs and sips his coffee.

"Agent Hanoverian, sir? You have a delivery."

Eddison blinks at his papers and looks up at the door of the conference room. Vic and Ramirez seem equally startled, judging from how long it takes Vic to get to his feet.

Then Vic starts laughing. "Ma sent us dinner."

"Bless your mother," groans Ramirez.

Shoving his notes to one side, Eddison accepts the Tupperware bowl of beef stew, still warm, and the tinfoil twist of the buttered dinner rolls. "She is an angel," he agrees.

For a time, they all focus on eating. It's been a very long time since lunch. Once Vic passes out the wedges of pecan pie, they turn back to their task.

"These girls become important to him," Vic says. "Whether he's preserving their perceived purity or punishing their wickedness, it's personal to him."

"So what was it about Darla Jean?" Ramirez starts pleating her tinfoil into a fan. "She wasn't just the first murder; she shaped his motive."

"All the interviews say she was a good girl. Her boyfriend said they'd only just kissed for the first time before she was killed. Everyone in town knew her, everyone in town loved her."

"But she was raped," she replies. "His pathology means he saw something he considered sinful. Maybe even that kiss."

Grabbing Darla Jean's file, Vic skims through the collected statements. "Boyfriend didn't notice anyone around until the pastor came out of his office. After the boy left to go home, the pastor didn't see anyone but Darla Jean, then he left to walk into town. As far as he knew, Darla Jean was alone."

"She didn't try to run," Eddison points out. "She didn't try to fight until it was too late. This isn't just someone she knew, this was someone she trusted."

"Even considering the rape, our first assumption would normally be family," Ramirez says. "Father, brother, cousin, *someone* sees the kiss, decides her sinful ways make her unworthy of being family."

"Father died two years before Darla Jean from a heart attack, and her male cousins were all either too young or not in town. She did have an older brother, though." Vic flips a few pages in the folder. "Jameson Carmichael; he was twenty-one at the time. Graduated at twenty from the University of Texas with a degree in Web design. Got a job with a small marketing firm in the city, commuted in from the family home in Holyrood."

"Is he on our list?"

Eddison shakes his head, but double-checks anyway. Tapping the name into his tablet, he starts sifting through search results. "It doesn't look like he's been on anyone's list recently. He quit his job and left the Holyrood/San Antonio area a few months after his sister died. He's mentioned in a few memorials and articles, but there's nothing else coming up."

"Well that sounds ominous."

Grabbing his phone, Eddison punches in a number and sends the call to the speaker in the middle of the table.

"What do you need?" asks Yvonne, skipping the small talk.

"Your wisdom and guidance," he answers. "Your mad computer skills, at least. Is there any chance you can come in tonight?"

"I'm alone with the baby, but I brought a secure laptop home, so I do have access to all my systems. Who loves me?"

"We do," laughs Ramirez. "We're looking for Jameson Carmichael; he's Darla Jean's brother."

"And can you hook us up with the most recent spreadsheet from the florist calls?" Eddison asks.

"Do you have any idea how many analysts loathe you right now?" They can already hear the swift tapping of keys in the background, as well as a baby's contented burbling.

"I know it's mind-numbing, but is calling florists really the worst thing we could ask everyone to do?"

"I know roughly the number of flower shops in the state of Colorado. Do you think this is something I ever wanted to know?"

"I'm sure there are any number of husbands in Colorado who would be very grateful for that spreadsheet."

"Cute, but it's called Google. Your man Carmichael, though— any chance he's a dead John Doe somewhere? Because he just disappeared when he left home. Closed out his bank account but doesn't look to have started another. Texas driver's license is expired, never renewed, but he didn't apply for one anywhere else. No bills, no tickets, no leases or titles, no passport, no hospital admissions in his name. He's not languishing in prison, either, unless it's as a John Doe or under a very convincing other identity. Your boy's probably either dead, suffering from amnesia, or he built himself a life under a new name."

"What about the car that was registered to him? You could track the VIN if he transferred the title or registered it elsewhere, couldn't you?" asks Vic.

"I could indeed, sir, but he did not. Car was totaled a few weeks after his sister died. Police and insurance both report that he hit a pair of deer."

"Deer totaled a car?"

"They do it all the time," Yvonne answers. "Bambi and his girl-friend can absolutely destroy your front end. Carmichael deposited the insurance payout about two weeks before closing account."

Eddison shakes his head. "You can get all that in seconds but it takes forever to find out if anyone has sold dahlias recently."

"Well, this time you gave me a name, sugar, not hundreds of businesses and owners who don't always pick up their phone or return calls."

"I deserved that," he says with a wince.

"Yes, yes, you did."

"I'm sorry, Yvonne."

"Hey, I know this case is important," she says gently. "If I could give the world a kick and a curse and make it go ten times as fast, I would."

"I know."

"Carmichael should have fingerprints on record from that investi-gation; can you run them, see if they pop up anywhere else?"

Ramirez glances at Vic, her curls falling out of her pencil arrangement. "We don't have the killer's fingerprints at any of the crime scenes."

"No, but maybe he's been printed under a different name. Names can change, prints not so much."

"Nada, sir."

"It was worth asking," he sighs. "Thanks, Yvonne, and please send us the updated spreadsheet."

"Will do, agents. Please try to get some sleep." She hangs up, and Eddison clicks off the speaker.

"She's right. Go home, both of you."

"Vic—"

"We are all exhausted," the senior agent reminds them, getting to his feet. "Go home. Sleep. Come to my place in the morning. Ma will love the chance to feed you, and we can check in with Finney."

Eddison hesitates, looking at the stacks of papers and folders on the table. He can hear Vic and Ramirez murmuring to each other, and then the door closes. A large hand grips his shoulder. "Vic . . ."

"Brandon."

He looks up. Vic only uses his first name when he wants to be very sure he's got Eddison's attention.

"It's Priya's birthday tomorrow," Vic says quietly. "You know it's a rough day for her. She's going to need you at your best."

"What if my best isn't enough?"

Rather than answer, Vic squeezes his shoulder and lets go.

MAY

Mum leaves to drive to Denver and her office a little before five, too antsy to stay still. Before she leaves, she hugs me so hard it'll probably bruise. "Be sure," she says again, "be smart, be safe." All in all, not the worst benediction you can give your daughter before she heads off to murder someone.

I stay sprawled in bed, not quite awake, but definitely not asleep, either. Sleep didn't happen last night; my brain wouldn't shut off enough to let me rest.

Thoughts of Chavi, chasing me through the sheet maze, swinging me around in a dance, laughing, bled out on the grey stone floor.

Thoughts of Dad, broken and numb and shamed at the hospital, hanging from the banister when I got home from school.

All those other girls, too, their names almost as familiar to me as my own now.

Darla Jean, Zoraida, Leigh, Sasha.

Mandy, Libba, Emily, Carrie.

Laini, Kiersten, Rachel, Chavi.

Natalie, Meaghan, Aimée, Julie.

I could live to be a hundred and ten, and I think I'd forget my name before losing theirs.

If I close my eyes, I can almost feel the weight of Chavi behind me, all those late nights scribbling in our journals side by side, falling asleep to curl around each other. Lazy mornings cuddling under the blankets, until Mum jumped on us. Literally jumped, and started tickling and laughing until we were all breathless. I can remember how it felt when my sister's hand moved over my hair, tucking it back away from my face or separating out the sections to help Mum re-dye the streaks. I can remember her breath warm against my ear, the way her fingers would draw designs against my hip before she was even awake, the way she never accidentally ate my hair but was constantly spitting out her own.

Eventually I get up and shower, drying my freshly touched-up hair with far more care than I usually give it. A large white rose, the biggest I could find in the tiny floral section at the grocery, goes over my ear. Wearing the full crown from my birthday felt a little too obvious. I don't usually look in the full mirror when I get ready, preferring to use my compact so I only have to look at whatever I'm working on, but this morning, I put on my makeup with all of me visible. I'm Chavi but softer, not as bright or as bold, my sister's bone structure and features through different-colored glass. I pull on the tiered white sundress, the royal blue sweater and leggings that I put out last night. A freak weather system that moved in yesterday means there's snow on the way, on the first of May. Still, with the coat I should be warm enough.

Downstairs, I can hear Sterling and Archer talking, the changing of the guard. When I come down, camera bag slung over one shoulder, Sterling is gone. Archer looks at me, his eyes a little wild. Second thoughts? But he gives me a shaky smile and opens the door, so I guess we're good. I can't imagine Sterling would have left if she had had any idea of our plans for the day.

I can still back out. Just tell him or any of the others about Darla Jean's brother, let them find and arrest him.

But I think of spending the next however long waiting for a court to tell me I have justice, when justice can't bring anyone back. Be sure, Mum said.

I'm sure.

We stop at Starbucks to get drinks for the road, and then we're on our way.

It's a long, quiet ride to Rosemont, both of us sipping at our drinks until they're gone. Music plays softly from the radio, hard to hear over the whirr and buzz of the heat. Halfway there, it starts to snow, fat, wet flakes that shush against the windshield and melt as soon as they touch the warm glass. Occasionally, Archer's GPS gives us a change in direction.

My hands won't stop shaking. I bury them in my gloves, even though they're starting to sweat. Right now, I think, it might be nice to be a religious person. It would be nice to have something or someone to pray to, with the relative certainty of being listened to. Then again, if I were a properly religious person, I probably wouldn't be doing this, so. You know.

The snowfall gets heavier as we go. When we drive through the tiny town of Rosemont, a cluster of orange-coated men and women are out with shovels and salt buckets. A trio of plows sits on a side lot by the fire station, ready to make sure folks can actually get out of their homes. Not many people live here in town; according to the articles I read about the chapel, Rosemont exists mostly so the area residents have someplace to market, mail, and educate their children.

Archer frowns at the open curiosity that meets us down the main road. "Is a stranger so shocking?"

"It's a small town."

Shiloh Chapel is a few miles outside of town. As small as Rosemont is, it manages to have four proper churches, but the chapel is left over from a wealthy mining family that used to own most of the land hereabouts. It's popular still for weddings, regardless of denomination. Archer parks the car a ways back, and for a moment I'm so enchanted by the view I almost forget why I'm here.

It's like standing inside a snow globe. White covers the sloped roof, more than a dusting but not quite thick enough to hide the reddish-pink terra cotta tiles. The walls are white as well, plaster or stucco or whatever it is that leaves thick swirls of texture like an oil painting. The small rosettes on either side of the ox-blood door are shades of blue, and there's something a little bit perfect about that.

There won't be enough sun to catch the other windows at their full glory, but there's magic in this too.

Checking over my camera, I sling the bag over my shoulder and climb out of the car, the camera itself cradled in my hands. My hip catches the door to swing it shut. I lean against the front of the car, where warmth seeps through my coat despite the damp of melting snow, and just take in the view for a bit.

Framing the picture comes later; you can't see context through the view-screen.

Archer is still in the car when I lift the camera and start taking pictures, the tiny chapel almost blending in with the snow except for its darts of color. I pace in a wide circle around the structure, finding the interesting angles. The east and west walls are, like the Methodist chapel back in Huntington, only as much wall as is needed to support the windows and roof. Even without beams of sunlight, without the way to track the shafts of color against the new snow, the glass is glorious. The western wall shows Jesus walking on the water through the storm, the disciples huddled in a rough boat in one corner.

Josephine was Episcopalian; we went with her to church sometimes out of curiosity, and afterward, Chavi would take the Bible stories and sketch them into windows like this. I haven't really thought of those stories in years.

The north wall is entirely solid except for a trio of rosettes in warm shades of yellow, amber, and brown. It's cleverly done, if you believe in a Trinity, each rose predominantly one color but containing all three, bleeding into each other around the inner edges. Maybe it's clever even if you don't believe.

I make another circle, stepping in for close-ups this time. A trail of green ovals shows where I've been, though fresh snow dusts the grass soon enough.

The east wall is its own sunrise, and I wish I could see it with all its warmth, the colors afire with light. There are colors I would never think to put into a sunrise, bright blues and soft greens blurring out from the indigo and lavender, but it works in a way Chavi could probably understand, if not explain.

When I come back around to the front, Archer is still in the car. "Coming in?" I ask through the closed window.

He shakes his head. "Far too cold for me. Take your time, though."

Right.

There are no chairs in the chapel, no kneelers, just space, empty even of the hum of electricity. I take my pictures, entranced more than I would have guessed by the simplicity of the northern rosettes, the colors warm and soothing like candlelight. There's a stillness to the air, the moment before a breath. It isn't simply silent, it's muffled.

Solitude, I suppose, when it's nature rather than choice.

Then I pack away the camera, setting the bag safely in a corner, and peel off my gloves, scarf, and coat. It isn't anywhere near warm enough, but I know what I look like in this dress, because I know what Chavi looked like in it. It was always one of her favorites, and even though she was an inch or so taller than I am now, an inch or so smaller in the bust, it fits well, sweet and innocent, the ruffled white tiers just a little bit flirty. There isn't a way for me to look like the too-skinny twelve-year-old I was, but I can look like a pale reflection of Chavi.

The rose is heavy against my ear, the weight fighting the pins holding it in place. It seems heavier than it should be, and I can't tell if it's just me, maybe, my body insisting on feeling the weight my mind wants to give it.

With my phone in my hand, I drop the coat in the center of the floor and sit down on top of it. Even with the heavy wool and my fleece-lined leggings, I can feel the cold seep through. Chavi used to sit like this, just captivated by whatever she was trying to draw.

I hear the rumble of the car turning back on and driving away. Of course no one's going to come if Archer's right there. So he'll hide a ways back, watch. Wait. I pull up a contact on my phone and hit "call" and "speaker," listening to the dull rings fill the small chapel.

"You're up early for a Saturday, Birthday Girl."

Something tight and terrible in my chest eases at the sound of Eddison's voice. I can hear chaos behind him, what would seem to be Vic getting roundly scolded by his ma. "It's snowing," I tell him, and he laughs.

"Goddamn Colorado. But you usually wait for me to call you on your birthday. Are you okay?"

Because as much as he's my friend, he's also an agent, or maybe more an agent at times, and he'll always look for patterns and the ways we break them. It's comforting, a little. Dependable. "I'm Chavi's age."

"Shit, Priya."

"Next year, I'll be eighteen, and logically, I knew it would happen, but I don't think I'm prepared to be older than my big sister."

I'm not fully prepared for a lot of things, but I'm pitching headlong into them anyway.

"Has your mother pinched you yet for being maudlin on your birthday?"

It startles a huff of laughter out of me. "She's stuck at work till later. Besides, I always get half an hour to be maudlin. It's a rule."

Because Dad killed himself on my birthday, and for all Mum refuses to mourn him, she never faults me for occasionally wanting to. She keeps a lot tucked away but has never asked me to live my own life that way.

"Did I ever tell you my mother chaperoned what should have been Faith's senior prom?" he asks. It's an offering of sorts, something private and painful, because he very rarely talks about his sister.

"Must have been hard."

"She was a wreck for weeks. But after that, she was a little better. It helped her accept that even if we got Faith back, we were never going to get those years and those events."

"So what I'm hearing is that I should have a blow-out party for my eighteenth and drink myself insensible to recover from it?"

"Don't you dare." He gives a soft grunt, and then I hear Mercedes's voice very close to the phone.

"Happy birthday, Priya!" she chirps.

"Thanks, Mercedes."

"Where are you?" she asks. "It's echoing."

"Shiloh Chapel," I answer. "It's in Rosemont, which is a pain, but it's got these amazing windows."

"If your mother's at work, are you there alone?" Eddison demands sharply.

"No, Archer drove me down."

"Can you put him on?" His voice is suddenly far too pleasant, which cannot spell out good things for Archer.

"He's outside. He said it looked too cold."

"Ramirez—"

"On it," she says. "I'll call you later, Priya."

"Okay."

"What the hell is he thinking?" Eddison snaps.

"That I asked nicely for my birthday?"

"A church, Priya. Of all places."

"I thought it would be safe as long as I wasn't alone."

"If he's outside, you are alone, and that isn't acceptable. Ramirez is calling him."

"Who are you talking to, Priya?"

251

And that is definitely not Archer.

I look up at the doorway. Even knowing what I'm going to find, my heart thumps in my chest. Sudden fear sits heavy, solid in my gut. "Joshua? What are you doing here?"

"Priya!" Eddison sounds pissed, or panicked. Both. "Who's there?"

"Joshua," I say numbly. "From the café. The one who poured a drink on Landon that one time."

"He shouldn't have been bothering you," Joshua says, his voice as warm and friendly as ever. He's in yet another fisherman sweater, sage green and lovely with his eyes, the sad eyes I almost remembered from Boston. At his feet . . .

Please don't let this be the biggest mistake of my life.

At his feet rests an enormous wicker basket, almost overflowing with white roses.

"You killed Landon?"

"He shouldn't have been bothering you," he repeats gently.

"Where's Agent Archer? What did you do to him?"

He laughs, and terror skitters up my spine. "I didn't have to do anything. I passed him in town, after he left you here."

In town? I knew he'd drive away from the chapel, that the idea of using me as bait would be too tempting, but I thought he'd come back along a side road, or through the woods. Why in the hell would he go all the way to town?

A very large part of my plan relied on Archer being close enough to rescue me.

I am so fucked.

"Why do you have roses?" I ask, my voice shaking from more than cold. Through the phone, I can hear Eddison's muffled swearing, like he's holding his hand over the mic. The only thing I can hear clearly is his yell for Vic.

"Oh, Priya." Joshua kneels, still several feet away, and smiles. "They're gifts, of course. My father taught me that you always bring a girl flowers. It's only polite. You're different from the others; you deserve more."

Carefully, slowly, so he doesn't panic and lunge at me, I push to my feet, phone clutched in my hand. "What are you doing here, Joshua?"

"I'm here to protect you." He sounds so sincere. How fucked in the head does he have to be to believe that? "You're such a good girl, Priya. I knew it back in Boston. And Chavi was such a wonderful sister to you. You were so loved, and so good."

"Then why did you kill her?" Tears burn in my eyes, form a knot in my throat. "Why did you take her away from me?"

"You don't know what this world does to good girls." He stands, and my fingers spasm around the phone. A phone isn't a weapon, though. He reaches out one hand, fingers tracing the air inches away from my bindi, the stud in my nose. "Chavi was a good girl, too, but she wouldn't have stayed that way. She was going away to college; the world would have corrupted her, and she would have done the same to you. I had to protect you both.

"And I did. You stayed good. I was worried after Chavi died, that you might act out, but you didn't. Aimée was exactly what you needed."

"I needed a friend," I retort, "and you killed her!"

"She was so sad after you moved away. I didn't want her to be sad." His fingers brush my cheek, and I flinch. "Don't touch me!"

"I promise it won't hurt," he says soothingly. "You won't even feel it. And then . . ."

I step away, scuttling backward, and smack into the wall. Oh God, this really is a tiny room, so much smaller than I realized before the serial killer stepped in. The serial killer who is much taller and stronger than I am.

Oh, fuck.

Still smiling, Joshua pries the phone from my clutching fingers. A hunting knife gleams in his other hand. "And then, Priya, you will always be good. I'll always be able to protect you." He ends the call and tosses the phone against the far wall.

"Please don't do this," I whisper.

His smile just grows. "I have to; it's for your own good. Now you have to hold still, or it'll hurt." He adjusts his grip on the knife, still held down by his side.

Taking as deep a breath as I can manage, I lunge into him, one hand at his wrist and the other in his hair, driving my knee into his crotch. As he tries to pull away, I kick and punch and scratch, trying to keep that knife away from my throat.

And I scream, even louder than I did for Chavi.

I scream, praying Archer's close.

I scream, and I may never stop screaming.

Eddison's heart stops when the line goes dead. Despite his training, despite the adrenaline screaming through him, all he can do is stare at the phone.

"Archer's almost back to the chapel," Ramirez reports, her work cell clamped between ear and shoulder. Her thumb flies over the screen of her personal cell. "He went to town for backup; goddamn asshole was using her as bait." She ignores the squawk of protest on the other end of the line. "I've got Sterling; Finney's calling the sheriff's office. Rosemont doesn't have a police force, so they're sending a couple of cars from the county seat. Archer has a pair of army vets from Rosemont. Stop talking and drive, you asshole!" she adds into the phone.

Vic also has both phones out, using one to arrange a flight to Colorado, the other to text Yvonne. They'd been going over the florist results when Priya called; Marlene scolded Vic for working at the breakfast table. "Yes, I'm still here. I need three tickets to Denver, and we need to be there as soon as possible."

Shaking himself out, Eddison grabs for his phone, pulling the Bureau-issued cell from the clip on his belt. He always thought it moronic to have six phones for three agents, but now he's grateful for it. He calls Priya back; it goes straight to voice mail. With the other phone, he texts Finney directly.

Ramirez pulls the phone from her ear and glares at it. "They got to the chapel and heard Priya screaming, and the asshole hung up!"

"Would you rather he hold the phone or the gun?" Eddison mutters.

"He should've kept the call open with the phone in his pocket so we could hear. Asshole."

Eddison isn't sure if she means him or Archer with that last one. He isn't about to ask.

"We need to get to the airport," Vic tells them. "Are your go bags at the office?"

"We've got backups in our cars," says Ramirez.

"Then let's go."

Marlene watches them leave, tight-lipped with worry.

Through some sorcery of too much experience, Vic gets them on a plane in barely an hour. They get an update from Finney just before boarding: Priya and Joshua—Jameson—are both being taken to the nearest hospital to get airlifted to Denver before the weather makes it impossible, and Finney will meet them at the hospital.

Sterling sends a postscript to Ramirez: the snow is turning into a full storm. It's possible they'll have to divert to a different hospital.

Eddison hopes the storm stays well west of Denver. Please, for the love of a God he's had issues with since Faith disappeared, don't let it fuck with the flights.

Then they're on the plane, and the phones are off, and Eddison's pretty sure time has never been so slow. He wishes, not for the first time and probably not for the last, that the Bureau was even half as well financed as shows and movies make it out to be. Then they'd be on a private jet, able to keep in contact with the folks on the ground, not stuck in economy on a relic of a plane that doesn't have Wi-Fi.

There also wouldn't be the incessantly screaming child kicking the back of his seat for *four straight hours.*

The taxi up to the gate is endless, and he jumps when he feels a hand on his bouncing knee. It's Vic's. Eddison flushes at the understanding in his senior partner's expression. Rather than a lecture, though, or a pointed comment, both of which he probably deserves for his impatience, Vic just pulls a picture from his workbag and hands it to Eddison. "This is why you'll find the calm as soon as there's something more you can do."

This . . . is a picture he did not know existed. It's taken from behind, at a bit of a distance, as Eddison and Priya look up at the statue in the Lincoln Memorial. They're side by side, his arm around her shoulders. Or, sort of; he's hooked over one shoulder, but then his arm is bent so his hand rests atop her scalp, their heads tilted into each other, his cheek against the back of his hand. Her arm is slung around his hips, fingers curled through his belt loop right next to his gun.

He takes a deep breath and stills his knee.

Vic is right. He usually is when it comes to people.

As soon as there's something he can do, he'll be doing it.

But goddamn it, can't this plane taxi any faster?

They get permission to disembark and he's got his bags and himself off the plane before most of the other passengers are even standing. Ramirez and Vic are right behind him. Near the baggage claim, there's a young woman holding up a piece of computer paper with *QUANTICO* written in messy black letters. She straightens when she sees them bearing down on her.

"SSAIC Hanoverian?" she asks.

Vic nods.

"Agent Sterling," she tells them. "Priya's alive, and she's going to be okay. She's got some injuries, I don't know how severe, but they got her to a hospital here in Denver, and I'll take you to her. Her assailant was airlifted to the same hospital; he's currently in surgery. Docs gave us an extra blood sample from their workup, it's at the lab and running with a priority rush on it. Fingerprints just confirmed as Jameson Carmichael. Agent Finnegan is at the hospital with Priya."

Vic gives another nod, slower this time, approving. "Let's get to the hospital, then. We'll check in with the Sravastis and Finney."

"Yes, sir." She walks briskly, either from her own sense of purpose or their radiating anxiety. A Bureau-issued dark blue sedan waits outside, defiantly straddling a lane of no-parking hashes. An airport security guard scowls at them.

Eddison scowls back. His is more impressive.

Vic shakes his head and mutters something about pissing on parking signs.

It's amazing, the sense of relief that Priya's alive.

Agent Sterling doesn't use the sirens, but she also doesn't exercise much respect for traffic laws. Eddison fully approves. She pulls up to the emergency entrance and idles, waiting for them to scramble out of the car. "Huntington cops are at Carmichael's apartment. I'll be in the garage here; call me when you're ready to head out."

"Thanks," Vic says absently. His attention is already on the ambulance screaming its way up the loop, and all three Quantico agents hurry onto the sidewalk so Sterling can pull away.

Ramirez shudders. "She nearly clipped a hearse."

Eddison rolls his eyes. "An empty one."

"How would you know?"

"No escort."

Vic ignores them. He frequently does whenever, as he says, they remind him more of his kids than his teammates. A harried-looking receptionist directs them to the second floor. Fortunately, they don't have to ask which room. At the room closest to the nurses' station, they can see two men leaning on either side of the door, one in the crisp black uniform of DPD, the other in a crumpled suit and off-kilter tie.

The one in the suit straightens when he sees them. "Hello, Quantico."

"Finney." Vic reaches out and the two men clasp forearms.

He nods at Ramirez and Eddison. "She got knocked about a bit. Some bruises, some concern with her ribs, her left wrist. She's got a gash on her throat that took a few stitches, but it wasn't too deep. She said it, but a nurse confirmed that she was not raped."

Vic lets out a slow breath. "That's physically. How's she actually doing?"

"Hard to say." Finney frowns and attempts to straighten his tie, but only succeeds in making the back longer than the front. "Aside from the shakes, she's fairly steady, but her eyes are a bit wild. She settled a little after her mother arrived."

"Is Deshani in with her now?"

The officer sneezes. Eddison's fairly certain it's a laugh. "Yes, sir, she is. Made two interns and a resident cry, until she put her foot down and demanded someone get a nurse so her daughter could be treated by someone who knew what they were doing. Never knew doctors could look so much like cats."

"Deshani has that effect," Ramirez and Vic say together, and both smile at the officer's surprise.

"Okay to go in?" asks Eddison. He shifts his weight from foot to foot, fighting the urge to bury his hands in his pockets. He's never understood how Vic can go so still when he's anxious.

"Yeah, go on. We can figure out a game plan after. Reassure yourselves."

He doesn't mention that they're far too close on this one, that they don't have the distance they should. He already knows they don't, and whether it's loyalty to Vic or just an understanding of how things can get, he hasn't said anything about it.

Eddison knocks on the door. "I come with Oreos," he announces. "Then get the hell in here," Priya calls back. "I'm starving!"

Vic and Ramirez both start laughing. Eddison just leans his forehead against the door and takes a deep breath. His hand is still shaking. He can feel Vic's grip on his shoulder and wants to snarl. Knows he could do it, too, and that his partner would understand the temper, the need to vent, and it's that more than anything else that keeps him from doing it. When the rage and relief are tamped down a little, he opens the door and leads the way in.

Deshani Sravasti rests against the foot of the bed, straight from the office. Her dark grey skirt and blazer are elegant but tailored severely, softened slightly by the dusky rose silk blouse and sheer, brightly patterned cabbage rose scarf around her neck. Her heels sit on the floor against the far wall with her bag, and she looks almost ridiculous with her nylons ending in bright blue hospital-issue ultra-grip socks, but Eddison's not brave enough to tell her that. He freely gives Deshani the same respect as the gun at his hip, unsure which is more dangerous.

Priya sits tailor-style on the bed, with a pillow on her lap and a bandage wrapped around her throat, and his heart skips at the amount of blood on the clothing bagged at her side. Seeing her faded hospital gown is not something he thinks he can get over anytime soon. She gives him a weak smile, mostly obscured by the fist that hovers in front of her mouth, the thumb tapping an urgent tattoo against the blue crystal nose stud. There are smears of makeup on her cheeks and around her eyes, left over from tears and sweat and, he guesses, blood and quick cleaning.

She looks like her sister. Christ but it's another punch to the gut to realize how similar their crime scene photos would have looked. Could have looked, if she hadn't been lucky.

"Blue," she says, the smile fading. Her hand drops to the pillow, palms and fingers wrapped in gauze and tape, and Inara's were like that, when he first met her—stop.

He takes a deep breath. "What?"

"The streaks, the jewelry. They're blue. Still blue. Hers were red."

He chuckles weakly and scrubs at his jaw, feeling the stubble he didn't bother to shave off this morning because he didn't have the energy. "Thank you." It helps more than it should—again—but not enough. She studies her hands, then looks up at him through her lashes, and he's moving before he's aware of it, thighs thumping against the side of the bed as he comes close enough to wrap his arms around her and just hold on.

She leans into him, her hands curling around his arm, and as she releases a great, shuddering sigh, he can feel her shoulders drop, the muscles in her back easing. He hears a click that's probably Ramirez taking a picture and he can't bring himself to care. Priya's alive. She's here and alive and he's more certain than he's been in twenty years that there might be a God out there after all.

"So do you actually have Oreos or was that just a way to get in the door?"

He reaches into the outer left pocket of his coat and pulls out a snack pack of Oreos, tossing it over her head so it lands on the pillow. He picked it up at the airport just in case, while Vic argued with the gate attendant to get them on the first flight out.

She covers it with one hand, but keeps the other on his arm, not moving away from him. "You got here fast."

"Next flight out. Vic kicked three people to standby so we could take their seats."

"Is he allowed to do that?"

"I don't know. Fortunately no one else did, either."

"Way to go, Vic."

The senior agent smiles and moves toward Deshani, hand outstretched. The woman takes it, holds it for a moment before letting it drop. Deshani isn't the type of woman to allow herself much comforting. "I'm glad you're all right, Priya," Vic says warmly.

"Aren't I always?"

"No. And that's okay."

She smiles at him, wry and small but there. Reluctantly, Eddison lets her go so she can sit up properly. He doesn't step away, though. "How are your girls?" she asks Vic.

"Holly's intent on having a magazine-worthy dorm room, so she and her mother have been plotting and crafting. I learned what a duvet is." He gives her a crooked grin, surprisingly young on his weathered face. "At least I'm fairly sure a duvet is made of fabric and goes on a bed."

Ramirez snickers and adjusts the strap of her messenger bag. "Now that I can see you're okay—or will be—I'm going to go find out what's going on. I'll see you both later."

"Doesn't Eddison usually do the scene thing?"

"There's a baby agent in the car; if I let Eddison ride down to the scene with her, she'll probably leave the Bureau."

"Sterling's tougher than she looks; she might ask him out."

If he was close enough, he'd be shoving Ramirez out the door right now. As it is, she gives him a mocking little finger wave before leaving.

There are exactly two chairs in the room, one a somewhat padded vinyl monstrosity, the other a faux-wood plastic contraption that looks so fiendishly uncomfortable they must use it to limit visiting time. Vic pushes the terrible one to Eddison, then shifts the armchair to the other side of the bed, near the foot. Neither man offers one to Deshani; they both know she's at the absolute stretch of her tether. The end of the bed is as far as she can make herself go, to give her daughter some space.

Eddison just spent four hours with the very real possibility that deplaning meant hearing of Priya's death. Space is not really one of his top priorities at the moment.

"They won't tell me anything about him," Priya says quietly.

"He's in surgery," Vic answers. "That's all we know so far."

She nods at that.

Eddison can't keep himself from cataloguing her injuries. Her left wrist is in an elastic wrap, the material already fraying around the bite of the metal butterfly clasps. He can see the beginnings of bruises on her arms, around her throat, on her face, especially on her jaw and chin. There's a deep pink scrape and welt between her eyes, and he wonders if the crystal bindi is on the chapel floor, or if it gave up the ghost in the ambulance. Finney mentioned there was worry about her ribs, but he can't bring himself to ask. Not yet.

Opening the pack of Oreos, Priya pulls one out, separates one cookie from the crème with a deft twist, and hands that one to her mother. Crumbs flake off against the gauze covering her fingers. After a moment's thought, she uses her thumb to peel the crème off.

"Really?"

She gives Eddison a sidelong glance. "There's no milk."

"If I call someone to fix that, will you stop eating it like a heathen?"

She rolls the crème into a neat, almost perfectly round ball and hands him the naked cookie. "There are more important matters on the table, aren't there?"

He considers that, then shoves the cookie in his mouth. "No."

"Children, behave," murmurs Vic, looking pained.

But Priya gives Eddison a small nod, not quite imperceptible, and he relaxes back into the chair. If she *needed* the Oreos, she wouldn't be remotely fussy about the way she eats them. She pops the crème ball in her mouth, brushes her fingers against the worn fabric of the hospital gown, and reaches up to push her hair out of her face. A moment later, it flops forward again, a heavy mass of blue-streaked black. "Mum?"

"I suppose the bandages would make it a bit difficult," Deshani agrees. She moves around the bed and up to her daughter's side, opposite Eddison, gently gathering Priya's hair into her hands. Despite the care, Priya winces once or twice. "There's some blood caked in there," her mother tells her, the bleakly practical words offset by the slight crack in her voice. "We'll wash it when we get home."

There's a knock on the door, and Finney pokes his head in. "They're still operating, but they sent out a resident to give an update, if you want to hear firsthand."

It should be Eddison getting up to go, but instead it's Vic hauling himself out of the sucking vinyl monstrosity. "Deshani, did you happen to bring any clothes for Priya?"

She shakes her head. "I came straight from the office."

"While I'm out, I'll see what the gift shop has to offer, and we'll get your clothes to the lab." He walks up the bed to get the sealed bag and drops a hand onto Eddison's shoulder, not squeezing, not gripping, just there for a moment and gone the next. A gift, in its way.

There are times Eddison knows how lucky he is to have Vic for a partner.

He's not sure he's ever felt it so keenly before.

"I'm going to get us some coffee," Deshani announces. "Eddison? If I promise to have them make it extra barbaric?"

"Some of us are strong enough to drink coffee the way the gods intended," he tells her, and she snorts.

"You're bitter enough, like calls to like." She nods to Vic as he holds the door open for her.

In the quiet of the room, Eddison watches Priya scrape the crème off the rest of the Oreos, tucking the cookies back into the packaging. "What happened, Priya?" he asks finally.

"I didn't think I was going to be able to get down to the chapel before we left," she says after a minute. "I'd only just learned about it, but it sounded . . . it sounded like something Chavi would have loved. I know it's stupid, but I can't help but feel like leaving the country is leaving her behind. We're taking her ashes with us and everything, but it's just . . ."

"It's a big move," he says neutrally. Waiting.

"Archer agreed to drive me down. When I went inside the chapel, he stayed in the car. Joshua said he saw Archer in town." She takes a slow, shaky breath, her eyes glassy with shock. "Why would he go to town?"

"We'll get the full account from him soon, but he went to get help. He thought the killer might follow you, so he left you alone as bait. He was looking for backup so he could get back and protect you."

"How could he protect me from town?"

He shakes his head. Archer may or may not lose his place in the Bureau—he did technically catch the killer, after all—but he'll be in a hell of a lot of trouble. Eddison's going to help make sure of that. "You were alone in the chapel, you called me, and Joshua came in."

"Joshua, of all people. He's always been polite. Kind. Charming without being creepy. He felt safe. I just thought—" She sniffs and rubs at the bloody dig between her eyes, blinking away tears. "I thought if I ever saw my sister's murderer, he would *look* like a murderer, you know? Like I'd be able to *see* all the things wrong with him. I never imagined someone like Joshua. Someone so freaking normal."

"His name isn't Joshua; it's Jameson. Jameson Carmichael. The first girl he killed was his sister, Darla Jean."

"He said Chavi was a good sister."

"I know."

"He said Aimée was a good friend."

Her eyes are still glassier than he'd like.

"What happened after the call dropped?"

She bites her lip, her teeth tearing at a scab, and he steels himself not to cringe at the beads of blood that well up. Her eyes are huge and tear-bright, and when he scoots to the edge of the chair and holds out his hand, she seizes it with a strong grip that makes the week-old bruises and abrasions sting. "He said he had to protect me from the world, had to make sure I stay good."

"He came at you."

"He had a knife. Well, obviously. He likes the stabby stabby."

"More like the slicey slicey."

"I love you," she huffs.

He gives her hand a careful squeeze.

"I don't think he was expecting me to struggle. Maybe his version of a good girl wouldn't? But I'm stronger than I look, you know?"

"Always have been." He shakes his head at her doubting look. "Twelve years old, Priya, after the worst days of your life, angry and scared and grieving, you threw a teddy bear at my head and told me not to be such a fucking coward."

"You were scared to talk to me."

"Damn straight. But you called me on it."

She's got both hands curled around his now, picking at loose curls of skin along his nails, and he doesn't try to stop her. "We fought over the knife, but he's a lot bigger. I got it, though, eventually, and I—I stabbed him." Her voice drops to barely more than a whisper, thick and heavy with pain. "I'm not even sure how many times, I was just so afraid he'd get up and come after me again. He didn't have a phone, and mine wasn't working. I think the throw killed it, and it shouldn't have, because we paid extra for the cases."

"Priya."

"I stabbed him," she says again. "And the knife—one side of it is straight, but the other edge is serrated and it makes this—this *tearing* sound when it comes out, and I don't ever want to hear that sound again. I shouldn't even have been able to hear it, because we were both struggling, and panting, and I might have been screaming, I don't know, but it was like it was the only thing I could hear."

"What happened next?"

"Archer ran in, just as Joshua fell. He had two men with him. One of them took me outside, tied his scarf around my neck to help with the bleeding. He said he used to be an army medic. Eddison, I'm sorry. I'm so sorry."

"For what?"

"For being so stupid." Despite her rapid blinking, the tears spill over, and he can feel the warmth when they drip off her chin onto the back of his hand. "It doesn't matter that I didn't suspect Joshua, I knew someone was after me. I shouldn't have put it on Archer to protect me without backup. I should have just forgotten the stupid windows and stayed home."

Fuck distance and professionalism.

He shifts up onto the bed, wrapping his arms around her again and rocking her slightly, and feels her break. She's almost silent as she sobs, gasping for breath as her body quakes. He doesn't try to calm her, doesn't try to tell her it's okay. He doesn't try to tell her she's safe now.

Safe, he's learned, is a very fragile, relative thing.

Slowly, the storm passes, and he reaches for the box of tissues beside the bed to help her clean her face. What's left of her makeup is a little terrifying, but he wipes off as much as he can without making it worse. He taps the bloody scrape between her eyes, leans forward to press a kiss just above it.

"Thank you for being alive," he murmurs.

"Thank you for letting me snot all over you."

That's his girl.

Vic and Deshani come back together, Deshani holding a triangle of cups aloft purely by carefully applied pressure, Vic holding his own cup of coffee and a sky-blue-and-white-striped bag with little blue footprints and a repeating *It's a boy!!!* banner. He looks so sheepish and exasperated holding it that it makes both Priya and Eddison dissolve into giddy, just-this-side-of-hysterical laughter.

Vic sighs and hands the bag to Priya. "They were out of 'Congrats, it's a tumor' bags," he says, not quite managing a straight face.

Eddison slides off the bed and over to Vic, while Deshani pulls the curtain around the bed to help Priya change. "Anything from Ramirez?"

"A text. Archer's still down at Rosemont; Finney's got a team of senior agents on the way to take over and haul his sorry ass back; Sterling and Ramirez are at Carmichael's residence. He keeps pictures."

"Of Priya?" he asks, gut clenching.

"Of all of them. They're bagging some of the card stock on his desk, pens, handwriting samples. Photos, clearly. It's fairly safe to say he'll be charged if he survives."

"How likely is that?"

"They're still working, but they don't seem very hopeful. His lung and ribs are pretty well torn up, some nicks to his heart, some pretty important blood vessels." His voice is quiet, that not-whisper that's clear but doesn't carry an inch farther than he wants it to. "Archer recovered the knife at the scene, so they'll cast it and test it against the previous murders."

"But without being willing to put it in writing or swear before a court of law, you're pretty damn sure our murderer is on an operating table right now."

"If he could survive long enough to make a confession, that would be lovely."

"Is Priya going to need to stay here in the hospital?"

Vic shakes his head, crossing his arms against his chest. "Once the pharmacy sorts out the medications they want to send her home with, you can head out with the Sravastis. If they need to make a stop or two along the way for essentials, that's fine, but only necessary ones. Once you're at the house with them, stay there."

Another gift. Normally that's Vic's job. Speaking with families, monitoring who comes to visit and what they say. The Eddison from college, from the academy, would be laughing himself shitless, but the man he is now—the agent he is now—knows to be grateful for true friendship wherever it can be found.

"Finney's got guards outside the operating room and in the scrub room, just in case," Vic continues before Eddison can decide whether or not a thank-you would be appropriate here. "I'll wait here with him for more updates and coordinate with Ramirez and the team down in Rosemont."

The curtain hooks rattle on their metal slide as Deshani pushes the plastic back into place against the wall. Priya settles back onto the bed, clad in fleecy, cheerful yellow pajama pants and a long-sleeve FBI T-shirt. "It's a very well-supplied gift shop," she says dryly, wrapping her hands gingerly around her hot chocolate.

"Isn't it, though?"

There's barely a second between the knock on the door and the door opening, and a woman in rose-pink scrubs enters. She gives Priya a con-spiratorial wink. "I got the drugs, man," she says, in a bad imitation of a television drug dealer. She waves a trio of white and blue paper bags, the tops folded over and stapled with long blue sheets of instructions.

Deshani pinches the bridge of her nose.

The nurse notices and laughs. "Oh, please let me play. I'm work-ing a double with a doc who can't ride herd on his interns. I need the venting."

"That I can understand," Deshani says. She rolls her head back, stretching until everyone in the room hears a soft crack.

"All right, ladies, here we are." She launches into a brisk but thor-ough explanation of each medication and how to treat the wounds, as well as what to look for and when to come back in. Clearly, she's had a lot of practice. When she finishes, she props her hands on her hips and regards both women. "The important thing, aside from remembering that I'm a nurse and therefore a font of wisdom, is to take care of your-self. You've got extra limits for a bit. Any questions?"

Mother and daughter examine the written instructions, then shake their heads in unison.

Both men smile.

"Then, unless these good agents need you to stick around, you are free to go. Would you like me to bring the discharge paperwork?"

Deshani glances at Vic, who nods a go-ahead. "Please."

The storm that was steadily covering Rosemont in snow is only starting to move into Huntington as Mum drives us back, and despite his
being a terrible passenger, Eddison insists I take the front seat. He
sprawls and fidgets in the backseat. When we stop at the drug store
for wound care supplies, he and I both stay in the car. At the grocery
store, however—not the Kroger near the chess island—I unbuckle
my seat belt.

"Are you sure?" Mum asks.

"I want something desserty. Something that is not an Oreo."

"Come on, then."

So Eddison ends up trailing us through the store with the basket
hooked over one arm, and I can't even imagine how we must appear.
Well, no, I can a little, because we are getting the strangest looks. There
he is in a Nats shirt and open FBI hoodie under his coat, me in my
pajamas and bandages, Mum in her suit, both Mum and me still wearing the hospital grippy socks instead of shoes. But there's the look on
Mum's face in return, the one that dares anyone to mention a single
goddamned thing.

Mum is very, very good at that particular look.

There is nothing resting about that bitch face.

We get subs from the deli because there's even less chance than
usual of things getting cooked at home, and some snacks and breakfast
stuff, and we detour through the ice cream aisle so I can find some
orange sherbet, which should be easier on my throat than the ice cream
Mum and Eddison quibble over until they each pick out their own pint.

The cashier stares at me as he moves our items across the scanner.
"What happened to you?"

Eddison bristles but I give the boy a bland smile. "Demon-possessed nail gun," I answer calmly. "We drew the diagram in the garage—more room, you know?—and did the ritual, and didn't even realize the power cord had fallen into the circle of summoning."

He looks about to protest, but Mum pats my shoulder. "Next time you'll know to double-check before you start chanting. At least you sent it back."

Eddison turns to fuss with the bags so the kid can't see his smile.

It's a terrifying shred of normality in something that is really, *really* not a normal day.

The couch is covered in a snow of linens, because tomorrow's task was going to be sorting them into keep, donate, and toss piles. Might still be tomorrow's task, knowing Mum. It's not like we can't do it while talking. What it means for today, however, is that even Eddison is sprawled on the floor with us to eat, and he manages to look not entirely disgruntled by that. We're almost done eating when he excuses himself to the kitchen to take a phone call from Vic.

Mum decides the timing is perfect, and we go upstairs to wash my hair. And, you know, the rest of me, but the hair is the really problematic part. I get back into the yellow pants and FBI shirt, though, partly because they're comfortable, mostly because they're comforting.

Everything aches. Several ribs are cracked—several, the doctor said, and didn't want to give me a solid number—and the muscles are tight and cramping. I'm not breathless or gasping, but I'm aware of every inhalation in a way I'm usually not. When you don't have any trouble breathing, it's really not something you pay attention to. It's not just in my chest, either, but in the bruises and swelling through my throat.

I didn't give adrenaline enough credit when I was trying to think my way through things. His, yes, but mine, too, making me stupid and desperate. It's the only explanation I can come up with for why I would grab for the blade, hold on tight. Not the handle—the blade.

My wrapped fingers are stiff and throbbing in time with my heart and they'll be fairly useless for a while.

If I'm not stupid, though—more stupid—I should recover fully. A few scars, maybe, but if I obey my limits and take care of myself properly, the doctors said I shouldn't lose any function. Only one doctor checked my ribs, but three of them looked over my hands. I have antibiotics and painkillers and sleep aids, and what I suspect is a rather strongly worded suggestion I get myself to a shrink for some antianxiety meds.

I probably should have been on antianxiety meds for the last five years, but now, for the first time since that terrible night we spent waiting up for Chavi, I think I'm actually okay without them. Mostly okay.

Will be okay.

That might be more disturbing than anything else, really.

Eddison is back in the living room, folding the linens we very purposefully unfolded to inspect. He doesn't even look sheepish when Mum scolds him for it. "I'm too old to sit on the floor," he tells her.

"I'm older than you are."

"You devour souls to stay young."

"True." She takes the stack of folded linens from him, shakes them all loose again, and dumps them into a box with everything else on the couch. "What did Victor have to say?"

"Still in surgery. The lab is doing its thing with the blood sample and everything Ramirez and Sterling pulled from the apartment."

"If he doesn't make it, do you tell the families?" Gently pushing me onto the couch, Mum flops to the floor and leans back against my legs, absently reaching for the Xbox controller. It's a way to keep her hands busy while we talk, because stillness is for when things go wrong. As long as she's moving, nothing can be wrong.

Or something like that, but it's Mum, and this is how she's been all my life, and Eddison knows her well enough not to give the stink-eye for it.

"It'll depend on how firmly the evidence ties him to the other murders. What he said, what we've found, is pretty damning, but may not be sufficient for the bosses to be comfortable declaring it. We'll find out." Picking up the blue-and-white envelopes for my drugs, Eddison reads through the instructions, then opens two of the bottles. One large pill, two smaller pills, all three of them white. He takes my hand and carefully transfers the pills to my palm. Then he gets up and heads into the kitchen, returning a moment later with a glass of milk. "I know you ate, but sometimes milk gives a better cushion for the drugs."

"Well acquainted with prescription drugs, Eddison?" asks Mum.

He shifts a little, uncomfortable but trying to hide it. "You get shot a few times, you learn some tricks."

Mum pauses the game so she can look over her shoulder at him. Whatever she gets from his expression, she doesn't comment on it. Just turns back to her game.

I take my pills. Drink my milk.

Thunder rumbles overhead, soft and rolling. There's snow falling outside, clean white flurries skittering in whorls and flips in the wind. It's the kind of night to stay safely inside, warm and curled up with those you love. I reach for Eddison's hand so I can pull him to the middle seat.

So I can lean against him.

He puts his arm around my shoulders and leans into me, too, and we sit in silence and watch Mum play. There are questions he should probably be asking.

Probably will ask once he figures out how to phrase them. The thing is, Eddison knows me.

He knows I'm only so many kinds of stupid.

So I think—I'm reasonably sure—he's waiting to ask until we know whether or not Joshua is going to survive. It changes the shape of things, doesn't it?

Probably not.

Legally not, in any case.

"What did you do to your hands?" I mumble into his shirt.

"It's a long story. Please don't ask Ramirez for her version of it."

As tired as I am, I can't help but snicker.

Eventually, the day catches up to us all. Technically, Eddison is here on guard duty just like Sterling was, but it doesn't feel right to put family on the couch, so we set him up in Mum's room. It's slightly less creepy than the idea of him sleeping in mine, and I suspect he feels the same way. Mum helps me get ready for bed, and for a moment, I can close my eyes and think it's Chavi bumping hips with me in the narrow bathroom, brushing her teeth next to me.

We curl together in my bed, the flickering illumination of the electric tea light casting shadows across Chavi's picture frame and the wall beyond. The teddy bear Mercedes gave me the first time we met usually lives on my dresser, but now he's cushioning my aching jaw. Mercedes has a seemingly endless supply of soft bears to give victims and siblings when she goes to a scene or home. It was a comfort then, and a comfort now.

It's also the bear I threw at Eddison's head when I first met *him*, so there's that.

"That did not go quite as planned," Mum says eventually, her voice little more than a whisper, and I can't help but giggle. And then I can't stop, and it sets her off, and we're lying there laughing our heads off, because fucking hell, is that ever an understatement. My ribs flare with pain even after we finally get our breath back.

"I knew Archer would leave," I tell her more seriously. "It honestly never occurred to me that he'd go farther than it took to hide. I thought he'd be out of sight but in range, especially of a scream. I was . . ." I let out a breath, hold the next, let it out. "I was terrified."

"I'd be very worried if you weren't." She stirs, shifts, settles so her cheek rests against mine and her chin digs into my shoulder. "Work was hell. I had to convince myself over and over not to drive down after you. I can't do that again."

"I have no more monsters to kill," I murmur.

"One and done?"

"Thank God."

"What would you think . . ." She falls silent, which is so unlike her I'd turn to look at her if my ribs wouldn't protest. Instead, I find her hand and tangle my fingers through hers, resting them on my belly. "For a long time, it's been me and you against the world," she continues after a while, "but we have our agents, and you have Inara, and your veterans . . . maybe it's time we open ourselves up a bit."

"I'm going to try to make friends in Paris. Not just grudgingly allow it, like with Aimée, but actively try."

"Good. And what would you think . . ."

Whatever the rest of that thought is, it seems to be impossible.

"Some of your cousins are at universities on the continent, or work there. A handful are even in Paris. Maybe we can start connecting with the outliers, work our way down to the older generations."

"Work our way up?"

"I said what I meant." Brushing a kiss against my ear, she matches her breathing to mine. "You could have died today, my love, and it occurred to me: I don't want to be all alone. I could do it, certainly, but I don't want to. And I realized, if anything happens to me . . . I know you'd be taken care of. Vic would adopt you in a heartbeat. I just thought . . . Save me, Priya-love, you know I hate leaking emotions."

Laughing softly, I give Mum's fingers a squeeze. "Cousins sound like an excellent place to start."

She's silent for a long time, her fingertips rubbing little circles against my shirt. "Was he scared?" she asks finally.

"Yes."

"Good."

Even with the adrenaline crash and the medications and the warm, comforting weight of Mum wrapped around me, I'm a little surprised at how easy it is to drift off, not quite sleeping but definitely not awake.

Then my phone beeps.

Mum props herself up to grab it from the nightstand. The number is Inara's, but the text is addressed to both me and Eddison. It's just a picture, no caption, but I can't make it out from the thumbnail on the lock screen. She hands the phone to me and I thumb it open, pulling up the picture.

Inara stands with another girl, about our age and significantly shorter, with Times Square screaming neon all around them. Both have half-size poster board signs and dangerous smiles. The shorter girl is on the left, her sign yelling *FUCK OFF* in gold glitter; Inara's says *BAD GUYS* in silver.

Across the hall, a muffled thump and curse is followed by a "Christ and goddamn, Bliss!"

Mum and I look at the picture a while longer, then Mum snorts softly. "I'm impressed," she admits. "Wandering around Times Square with a sign that says fuck off. Lovely."

"Fuck off, *bad guys*," I tell her, aiming for prim but landing somewhere next to a laugh.

"You did your best to drag ours straight to the gates of hell; we'll see if it sticks."

I turn the phone to silent and set it back on the table, but as I drift off again, I can hear the buzzing vibrations against the wood that says Eddison and Inara are back-and-forthing. It's a strangely welcoming sound.

Jameson Carmichael—also known as Joshua Gabriel—dies Thursday, May fifth, at eight forty-seven in the morning, mountain time.

He never woke up.

Eddison can't decide if that's a good thing or not. A confession, or even a chance to question him, would have helped immensely, but there's a part of him that's glad they never had to hear him try to further justify what he did. There's more analysis to be done before anyone will sign off on informing the other families, but there's a sense of completion there.

Vic and Finney go down to Texas to talk to Mrs. Eudora Carmichael, and Vic comes back looking a kind of haunted that makes Eddison's skin crawl. Vic's daughters take one look at their father and practically nail him to the couch, sitting around him with snacks and a nearly endless stream of animated movies at the ready. It's what he's always done for their bad days; his girls are too bright not to realize that it works both ways.

Once the girls are asleep, Vic squirms out from under them, adjusting the blankets so they're covered, their limbs so they're not about to fall off the couch, and motions his partners outside. They follow him, but not until Eddison snaps a picture to send to Priya.

After all, she's been part of that puppy pile in the past.

Outside, they walk down the driveway to a little playground. The benches there have seen any number of impromptu conferences or post-case wind-downs. Vic sits heavily, looking older than he is, while Ramirez perches atop the back and stretches her legs along the length of the bench. They don't bother leaving room for Eddison; he almost never sits during serious conversation if pacing is an option.

Vic reaches into his pocket and pulls out a pack of cigarettes and a lighter. "Not a word to my wife or ma," he warns them, and holds it out.

Eddison takes one immediately. Ramirez shakes her head.

"Your gal in Counterterrorism not like the taste?" Eddison asks her.

"She has a name, you know."

"Now where would the fun be in that?"

She takes a cigarette before Vic can put the pack away.

"Mrs. Carmichael was devastated," Vic tells them, releasing a long, thin plume of smoke. "The last time she heard from her son was when he drove away a few months after his sister's death. At first she was in hysterics, but once she calmed down . . ."

"She started to reframe how she saw him," Ramirez finishes for him.

Vic nods. "He'd always been very protective of Darla Jean, she said. A very attentive older brother. He didn't like boys paying attention to her, or her paying attention to boys. Didn't like it when she dressed certain ways, or said certain things. Looking back, Mrs. Carmichael thought he was more physically affectionate than most brothers, but she was so glad they weren't fighting she didn't think too much of it."

"So Darla Jean kissed a boy in a church," says Ramirez, "a flower on her dress, and her brother saw. Felt betrayed?"

"Rapes her, kills her, runs back home before anyone can find her. Rural Texas, I bet most of the men know how to hunt. Any number of them have knives like his," Eddison continues.

"He doesn't run right away, not until the investigation's stalled. Not until his leaving won't be suspicious. And it's a small town, he's a smart young man, grieving his sister, is it really a surprise that he doesn't come back?"

"And everyone pities Mrs. Carmichael, to lose both her children so close to each other." Eddison flicks the ash onto a bare patch of soil, stepping on it just to be sure. "No one thinks twice about Jameson, so he becomes Joshua."

"He goes somewhere else, can't settle without Darla Jean, moves on again. He sees Zoraida. Everything a sister should be."

"He remembers Darla Jean was a 'good' sister, a good girl, until that boy, and he resolves to protect Zoraida from the same fate. Kills her to keep her innocent, but treats her gently."

"But every spring, he remembers Darla Jean, and when he sees the combination of pretty girl, church, and flowers, it triggers him. He stalks them to see if they're his definition of good or not."

"I hope you both realize that neither of you is ever getting promoted as long as you finish each other's thoughts," Vic points out. He stubs out the remains of his cigarette against the bottom of his shoe, then peels the paper away from the filter and drops both pieces back into the pack.

Ramirez hands him her cigarette to finish. "He learns Priya is in San Diego because of a photo contest; we found the magazine at his apartment. Priya, fifteen, San Diego. He takes it on faith, goes after her."

"But he finds her just before she leaves, and he has to look for her all over again. It takes him a while, but then Deshani's profile runs in the *Economist*, and she mentions that she and Priya are moving to Huntington. He decides to get there first."

"And the rest is history."

There's a question—a thought, maybe, or a possibility—that hangs heavy between them. Eddison remembers that feeling coming back from Denver the first time, that itching sense of something being out of place about the Sravastis' reactions. He snorts softly. "We're not saying it, are we?"

"No," Vic answers immediately. Firmly.

"Should we be?" Ramirez asks.

There isn't an easy answer to that, and they all know it. There's the law, their oaths to the FBI. There's the much murkier territory of right and wrong.

But there's also Priya, the laughing girl she used to be, and Deshani, too strong to stumble even if it kills her. There are all those other girls.

Eddison's never been sure what he thinks of the afterlife, if there are lost souls waiting for answers before they can move forward to the light or heaven or whatever. There are too many lost souls still living. But however much he wants to deny it, there's a part of him that will always tell the dead to rest in peace when they solve a murder. As if the knowing can give them that misty satisfaction and let them move on.

From Darla Jean Carmichael to Julie McCarthy, are those girls able to rest now?

And he thinks of Faith. Always, forever, of Faith. If he ever finds the bastard who took her . . .

"Priya's more her mother's daughter than ever," he says finally.

"Once we get the new round of lab reports, Finney and I are both recommending the case be officially closed," Vic tells them. "Priya Sravasti is a victim of Bureau ineptitude. An overeager agent charged with her protection used her as bait because the section chief was more concerned with politics than with the facts of the case. Section Chief Ward will face a full internal investigation regarding her actions."

"And that's an end to it?" Ramirez asks.

"Are you okay with that?"

She looks off into the stretch of trees that backs the playground, running along in a thick strip between this row of houses and the ones behind them. She hates the woods, and it took almost two years and a night of far too much tequila for her to tell them why. Vic might have already known, actually, if he had access to her background, but he'd never made mention of it if he had. Most of her nightmares were born in the woods, something that may never leave her.

It's never stopped her from running straight into the trees if there's a chance in hell the kid they're looking for is alive in there.

"Yes," she says eventually, drawing out the word. "I suppose I am."

Because there's the law, and there's justice, and they're not always the same thing.

The night before Mum and I leave the country, the Hanoverian living room is full of laughter and arguments and noise. So much noise, and it's amazing, the vitality of it. Vic is thoroughly outnumbered by his mother, wife, and three daughters, and because Inara and Bliss are in the room, Eddison stays on the opposite side of it and doesn't even try to help his senior partner. Mercedes just teases both men.

It's home, and family, and all kinds of wonderful things.

Eventually, though, everyone heads to bed, Marlene and Jenny kissing everyone on foreheads or cheeks. They get Eddison's cheeks at the same time from either side, and doesn't that just make him squirm?

The picture is wonderful. Inara and Bliss both promptly ask me to text it to them. So do Vic and Mercedes, when Eddison can't see them.

I have a feeling Mercedes will be putting it on her desk at work at some point, just to fuck with him.

Mum shoos me upstairs, where we're sharing Brittany's room, but she stays in the living room with the adults and I know it'll be a while before she's up. So I head into Holly's room with Inara and Bliss.

They came down a few days ago from New York, with a detour to Sharpsburg to check on the youngest Garden survivor. The best part of meeting them may have been watching Eddison try not to crawl out of his skin. He kept hovering in the doorway of whatever room we were in, clearly torn between wanting to run the hell away and wanting to make sure we don't accidentally take over the world.

I'm fairly sure it wouldn't be an accident if we did.

Bliss is as prickly as Mum and me, if a bit more aggressive with it. I generally keep my snarls as an answer; she uses them as a challenge. I can't say I blame her. What happened to her was a lot more public than what was done to me, even when the news took up Chavi and her place in the string of unsolved murders.

Inara is quieter than Bliss, not shy or withdrawn, just . . . more patient, I suppose. Bliss explores a situation by lighting a match and letting it explode. Inara watches first, observes. She waits to speak until she knows what she wants to say and has a healthy guess as to how others will react to it. It's easy to see why the Hanoverians have taken them in.

"I hear your parents and siblings are in Paris," I say to Bliss, my fingers buried in Inara's hair to help her braid it for bed.

Bliss growls, but Inara glances back at me over her shoulder. "Most people would just say *family*."

"Your family's here, and in New York. I may not know you two that well, but that's clear enough."

Inara laughs at the fierce blush that lights up Bliss's pale skin.

"Yes," Bliss manages after clearing her throat. "They're in Paris. My father's teaching."

"They've been bugging you to come visit?"

"Yes."

"Well, if you do . . . we're going to have a couple of guest rooms. If you want to get together, or if you need to escape for a night. Or if things go south and you need to say fuck it. Safety net's there. And you wouldn't have to listen to your parents pout if you bring Inara."

"They have been bitching about it," she agrees. Without warning, she pulls off everything but her underwear and rummages through her bag for sleepwear.

"Our apartment is one giant room," Inara explains. "Even after the Garden, modesty isn't so much a thing there."

"Eh. I had a sister." I tie off Inara's braid, hand her the brush, and turn around so she can return the favor. Her strokes are smooth and sure, never tugging too hard but letting the bristles scrape gently along my scalp.

"Does it ever stop, do you think?" Bliss asks suddenly.

"Does what?"

"That sense of being a victim."

It's a little strange, the way they both focus on me at that. They're both older than me, if not by very much, but then, my world exploded five years ago. In a sick sort of way, I guess I have seniority. "It changes," I say finally. "I don't know that it ends. Sometimes it flares, for no reason at all. The more choices we make, though, the more we live our lives . . . I think that helps."

"We heard Eddison say you killed the bastard. The one that was after you."

"I did." My hands are in my lap, free of heavy-duty bandages but still more Band-Aid than skin. Inara has pale, rippling scars on her hands from burns and gashes. "He came after me, we struggled over his knife, I stabbed him. A lot. Adrenaline, you know?"

"I shot Avery. The Gardener's older son, the one who liked to maim. I don't know how many times."

"Four," Inara says, her voice soft.

"Sometimes I shoot him and there are no bullets in the gun. Sometimes I shoot and shoot and shoot and never run out of bullets, but he doesn't stop. He just keeps coming forward."

"Sometimes I wake up and have to strip down so I can lie naked in the tub, because clothes and bedding feel too much like flower petals," I reply. "Because in my nightmare, I'm alive but bleeding out, can't move, and he's surrounding me with white roses, like the Lady of Shalott's bier down the river."

They both laugh, even as Bliss groans. "You like classics?" Inara asks.

"Some of them."

"Don't ever get this one started on Poe," Bliss tells me. "She can quote all of it. And by quote, I mean recite. All of it. Every goddamn word of it."

The braid thumps against my back as Inara ties it off. "It kept my brain busy."

"That's the trick, I think." I stretch out across the bed. Inara and Bliss aren't anything like Chavi and Josephine, but the feeling is there. I'm comfortable with both of them in a way I didn't expect to be right off. "Things don't just magically get better, but we can make them better."

"Slowly," adds Inara.

"So fucking slowly," sighs Bliss.

"I take pictures of Special Agent Ken and send them to Eddison. When we get to Paris, I'm dressing the doll in mime gear at a café, and I can almost guarantee Eddison's response will be *That's horrifying* or something very similar." They laugh again, Bliss easing down gently across my back, careful with my battered and wrapped ribs. Her hair is all wild curls, not something you can braid dry, and it spills around her. I can see their wings, or parts of them where the tank tops don't hide them.

They're beautiful, and awful, and I get the feeling they see them largely the same way. At least Inara, anyway, but then, I think she's had more practice than Bliss at reframing perspective.

Inara stretches out beside me, her legs thrown over mine and her cheek against the back of Bliss's shoulder. "How many times did you stab him, Priya?" she asks softly.

"Seventeen. Once for each girl he killed, and once for me."

Her slow, satisfied smile is both terrifying and wonderful.

I don't remember falling asleep that way, but Mum shows me the picture in the morning. Over Marlene's amazing cinnamon rolls, Eddison teases Bliss about being cuddly. He takes a little too much delight in setting her wrong-footed, at least until Inara hands me a little blue dragon made of clay and tells me to mail it back once Special Agent Ken is done with him.

Seeing Eddison try not to blush is always a good thing.

We say goodbye to the female Hanoverians at the house, laden down with plastic bags of treats from Marlene. She swears there won't be a problem getting through security with them, and standing safely behind her where she can't see him, Vic rolls his eyes.

"Victor."

He freezes, sighs, and shakes his head.

Mum watches him with amusement. "You didn't really think you'd grow out of that, did you?"

"Did you?"

"It never worked on me to begin with."

Eddison nudges Vic in the side. "I can believe it. Can you?"

"I absolutely believe it."

Inara and Bliss ride with us to the airport, sitting in the back with me while Mercedes and Mum sit in the middle row. Suitcases fill the trunk space. Our stuff left Colorado last week, professionals loading it into the shipping container to guarantee even distribution. They were significantly better at their job than the ones who dropped the container off. Still, it's going to take another two to three weeks before it actually arrives at the new house, so until then we're living out of suitcases.

There's an entire suitcase dedicated to Mum's coffeemaker, the box wrapped in most of the towels we own for extra protection.

Eddison and Vic grab most of the bags between them, save for the carry-ons and the enormous orange-and-yellow knit blanket Hannah gave me when I said goodbye to my vets. She gave me her address, so I can write, and I have a feeling she'll chivy the men into writing me occasionally. The blanket is warm and soft, eye-smartingly sunny, and she had to yank it away from the unabashedly weeping Happy when he looked ready to blow his nose in it.

Officer Clare was there, his partner watching him closely, to apologize. He's on suspension until the department psychologist clears him for duty. Some cases hit unexpectedly, especially if your wife leaves you just before. It's no excuse, but the situation is what it is, and it's not my problem anymore.

Gunny looked at me for a long time, then gently folded me against him. "Armistice, Miss Priya?" he'd whispered.

Something like.

Then Corgi clapped me gently on the back and announced my smile didn't make him want to piss himself anymore. So, you know. There's that.

I'm going to miss them, and it's weird, kind of, that I find that comforting, but for so long, I haven't really missed people. I missed my agents, but I was in such close contact with them that it wasn't really missing them so much as wishing they were nearby. I missed Aimée, but missing her was caught up in everything else about the murders, tangled and complicated and really not fair to her.

We get the bags checked, and thankfully Mum gets to use the company card for the baggage fees because holy shit, and walk in a mass toward the security line. It's insane, which isn't surprising for Reagan midmorning.

"All right, you three," Eddison says, pulling out his phone and using it to point at me, Inara, and Bliss. "Stand together, give me fuel for my nightmares for years to come."

Snickering, Inara and Bliss lean into me on either side, our arms wrapped around each other, and smile for the camera. Eddison actually shudders.

"Three of the most dangerous human beings on the planet," he mutters.

"What am I?" asks Mum.

"Their demonic leader." But he kisses her cheek.

"We'll write," Inara tells me. "We'll definitely let you know when this one's parents wear her down."

"Door's always open."

"So's ours," Bliss says. "You ever want to come on a holiday, we've got a bed for you. We'll take New York by storm."

"But will it ever recover?" Mercedes asks with a laugh, wrapping me in a hug from behind.

Goodbyes haven't been this hard since Boston, but I'm grateful. God, I'm so, so grateful to have people who mean this much to me. Mercedes passes me back to Inara and Bliss for hugs, and they hand me off to Vic. He holds me close for a long moment.

"I am so glad you're safe," he whispers, "and that you're starting to be happy again. You're one of my own girls, Priya, you know that."

"I do," I whisper back, giving him a squeeze. "You're not rid of us that easy."

Eddison pulls me a little ways away as Mum gives her round of goodbyes. Inara and Bliss are a little in awe of her, I think, less in the you-make-me-speechless way than "I want to be you when I grow up." When there's a good bit of distance between us and the group, he pulls me into a hug. "So this thing that I've been very carefully not asking," he says quietly. "Can you live with it?"

I've been thinking about that for weeks, even before my birthday. "Yes, I think I can," I answer. "Not easily, perhaps, but that might be for the best. And you told the rest of the families; no one has to wonder anymore. I can live with that." I rest my head against his shoulder, smelling the spicy cologne he uses when he can't be bothered with aftershave. Or shaving. "Mum and I talked it over, and we're going to spread Chavi's ashes. We're thinking a lavender field, with one of the castles and the river in the background? That should appeal to Chavi. We're going to make this a good move."

"Okay."

I look up at him, and his stubbly cheek scrapes against my forehead as he drops a kiss between my eyes, just above the bindi. It's only in the past week I've started wearing it again, the skin fully healed. "I'm going to miss you, you know?"

"Nonsense," he says gruffly. "I fully expect Special Agent Ken to be giving regular reports. And, ah . . . you know, I keep accumulating a ridiculous amount of paid time off. Maybe I'll finally dust some of that off one of these days."

"There'll be a room. Always."

He kisses me again, then releases me with a slight push back to the group. Another round of hugs and goodbyes, and then Mum and I are in the security line. I clutch the folded blanket to my chest, and after fighting with myself for a moment, I look back over my shoulder at them. Inara and Bliss are leaning against Vic, comfortable and casual, and Mercedes is poking a blushing Eddison in the shoulder, the girls egging her on and Vic grinning like a loon as he pretends to be the adult.

The line shuffles forward and I follow, and Mum wraps her arm around my shoulders to bring me in for a kiss on the cheek. "Ready for this, my love?"

"Yeah." I face forward and take a deep breath. "I'm ready."

Your name was Jameson Carmichael, and Darla Jean was your everything.

You were just waiting for her to grow up, weren't you? Old enough to leave your tiny Texas town and never come back, go with you somewhere no one knew you were related so you could start your proper life together. You never told her that, of course. You never thought you needed to.

Darla Jean loved you as her brother but that could never be enough for you.

You've punished us all for it over the years, for her perceived sins. So many lives you've destroyed, mothers and fathers, sisters and brothers, cousins and friends, the pain spiraling out to all those touched by us.

My mother gardens, but then, you know that, don't you? Because you watched us back then, in Boston, and again in San Diego. She plans her gardens, sketching out the beds so she knows what she wants to plant where, and they're always balanced. Here are the annuals, planted fresh every year.

Here are the perennials, blooming and resting and blooming again. With the proper care, they keep living, keep thriving, as others die around them.

I've been alive the last five years, resting or hiding or whatever we want to call it. Grieving. Now, I think, finally, I'll know what it is to bloom again.

And all it took was your blood, warm and heavy and sticky on my hands.

Do you like that, Joshua? That in your own, special way, you might finally be the thing that helps me heal from what you've been doing for so long?

The knife tore and ripped each time I pulled it out of you, and I think I understand why you always sliced and slit, never stabbed. Such a terrible sound, and the feeling of the flesh catching on those points. I hope you felt each one. Your favored ones, your good girls, you studied the body to make their deaths as painless as you could, but anatomy was never really my thing. If it had been, maybe I would have realized how easy it is to slam against ribs, the strength it takes to try to drive a knife through bone. Maybe I would have learned how tough muscle is, but how easily the lung gives way to a blade, with a wet, sucking gasp that announces its weakness. Maybe I would have read somewhere that blood is darker closer to the heart, or maybe it only seems that way.

But strangely—or not—I find myself thinking of the roses. You brought so many with you, filling your car. I didn't realize until I was outside that you had so many more you hadn't carried in with you. You would have made me a rose bower inside the chapel.

But the roses didn't fall around me. I bled, true enough, but not enough to fall, to pool. That was you. It was your life painting the white petals, your own little Wonderland garden, and you never expected that your rules could change, be overthrown.

There were things I wanted to ask you, but even at the end, didn't dare. You could have woken up, after all, could have said something that made it obvious—more obvious—that I knew who you were.

That's okay, though, because you know what I realized, Joshua, there in the cold and the falling snow and the blood warm and wet and heavy on my clothes just like that long-ago morning with Chavi?

I realized your answers couldn't matter. It doesn't really matter why you did it, why you chose them, chose us, chose me. It doesn't matter how you justify it, because the answers were never going to make sense to anyone else anyway. They were yours. And they were wrong.

They were always, always wrong.

You were one of the sick, terrible things in the world, Joshua, but no more.

My name is Priya Sravasti, and I am no one's victim.

ACKNOWLEDGMENTS

To all the people who have stuck by me and supported me as I spent most of a year freaking out about how this book was doing its best to kill me by way of a nervous breakdown: *thank you*. I could not have done this without my cheering sections, all the people who kept telling me not to get discouraged, everyone who listened to me panic and complain and just generally lose my mind.

To JoVon, who bought the book when it was nothing more than a *very* different synopsis, and Jessica, who absolutely believes in it, and Caitlin, who deserves a freaking medal for our edit process. Caitlin, you have a gift for making the impossible seem manageable, and your calm confidence definitely pulled me through. Agent Sandy, for finding a home for the Butterflies that opened its doors to more of the story.

Isabel, Maire, Kelie, Roni, Pam, Allyson, because there wasn't a single part of the process you didn't hear about and yet you're somehow still my friends. A massive thank you to my family for being so excited about every milestone and success, and understanding when I spent Thanksgiving staring at edits. Everyone at Crossroads, for talking up *The Butterfly Garden* and celebrating with me whenever we had to order more into the store (and for never telling me to shut up when I couldn't stop talking about how much everything was stressing me out).

You know, I'm sensing a theme here.

And to everyone who's read and loved *The Butterfly Garden*, everyone who's shared a review or talked about it online, everyone who's picked it for book club or pushed it on friends, thank you. Thank you for your enthusiasm, for your support, and for staying with me this far.

ABOUT THE AUTHOR

Photo © 2012 Arabella Blizzard

Dot Hutchison is the author of *The Butterfly Garden* and *The Roses of May*, the first two books in The Collector Trilogy, as well as *A Wounded Name*, a young adult novel based on Shakespeare's *Hamlet*. Hutchison loves thunderstorms, mythology, history, and movies that can and should be watched on repeat. For more information on her current projects, visit www.dothutchison.com or connect with her on Tumblr (www.dothutchison.tumblr.com), Twitter (@DotHutchison), or Facebook (www.facebook.com/DotHutchison).